The world's greatest theme attraction!

When on old friend calls for hel home town he tried to leave apparent there is something l everybody wants a piece of it. Aston and adventure television show host, Jo Slater, find themselves in a race against local criminal elements, environmental extremists, and mysterious mercenaries to find the creature before it kills again. Sam enlists the aid of his old rival, park ranger Rusty Crews, and Ned King, a naturalist with a flair for self-promotion, who would like nothing better than to find the perfect main attraction for Crocalypse, his new bio theme park.

Crocalypse - An action-packed monster thriller with bite!

Praise for David Wood and Alan Baxter

"*Crocalypse* is Jurassic Park on steroids!" Melissa Bowersock, Author of the *Lacey Fitzpatrick and Sam Firecloud Mystery Series.*

Renegade marine biologist Sam Aston is back for a second outing in what is shaping up to be a must-read aquatic adventure series! Danger and intrigue lurk both above and below in this action-filled, white-knuckle romp with a breathtaking conclusion!- Rick Chesler, author of *SAWFISH*

CROCALYPSE

A Sam Aston Investigation

DAVID WOOD
ALAN BAXTER

Crocalypse by David Wood and Alan Baxter
© 2021

Edited by Melissa Bowersock

Published by Adrenaline Press | www.adrenaline.press
Adrenaline is an imprint of Gryphonwood Press
www.gryphonwoodpress.com

ISBN: 978-1-950920-20-4

Books by David Wood and Alan Baxter

Jake Crowley Adventures
Sanctum
Blood Codex
Anubis Key
Revenant

Sam Aston Investigations
Primordial
Overlord
Crocalypse

Dark Rite

Books by David Wood

The Dane Maddock Adventures
Blue Descent
Dourado
Cibola
Quest
Icefall
Buccaneer
Atlantis
Ark
Xibalba
Loch
Solomon Key
Contest
Serpent
Eden Quest (forthcoming_

Dane and Bones Origins
Freedom
Hell Ship
Splashdown
Dead Ice
Liberty
Electra
Amber
Justice
Treasure of the Dead
Bloodstorm

The Myrmidon Files (with Sean Ellis)
Destiny
Mystic

Stand-Alone Novels
Into the Woods (With David S. Wood)
Callsign: Queen (with Jeremy Robinson)

David Wood writing as David Debord

The Absent Gods Trilogy
The Silver Serpent
Keeper of the Mists
The Gates of Iron

The Impostor Prince (with Ryan A. Span)
Neptune's Key
The Zombie-Driven Life
You Suck

David Wood Writing as Finn Gray

Aquaria Falling
Aquaria Burning
The Gate

Books by Alan Baxter

The Roo
Devouring Dark
Hidden City

Alex Caine Series
Bound
Obsidian
Abduction

The Balance
RealmShift
MageSign

Served Cold- Short Stories
Crow Shine- Short Stories
The Gulp- Short Stories

Manifest Recall
Recall Night
The Book Club
Ghost of the Black: A 'Verse Full of Scum

Prologue

Five years ago.

Jo Slater shone a flashlight into the depths of the tomb. "Never seen before," she whispered. "Can you believe it?"

"It's always such a thrill," said a soft voice behind her. Jade Ihara stepped up beside Slater and clicked on her own flashlight. "Let's go carefully. There may be traps. And don't touch anything." She directed the last toward Dave, the cameraman, who was looking around in wide-eyed amazement.

"Dave, Carly, you getting everything?" Jo asked.

Her cameraman and sound engineer both made quiet noises of confirmation. She heard the nerves in their tone and couldn't blame them. This was some creepy stuff, but perfect for her show. Viewing figures would go stratospheric with this. And if they found something genuinely valuable? Well, she would hit the big time, for sure. Still trying to find a good direction for her show, the general idea of discovery was currently driving her forward. But a previously unopened Egyptian tomb? This was a dream come true. She swallowed her nerves and moved aside to let Dave get a good shot through the new opening.

Sweat dripped down the thickset cameraman's face. He'd had a few too many the night before and now he was paying for it. Karma.

"Let me go first," Ihara said.

Carly nodded eagerly. Despite her diminutive size, she was courageous, and she appeared to have developed a bit of a girl-crush on the intrepid Ihara. Slater cleared her throat, and when she had their attention, gestured Dave and Carly to follow, then she brought up the rear. Being in front of the camera was a privilege, but it was equally important to know when to stand back and let the lens go first. A basic rule of documentary-making she always remembered was to always keep the viewer front and center.

They moved slowly along a low, dim passageway, lit only by the dancing beams of their flashlights. Many people believed there wasn't much left undiscovered in Egypt, but Slater was not one of them, and teaming up with archaeologist Jade Ihara for this episode had proven worthwhile. The previous chamber had contained a wealth of grave goods: canopic jars, scarab beetles made of lapis lazuli, and mummified creatures of all sorts. Fascinating stuff, but the usual fare. Now she needed something climactic, a way to end on a high note.

Come on, she thought to herself. Give me something amazing!

"Look, here," Ihara said, aiming her light at the ground. "See that flagstone is a little higher than the rest?" She moved her light slowly. "And that one, that one, that one, and right there at the end? Each of those is a pressure sensor. Don't step on them."

Slater swallowed. She'd been so busy hoping for something she'd let her attention wander. That was no good. But a smile played at her lips. If there were pressure plates here, surely they were protecting something special.

"Jo, I don't know about this…" Dave's voice wavered.

"I understand," Slater said. "But look. There's an opening at the end. A doorway, maybe? Let's get that far, see what's through there, then take a break. We can head back above ground and consider our next steps, okay?"

"I'll light the ground," Carly said. "Dave, you watch your step."

"Tread carefully," Ihara said, and led them on.

The doorway Slater had mentioned was high and wide, the narrow passage opening out to accommodate it. Large sandstone blocks made a frame, nothing but darkness beyond. Ihara reached it first.

"Hang on!" Slater said. "Dave, go alongside Jade so we get footage of her light falling inside. I want viewers to discover what's through there with us."

"Ah, damn," Dave muttered, but he moved carefully alongside Ihara, Carly shining her light at the ground for him. Ihara glanced at Dave and he nodded, so she slowly panned her flashlight through the doorway. He followed it with his lens.

Carly let out a little squeak and Dave sucked in a sharp breath as the beam fell on a towering figure. It took Slater a moment to realize it was a statue of a powerfully-built man with the head of a crocodile. He clutched a staff in his right hand.

"What the hell is that?" Dave said.

"Sobek," Jade replied as if that explained everything.

"Could you elaborate?" Slater hated prompting Ihara, but they were making a television show, after all.

"Sobek is an aggressive, animalistic ancient Egyptian deity associated with military prowess, power, and fertility. He is also called the Lord of Semen. Is that something your audience would enjoy learning?"

Carly choked with laughter and Dave's chest trembled as he struggled to hold the camera steady. Even Slater had to grin.

"Probably, but I'm afraid the network will force us to edit it out."

"Sorry," Ihara said. "There's something wrong about this place."

"What do you mean?" Slater asked.

"First of all, there were no personal effects among the grave goods. Nothing that a person would want to take into the afterlife. In King Tut's tomb they found things like golden sandals, linen gloves, the crook and flail that symbolized royal power, and treasure. There's nothing like that here."

"So, whoever is buried here went to the grave broke?" Carly asked.

"That's one possibility," Ihara said. Before they could follow up on her cryptic comment, she turned and shone her light off to camera left. "There's also this. If you look closely you can see the wall has been patched."

Once she knew what to look for, Slater spotted it right away. "It looks like a large tunnel was blocked off."

"I think that's exactly what it is," Ihara said. "My gut says this place was built to hold something large—too large to come through the way we did. So, they cut a shaft to the surface, brought it down, then sealed it up again."

"But where?" Slater asked. Aside from the statue, the chamber was empty.

Jade smiled. "Everybody stand back." She made her way over to the statue of Sobek and sprang nimbly up onto the plinth that supported it. "This staff is actually a lever." She shone her light onto the plinth. The staff disappeared into a dark slit cut into the stone.

Ihara took hold of the staff with both hands and pulled it toward her. It slid forward, and then a low rumble filled the chamber. Slowly, the floor began to sink. Ihara smiled and waved goodbye as she disappeared from sight. Slater watched in rapt amazement as a ten meter wide hole formed in the floor. Around the edge, stones fell into place, forming a spiral staircase that wound down to the floor below.

Slater wanted to jump for joy. Here was the high point she had been hoping for!

"Come on down," Ihara said. "It's really quite something."

They hurried down the staircase to find themselves in a huge chamber. A few meters in front of them, a line of mummified crocodiles barred their way. Ihara shone her light around the large chamber, briefly highlighting urns and leather bags. Dust covered everything, the place clearly undisturbed for centuries.

"Wow, this place is massive," Ihara said quietly, almost as if her voice might disturb something. "And what the hell is that?"

Slater trembled instantly at Ihara's tone. If the stalwart archeologist was troubled, it could only be something serious. She pushed closer behind Dave to see better. Ihara's light panned back and forth across what looked like a rough statue of a gargantuan crocodile stretched out across a plinth hewn from native stone.

"That is one hell of a sculpture," Dave said.

"Look again," Ihara said. "It's been mummified." She was correct. The thing was wrapped in old bandages. "Mummification is intended to preserve the remains of a once-living thing."

"Clearly dead now," Slater said. "But I've never seen a croc that size." She frowned. Surely it wasn't real.

"Looks mummified," Ihara said. "It's possible crocs used to get that big, I suppose."

"I guess that's what was brought in through the shaft you spotted," Carly said to Ihara.

"That thing has to be fifty feet long!"

Ihara sniffed and stepped back, forcing Slater and Dave to retreat as well. "We're done for today. This is too important. We need to have better lighting, more gear. And we need to make sure we do everything to preserve that beast. Already we've triggered changes by opening this place up. We're not prepared to move into that chamber yet. There's some people I know, experts in this sort of thing. I'll call them in."

"Really?" Slater was disappointed. "Not even a quick look around?"

"It's been hundreds of years," Ihara said with a smile. "It can wait another day. Trust me, I've long since learned that patience is key in this game. Preparation is everything. Let's get back topside. I'll make some calls and we'll come back down tomorrow, better prepared. Watch your step on the way back."

The next morning Slater woke a full hour before her alarm, too excited to sleep any longer. After restlessly shifting around for a while, she got up, showered, dressed, and went downstairs. In the hotel lobby she heard raised voices and emerged from the stairwell to see Jade Ihara, Dave, and Carly arguing with local police and two men in suits. Standing alongside was Mr. Hunter, the wealthy benefactor of this expedition and the finance behind the episode in question. Slater's stomach dropped. This couldn't be good.

"Not the bloody camera!" Dave was saying.

"The camera will be replaced," Mr. Hunter said, patting the air with both hands to try to calm the cameraman down. "I'm sorry, I've tried everything, but they're completely insistent. I promise you'll be fully reimbursed for any and all losses."

"We've been calling up to your room," Ihara said when she saw Slater approach.

"I was in the shower. What's happening?"

"I'm afraid we're having to shut it all down," Mr. Hunter said. "All footage and information related to this project is being confiscated. Thank you enormously for your work so far, but—"

"That's bullshit!" Slater spat. "You can't just pull the rug out from under us like that. Nearly six weeks we've been on this, we have hours of footage. It is ours, you can't simply confiscate it!"

"Not any more, I'm afraid. You can check the small print of your contract if you like, but this is the call we're making." Hunter looked genuinely aggrieved, but he also looked like someone who would not be convinced otherwise. Why had he even included language like that in the contract? Had he suspected something? Maybe Slater and Jade Ihara had both been used here.

"I would advise you make no trouble," said one of the suited men in heavily-accented English. The two uniformed police officers stood a little straighter.

Slater instantly felt the tension rise.

"You will be fully compensated," Mr. Hunter said. "With a kill fee bonus added on. That's in the contract too."

"It's not about the money!" Slater said. "My show…" This was supposed to be the one that really cracked the big time.

"I'm sorry, I'm afraid there is no show this time."

Jade Ihara moved over and put a hand on Slater's forearm. "This happens sometimes. Not often, but it's not unheard of. I'm really sorry, Jo, trust me. Take the money and walk away. Use the fee to finance another expedition. I'd be happy to work with you again. Call me any time."

Slater looked around the small group, clenched fists trembling in rage. Ihara was angry too, it was clear in her eyes and clenched jaw, but she appeared to be a realist too. Slater knew if the archeologist had decided the cause was lost, there was not point in pushing harder. "Dave, give him the camera." She turned to Hunter. "I want his camera replaced immediately, and the full fees transferred by the end of the day."

Hunter smiled, nodded. "Of course."

Slater turned and strode from the room before she said something else that she might live to regret.

"Jo!" Ihara hurried to catch up with her. "I don't know what's going on here, but whoever is behind this pulled more strings than a harpist. And between what they paid us and the palms they must have greased, that's a load of cash."

"What are you trying to say?" Slater snapped.

"I'm saying this is a situation we're all better off simply forgetting about."

Chapter 1

A full moon hung low over the Blacktooth River, casting glittering silver across the slowly moving water. The night was close, humid, as far north Queensland pushed inexorably towards summer. Bugs flitted through the hot air, cicadas sang loud, somewhere across the river a fruit bat took flight with leathery slaps of its wings.

Isabella Martin, Izzy to her friends, sat and swung her feet over the edge of the dock as she waited. It wasn't like Coop to be late. She hoped he hadn't got sidetracked. Maybe his dad had sidetracked him. Disabled from a work accident a decade ago, Cooper's father had experienced a rapid decline in health, mostly due to drink and depression. He was a master of guilt trips, and knew how to push all of his family's buttons, especially Coop's. She sighed at the thought. Sometimes it sucked to still be living at home and treated like kids. But Cooper's apprenticeship was starting soon and he'd be earning money. With her job at the supermarket they'd have enough to rent somewhere. A small unit, probably, but something of their own. Rental prices in this arse end of nowhere town were not high, after all.

Her mother would kick up a fuss, of course. She was a Yirrganydji woman and all about family, staying together, sharing space. Izzy thought perhaps her Irish-Australian father sometimes resented his in-laws living with them, her Aunty right next. It was a bit claustrophobic sometimes. But Nan and Pop were lovely, and helpful around the place, and Aunty was always bringing food around. She was a great cook. Plus, their house was big, on a good acre and a half.

Regardless, Izzy had had enough. She wanted to spread

her wings, and spread them wide. One day before too long she wanted to not only leave the family home behind, but Blacktooth River entirely. The town, named after the wide, muddy river that wove through it, was a good place for a kid to grow up, but not for a young adult with dreams and aspirations. She and Coop would rent for a year or two, save up enough to get a car, then hit the road. Maybe Townsville or Cairns first, nothing too dramatic. But from there, the world would be open to them.

Long, strong arms grabbed her around the body, pinning her arms to her sides. She squealed and kicked, then broke into laughter as Cooper planted hot kisses across the back of her neck.

"Scared the crap out of me, you asshat!" she panted between laughs.

He let go and sat next to her, long legs swinging, one hand brushing back his shaggy, sandy hair. "You were in deep thought, huh? I didn't exactly sneak up on you."

"Didn't hear you coming."

"Obviously. What were you thinking about?"

"Nothing much. Just wishing we could get out of this place sooner rather than later. I feel… I don't know, Coop. I feel like I need to change things up. I'm stagnating here."

Cooper slipped a hand under her long, black ringlets, his palm hot against the back of her neck. He pulled her in for a kiss. "We will," he said as they moved a little apart again. "We've got a plan, remember?" He ran one thumb gently over her lips, his blue eyes lost in her brown ones. Then he leaned in for another kiss and for a while time stood still. Blacktooth River didn't exist. All that mattered was Isabella Martin and Cooper Cook, lost in each other.

Izzy put a hand on his chest and pushed him back, sucking in a breath. She smiled, glanced back behind them to where the dock met the road. To one side was the small car park, then the road headed back away from the river, leading eventually to the highway and freedom. The other way, the street led into town and the shops beyond. Everything was still and quiet.

"No one's watching," Coop said. "We have the night to ourselves. Here." He pulled a hip flask from his pocket and handed it to her.

"What's in it?"

"Dad's Bundaberg rum."

Izzy laughed. "Bundy? Could you be more of a cliché?"

"You want a drink or not? It's why I'm late, I waited for Dad to doze off in his armchair, then snuck it out. It's grog and it's free."

"You make a good point." She unscrewed the cap and took a long slug, the sweet dark rum burning gently on the way down. She held it out to Cooper.

"Have another. I already had a few on the way."

She smiled crookedly. "That's why you're so horny?"

"I'm always horny."

Her smile turned into a laugh. "That's true!" She slugged again, then handed it over and Cooper took a long drink despite his refusal only moments before.

He pocketed the stainless steel flask and moved close again. They fell back to kissing, pressing themselves together. Cooper's hand slid under her light singlet, across the soft brown skin of her stomach. She matched the movement, her palm against his hard, well-defined abs, but then pushed him away. They were sitting in full view of anyone who might be passing. Sure, Blacktooth River was dead at the best of times, especially late at night, but her mother would be disappointed if people gossiped about Izzy canoodling at night, and her dad would be furious. He'd probably come after Coop with a tire iron. She loved her dad so much, but he still acted like she was a little girl. Another reason she needed space.

"Cool your jets, cowboy."

"Aw, come on, Iz. No one's about."

"Not here, Coop! Not now."

"I wish we had a place of our own already," Cooper said, face twisted in frustration.

"I know. Me too. But my folks are sleeping. Soon enough we'll have our own place."

Cooper grinned, but made a noise of disappointment. He stripped down to his boxers and turned towards the end of the jetty.

"Cooper, are you mad!" Izzy said, jumping up to grab his arm.

"Gotta cool my jets somehow!"

"Are you mad? There could be crocs."

"We've swum here so many times," he scoffed.

"I know, but not at night."

Cooper winked. "We'll see anything, it's a full moon." He turned and jumped in before she could say more. He swam a small circle and sighed loudly. "Izzy, it's so good. Come on in."

"No!"

He splashed cool water up at her, his face bathed in moonlight, hair slicked back. "Come on. What are you, chicken? We'll stay right here near the jetty. It's so nice in here, Izzy." He gave her a sly smile. "You really don't know how to loosen up, do you?"

She looked down at him, a smile playing at her lips. He was so desperately child-like sometimes. Or no, perhaps more like a puppy. She glanced around once more, then quickly stepped out of her thongs, pulled off her singlet and denim shorts, and moved to the end of the jetty.

"Yes!" Cooper said, looking up at her with wide eyes, filled with longing.

She paused a moment, let him drink her in, then jumped into the water. It was warm, but much cooler than the late-spring air. It chilled her skin and her blood, filled her with vigor. Cooper grabbed her hips and pulled her into him, kissing her. She pushed him back and dunked him. Her laughter rang out as he came up spluttering.

She turned and swam away, Cooper in hot pursuit. Her foot clipped something. She stopped and turned, looked down, but the water was brown and muddy, impenetrable in the night. Cooper caught up and pulled her into an embrace, but she pushed him away.

"Wait, there's something down there." She cautiously moved her feet as she trod water, arms moving rhythmically to keep her in place. "I can't feel it now."

"Just a log probably, or a rock," Cooper said, reaching for her again. "We're right near the bank."

She shook her head, backed away from him. "No, I definitely felt something but now it's gone. So that means it was moving! You know there are crocs in this river."

"Izzy, come on–"

"No, Coop, I don't like this. It's stupid." Izzy turned and swam back towards the dock, skin tingling with the sensation that something just under the surface swam with her, right behind, just below, catching up.

"Come on, Izzy, it's okay! Come back!"

"We should get out, right now." She reached the dock and grabbed the edge, pulled herself up. She couldn't help wincing as her legs came up out of the water, imaging a long, scaled snout shooting up with her, snapping shut, teeth crushing into her flesh.

But she rolled onto the rough, weathered wood and turned around, water dripping off her. She pulled her knees to her chest, arms wrapped tight around them. "Coop?"

He was nowhere to be seen.

She stood. "Cooper! Stop playing about!"

She imagined him ducked under the water, ready to pop up laughing, deliberately scaring her. She waited.

"Cooper!"

She turned and looked down either side of the jetty, remembering him grabbing her from behind earlier. It would be just like him to swim underwater, come up elsewhere and try to scare her.

"Cooper Cook!" she yelled, heedless of who might hear her, appalled at the terrified waver in her voice. "Do not mess with me, Cooper! I'm not in the mood." Still staring over the water, she dragged her shorts back over her wet legs, pulled her top back on and stepped into her thongs.

"Cooper!" She hurried off the jetty, along the bank to where she'd felt… something. "Cooper!"

No answer. No movement but for the river's sluggish crawl towards the Coral Sea miles and miles away. She startled at a ripple out towards the middle of the wide, deep river.

"Coop?" Her voice was weak now, hopeless. Despite the near-summer warmth, Izzy began to shiver. Her knees gave way and she sank down to the dock, trembling with fear, eyes locked on the black waters.

Chapter 2

Sam Aston paused his slicing of fish and looked out over the main tank of the new Sea Life Aquarium. The sharks and rays in the big tank with tunnels running back and forth underneath would be hungry. Tourists walked through the tunnels, their forms distorted by the curved glass, staring up in wonder at the underwater world all around them. They looked strangely captive from this vantage point, the sharks and other fish the free and unfettered ones. Aston loved this aspect of a public aquarium, parts the public never saw. Maybe he'd put on the mail suit and swim with the sharks today, feed them by hand, entertain the crowds. It had been a while since he'd done that, and he always enjoyed it. He found it calming, therapeutic even. And this new facility on Kangaroo Island in South Australia had all the best gear. It might not be the real marine biology he was trained for, but it was a good job, the right kind of environment. He'd work towards more scientific and conservation work as the place became better established. He already put forward several research proposals and applied for some grants. He had every intention of turning Sea Life Aquarium into Australia's premier tourist and science aquarium. They'd hired him for his greater knowledge, after all.

But above all else, he was glad to be home. Well, not home exactly. South Australia was a long way from the Queensland coast he considered home. But he was back in his country and finally out of debt, out of trouble. For the moment, he chided himself with a wry smile.

"Hey, Sam!" Greg Chanter said as he walked by behind.

"Hey, Greg!"

Home and using his real name again too, a double pleasure. He'd spent a long time pretending to be a man called Pete Cartwright while hiding from Chang, and the mountain of cash he owed the man and his criminal organization. All that was done with now. He hadn't felt so relaxed in as long as he could remember.

Footsteps rang softly on the metal gantry behind him and before he could turn, someone grabbed him around the waist.

"What the hell…" he managed, as he twisted in the grip, then he was smothered by a kiss, long dark hair swinging into his face. Happily, heart hammering, he returned the kiss, then leaned back to look into Jo Slater's deep green eyes. She was only a couple of inches shorter than his six feet.

"Hi," she said huskily, smiling.

"I didn't think you were back until the end of the month."

"We wrapped early. Sometimes it goes like that. You want me to disappear again and come back in two weeks?"

"Hell, no!" Aston leaned forward, kissed her again. "It's so good to see you."

"You should have come along, Sam." Slater stepped back, looked out over the water of the huge aquarium habitat. "It was so beautiful there and we saw some crazy stuff."

"Crazy?"

She laughed. "Well, not Sam and Jo crazy like Kaarme or Alpha Base. Let's hope we can avoid that kind of crazy for a long time. But cool stuff. You ever seen a Komodo dragon for real? They're huge!"

"They really are, huh. But I'm happy here. For the first time in a long time, Jo, I feel like I belong. Like I have a new purpose."

She nodded, smiled. "I get it. I guess you'll just have to put up with me disappearing frequently on shoots. You'd better behave every time I'm away."

Aston kissed her again. "I will. I love you, you mad intrepid adventurer."

"Love you too! And you'll come with me sometimes, right?"

"Of course. As often as my leave from this job allows."

"Good. What time's your break? Want to get lunch?"

Aston glanced at the Victorinox dive watch on his wrist. "Another forty-five minutes. You want to wait around that long? We can head to the canteen then. They do some pretty good stuff and I'm staff, so it's free."

Slater opened her mouth to answer but was interrupted by Aston's phone ringing. He pulled it from his pocket and though there was no name attached to the calling number, his heart skipped. He recognized it all the same.

"I'm sorry, Jo, but I need to take this."

Slater nodded, though her eyes were narrowed. She must have caught his reaction.

He tapped the call answer icon. "Hello, this is Sam Aston."

"Sam, hi. It's Sophie." There was a slight pause. "Cook."

Aston felt like he'd been doused with ice water. His Sophie. From the old days. "You okay?" he asked. "You sound rattled. Gotta say, I didn't really expect you to call any time."

"I need your help, Sam."

Aston frowned. "Okay," he said cautiously. "What's up?"

Slater tipped her head to one side, narrowed eyes sinking into a frown of concern.

"It's Cooper," Sophie said. "He's missing."

"Your kid brother?" Aston remembered Cooper as little more than a snot-nosed adolescent, annoying as hell, but the kid was probably close to an adult by now. "Missing?"

"I need you to help me find him, Sam. The authorities are… Well, they're not helping."

Sophie sounded at her wit's end. But why the hell was she calling him? "Isn't this something for the police?" he asked, watching Slater's frown deepen. "The parks department, at least? How can I help you?"

Sophie barked a derisive laugh. "You know what the cops are like up here, Sam. But that's not the point. Cooper went missing in the river. The authorities have sent out a couple of rangers in a tinny but they don't have the resources to make a proper search. And the police have listed him as a missing person, but he's got a history with them. Just a few drunken spats, nothing really, but they're acting like he's just run away. But he hasn't, Sam. He was swimming with Izzy and she said he vanished."

"Okay, okay, slow down." Aston had no idea who Izzy was, but the whole thing sounded like a debacle. He had no idea how he might help really, but if Sophie had resorted to calling him after all this time, she had to be desperate. "You called anyone else?"

"Only people in town, Sam, and you know what that's like. Please, I would never call if I though there was anything else to do. I need your help. I need someone who can dive. And I need someone who cares. You still care, right?"

"Yes, of course I do." He wasn't sure how he felt, if he were honest. Sophie and Blacktooth River were ancient history, best forgotten. He hadn't considered his hometown home since he'd moved to the coast. But it was history nonetheless and there was a time he cared a lot for Sophie. "Okay, sure, no worries. I'll come."

"Today?"

Aston blew out a breath. He'd hardly been in the new job five minutes, could he take time off so soon? He had already built up a lot of good will, maybe he could spin it. "Sure, as soon as I can, okay. I'll call you when I have more plans."

"Thank you, Sam! Thank you! Come quick!"

"I will." He hung up and turned back to Slater. "Sorry, I'm going to have to take a raincheck on lunch."

"Yeah, I gathered that. What's going on?"

"I have to go home." Funny how he'd only been thinking moments before that Kangaroo Island was Australia but not really home. Now he was suddenly planning to head up to far north Queensland after all.

"Home? Queensland?" Slater's face fell. "I only just got back," she said.

"I know, I'm sorry. It involves an old friend."

"More than a friend, I'd say, judging by how that call went and the look on your face."

Aston nodded. "Yeah. It's complicated. But hey, I reckon I could use some help if you're willing to come along. If I'm honest, I could use your support."

Slater hesitated. "Well, I was going to talk to you about this over lunch, but another reason we wrapped early is because a possible job came up in Chile that I don't want to miss out on. I'm waiting for a call about that later today or tomorrow."

"Oh, okay. I guess I wasn't expecting to see you for a couple more weeks anyway."

Slater laughed, but it was good-natured. "Sam Aston, you look like a whipped puppy."

He couldn't help a grin. "I miss you, that's all. And it would mean a lot to me. Things always go bad one way or another when I go back home. I promised myself I'd never go back again, but... You can take that call anywhere, right? And if you have to rush off, I get it. Your job is important."

Slater nodded, kissed his cheek. "Of course, I can take that call anywhere. And if necessary, work can wait. Let's plan a trip."

Chapter 3

Aston and Slater stepped from the air-conditioned comfort of their hired Nissan Pathfinder 4WD and into the thick heat of Blacktooth River. Humidity slammed around him like a hot, wet blanket. It was strangely nostalgic.

"Oof!" Slater glanced at Aston, one eyebrow raised. "This is hotter than Cairns."

"Yeah, well, we've driven six hours from the airport, and most of it north! Welcome to the tropical top end."

Aston still felt like Cairns and the coast north and south of it was home to him. The home he'd chosen. But there was no denying this was ancestrally his home. Where a person grew up would always be encoded in their being. This even smelled like childhood. He shuddered, despite the heat. He really didn't want to be here. With any luck, they'd get away again very soon.

Slater looked up and down the long, wide street. There were no curbs. Wide-bladed grass grew right to the edge of the bitumen on both sides. Palm trees lined the road a few meters back, with more trees – gums, mango, avocado, numerous others – dotted here and there in between the weatherboard buildings, corrugated steel roofs reflecting the mid-afternoon sun. "So this is where you grew up," Slater said.

Aston nodded, lips pursed. He'd never stated it outright, even in the privacy of his own mind, but he realized he'd made a subconscious pledge to never return to Blacktooth River. Now he'd been called in and the place hadn't changed a bit. "Yep. This is what made me. And it's what made me leave."

Slater laughed, but it was a slightly uncomfortable sound. "You going to be okay?"

Aston shook himself, smiled. "Yeah, I'm good." He wasn't a kid any more. The ghosts of the past were just that. Ghosts. Ephemeral and harmless.

Several shops lined the street, starting just after where Aston had pulled up. A crossroads a little further along was just visible. A few battered utes and SUVs were parked here and there, a handful of people walked the pavements. Aston pointed to the crossroads. "Dock is that way, just past the other end of town. Come on." He climbed back into the Nissan and when Slater had sat beside him, he started it up and drove to the crossroads, turned right. Another short street of interspersed houses and shops led them to another T-junction, the road ahead running along parallel to the wide, brown Blacktooth River itself. Aston turned left and a couple of hundred yards along there the old wooden dock stuck out into the sluggish water for about ten meters. A couple of tinnies were tied up there, and a Queensland National Parks boat, that one sleeker, fiberglass and chrome and quite new-looking. It was a hell of a boat for a sleepy backwater like Blacktooth River. Diagonal parking bays lined either side of a small car park on the other side of the dock before the road curved away from the river, back into the rainforest. All the parking bays were empty except for one with a battered old Mazda ute parked in it, and next to that a Toyota Landcruiser with a Queensland National Parks logo on the door.

Aston couldn't help a laugh. Slater looked at him, one eyebrow raised. He pointed. "That ute, it's Sophie's car. Still the same one. She must have had it more than a decade. See that dent in the driver's door? That's when she lost control on a wet road one rainy season and went sideways into a power pole."

"Why do you call them utes?" Slater asked.

"It's short for utility vehicle. You call them pick-ups, I suppose?"

Two people stood at the end of the wooden dock, watching as the National Parks boat cast off and moved slowly out into the middle of the river. Aston and Slater sat in the Nissan looking towards the dock. The two figures turned and Aston's heart skipped a beat, seeing Sophie Cook for the first time in a long time. She looked good, but her eyes were distraught. That was obvious even from this distance.

"That's my friend," he said. "It's her brother who's missing."

From the corner of his eye he saw Slater smirk at the word 'friend'. Sophie had brown straight hair, cut into a shoulder length bob, brown eyes to match, and her figure was as good as Aston remembered. She wasn't especially tall, but had curves in all the places he liked.

"Who's the other one?" Slater asked.

Beside Sophie was a young girl with a waterfall of black ringlets and chestnut brown skin. She was young, beautiful, but her large brown eyes were sad too, her mouth downturned. She would be about the same age, Aston estimated, as Sophie's brother, Cooper.

"I'm guessing that's Izzy."

"And who's Izzy?"

"Don't know. But Sophie mentioned her when she called."

"You are just full of useful information, aren't you? Come on, let's go," Slater said.

They climbed from the hire car and walked along the wooden dock, faces immediately sheened with sweat from the close humidity. Sophie smiled, then her eyes widened and she took a half-step backwards as she saw Slater walking alongside Aston. Slater made a soft huff of… what? Aston wasn't sure if it was amusement or annoyance. Maybe both.

"Sam," Sophie said, overcoming her surprise. She came to meet him and they hugged, a little stiffly. Aston was intensely aware of Slater standing right behind him. He suppressed a grin at the absurdity of it all.

"Hi, Sophie. This is Jo."

The two women nodded and smiled at each other and Aston looked away, determined not to be entertained by their wariness. He should probably have made it clear that his friend who was in trouble was his ex. Well, hindsight was 20-20 and all that.

"Nice to meet you," Slater said. "I'm really sorry it's under circumstances like this."

"Me too," Sophie said. "But good to meet you too."

The moment of tension had passed, Aston realized, at least between Jo and Sophie. But his ex still looked at him with guarded caution.

"Thanks for coming so quickly," she said.

"You're welcome. A friend in need and all that."

Sophie half-smiled, awkward.

"You want to fill us in on the details?" Slater asked.

Aston glanced quickly at her, then back to Sophie. How had it so suddenly become difficult between him and his ex while Slater was cool as a cucumber?

"Let's talk to Izzy," Sophie said.

They walked together back to the young girl at the end of the dock as she watched the boat trawling slowly back and forth.

Sophie put a hand gently on her shoulder. "Izzy, this is the friend I told you about, Sam Aston. He's a diver, a real pro. And this is his friend, Jo." Sophie seemed entirely comfortable introducing Slater as his friend, without needing any other information. Aston supposed that was probably entirely natural. He chided himself at how unnecessarily difficult he often made things when it came to people, especially women.

Izzy smiled at them both, but it was a small, sad thing. "Thanks for coming."

"Why don't you tell us what you know and we'll see what we can do?" Aston said.

Izzy explained about meeting with Cooper two nights before, how they'd ended up cooling their passion in the river. Aston said nothing about the foolishness of swimming in the Blacktooth at night, especially this near to summer. He'd done the same things himself as a kid. People in croc country somehow managed to get incredibly blasé about the dangers and it was usually tourists who were taken if anybody was. This close to town, to the dock, they should have been fairly safe. At least in the daytime. Night swimming? Maybe not so much. But it was well past the point of assigning blame. Twenty-twenty hindsight again.

"The only thing I saw once he disappeared was a big ripple in the middle of the river," Izzy said, finishing her tale with a gasp and half-suppressed sob. Her eyes were wet with unshed tears.

"Have any divers been out?" Aston asked.

"National Parks came out with a police diver yesterday," Izzy said. "They did a brief dive right around here, but didn't find anything. Sophie called Parks back and insisted they search more, but the police haven't come back. They don't care about us." She gestured to the Parks boat slowly plying the water near the far bank. "He's been cruising up and down, but I think he's only humoring us, mainly because he likes Sophie. What does he expect to see from there?"

Sophie made a humorless sound of derision. "That's probably true. Says he's looking for evidence, but he's just killing time. I think everyone's given up already, Sam. It's why I called."

"We really want someone who gives a damn to take a proper look," Izzy said. "A professional."

Aston gave what he hoped was a reassuring smile, then gestured to Slater standing beside him. "Well, you've got two of them," he said. "My girlfriend and I make a good team, I promise. And we're both experienced divers." He wondered why he phrased that so awkwardly the moment it was out.

"Sam's the pro diver," Slater said, flicking him a sidelong look. "But I'm good backup. We'll do whatever we can to help."

"Thank you!" Izzy said. Aston was pained at the hope in her voice. Honestly, he thought the most likely thing they would find would be remains if they found anything at all. The rivers and surrounding forest teemed with scavengers that made short work of remains, human or otherwise. Maybe Izzy knew that too. She was local, and smart enough, it seemed. Perhaps she just needed closure. He couldn't blame her for that. And hope sprang eternal, until it was dashed with evidence.

"We'll get out of your way," Sophie said, throwing a quick glance at Slater. "You know where to find me."

"You haven't moved?"

"No, I'll be at home. Izzy will be with me, or at her house which isn't far from mine." She patted Izzy's arm and the women walked away, climbed into Sophie's Mazda.

Slater watched them go, then turned to lock eyes with Aston. "Did you bring me here just to get one up on your ex-girlfriend?"

"No!" Aston said, confused by her crooked smile. Was

she enjoying his discomfort? He'd expected her to be the uncomfortable one, but he had been nervous since they left Kangaroo Island. "I really wanted you to come along. Honestly. Everything's better when you're around." He paused, allowed a cheeky grin to spread. "But I did enjoy seeing the look on her face when you came walking up."

Slater slapped his arm. "Men!" she said, and stalked off back towards their car.

Chapter 4

Russell 'Rusty' Crews sat in his office, heels resting on his desk, and stared disconsolately out the window at the late afternoon sun slowly sinking behind the high, rainforested hills to the west. He sighed. Nothing ever happened in this backwater town, his life was draining away like swamp water, and what did he have to show for it? Basically nothing. He rested his hands, fingers interlaced, on his round belly, straining the buttons of his Park Ranger's shirt. He was still a strong man, still as large as he'd ever been… well, larger, if he was honest. But there had been a time when he'd been powerfully muscled, a rugby league legend, heading for the big time. He'd been scouted, signed up to train with the Townsville Blackhawks. He knew, somewhere deep inside, that he'd wear the Queensland maroon one day, clash with the Blues in a State of Origin match. He was be a big deal, headed for glory.

Then a sideways tackle, that big bastard coming in low, popped his knee out. That sound, the sharp crack of tearing cartilage followed by the searing rush of pain, and that was it. He'd literally heard his career end. He walked with a barely perceptible limp these days, but the major leagues fled from his future at that awful moment. He should have been someone. And now here he was, still in Blacktooth River, chief ranger sure, but of the smallest and most poorly funded park in Queensland. Most people had never even heard of it. His knee ached, like it always did when he thought about what could have been. What should have been.

And all this melancholy, he knew, was because that idiot Cooper Cook had got himself taken by a croc. That was the most likely explanation, at least. Something finally happened in Blacktooth River and there was not a damned thing he could do about it. It would only drive a wedge further between himself and Sophie, probably, which was the last thing he needed. Every time he thought maybe they were finding common ground again, something stupid happened. And well, things didn't come much more stupid than Cooper Cook. Maybe he could use it to offer sympathy to Sophie, though. Find a way to turn it around, get back into her good graces. At the very least he needed to stop lamenting his lost past. He'd had the boat driven up and down all morning to appease her, but what did she expect them to find? The river was so muddy you could hardly see the bottom in most places.

There was a rapid knock at the office door and before he could say anything, it swung open and Craig Gomzi stepped in. Talking of stupid things, Rusty thought tiredly.

Blacktooth River National Park, home to the river and town of the same name, had a two-man team on its National Parks roster. Literally one other person aside from Crews himself, and it had to be this idiot. Oh well, at least he'd find out where things stood with the Cooper Cook situation.

"Rusty," Deputy Ranger Gomzi said. "How ya goin'?"

"Same as ever. You got an update for me?" He took his feet down and sat forward, elbows on the desk.

"Steve Jackman is missing half a goat," Gomzi said, slumping into the chair on the other side of the desk.

Crews winced, looking away from the half-exposed ball sack visible up the leg of Gomzi's overly loose Parks-issue khaki shorts. The man's clothes were always a size or so too big and Rusty had no idea why. Surely Gomzi had mirrors at home. "Half a goat?" he asked, doing nothing to mask his confusion.

Gomzi nodded, ran one hand back over his short-clipped blond hair. He was a wiry man, short and skinny, but with a kind of corded strength about him. But there wasn't a single thing about the man that wasn't as annoying as hell. "The man says he found one of his goats cut in half. Everything behind the front legs was gone. Looked like it had been bitten in two, according to Jackman." Gomzi grinned, crooked teeth on display, and lifted his palms as if to say, What are you gonna do, eh?

"A damned goat bitten in half?" Crews asked.

"That's what he said."

"An adult goat?"

"Apparently."

Crews had been expecting an update on the search for Cooper Cook. Gomzi had been out in their one boat all morning and again all afternoon, supposedly searching. What the hell was he on about half goats for? "When did you talk to him?"

"Rang me just now while I was driving back here. Said he was pretty concerned and what are we gonna do about it?"

"What are we gonna do about his half a goat?"

"About whatever it was that bit it in half, specifically." Gomzi shifting, fully exposing the other half of his saggy scrotum.

Crews sighed, looked away again as he scratched the top of his rapidly balding head. "I suppose I'll have to think about that," he said eventually. Even a croc, a big one, wouldn't bite a whole goat in half. Take a goat, sure, if it was close enough to the water. Grab it, roll over with it then jam it under a fallen log to tenderize it, eat the poor animal later. Which is probably exactly what had happened to the unfortunate Cooper Cook, for that matter. But bite it in half? No croc was big enough to do that even if it was so inclined.

"Apparently one of the Abbott brothers is missing too," Gomzi said around one finger as he absently chewed on the nail.

"What?"

Gomzi took the finger from his mouth. "Apparently one of the Abbott brothers is missing too."

"Yeah, I heard you. What do you mean by missing?"

Gomzi shrugged. "Bob Daley said Mary Collins told him in the pub that Terry Abbott has been missing for two days."

"Two days?"

"Yep."

"Well, that's a concern for the police." Crews laughed. "I'm guessing they won't be calling the cops though. Not really their people, after all." The Abbots were meth cookers and dealers who lived in the bush right at the edge of park property. They kept largely to themselves, so Crews didn't care about them. If the cops ever cared about them, it was unlikely to involve Parks anyway. "I expect Terry was probably killed in a deal gone bad. No loss to the world there. A shame, it wasn't his brother, Rhys. He's the real SOB out of that lot. But what about the search for Cooper Cook? Coming in here talking about half-goats and missing meth-heads!"

Gomzi nodded, took a deep breath. "Well, we had a good look yesterday. Police divers checked the immediate area in the afternoon but found nothing. They've issued a missing persons, said it will almost certainly end up marked as accidental death after the requisite amount of time has passed. They don't give a hoot any more. I spent this morning with a couple of local fishers and we dragged the river as best we could about five hundred meters downriver from the dock. Got nothing but logs and a couple of rusty

IGA shopping trolleys. I spent all afternoon searching the far bank, looking for any clues or signs, but found nothing. Not even really anything croc signs, to be honest, but of course, one could easily have just swum downriver to the jetty. I don't reckon we'll ever find anything. The body has probably been washed away on the current and predators or scavengers have already gotten to work on it, or if a croc did take it, he's wedged in an underwater locker somewhere, getting nice and decayed for the croc's lunch another day. Idiot should know better than to swim at night."

Crews scowled. He hated to admit it, but he agreed with everything Gomzi had just said. It sound like his deputy had done everything and done everything right. This situation was bad. He'd never liked Cooper but he didn't wish the kid dead. Cooper only had himself to blame though, really, even if he was just bloody unlucky. How was Crews supposed to talk to Sophie about it? He'd loved Cooper's sister once. Hell, maybe he still loved her. She'd loved him too, but he felt fairly certain that ship had sailed. He wondered if he'd ever be able to win her favor again. If he was stuck in this arse of a town, he should at least have one of the best lookers for a wife. Didn't he deserve that? Sophie was smart and interesting too. Surely there had to be a way to turn this to his advantage?

Gomzi unfolded a tabloid newspaper, the North Queensland Gazette, and flattened it out on the desk, then turned it to face Crews. The headline on the front page was about a new development north of Cooktown and the furor around its environmental impact. Under that was a picture of a huge red kangaroo and the headline, What Really Happened in Morgan Creek?

"Why are you showing me this garbage rag?" Crews asked. "It's all bullshit and conspiracy theories."

"It's not!" Gomzi said vehemently. "My brother was killed by that feral roo. I told you all about it."

Crews nodded, remembering. The entire town had apparently been decimated by some monstrous kangaroo gone rogue. The whole thing was ridiculous, but Gomzi's brother had indeed died. Crews suspected it was a mass murderer and the local authorities were covering it up with the insane roo story because the killer was still on the loose, but what did he know? Or care? It wasn't even in this state. "Yeah, I'm sorry for your loss," he said perfunctorily. "But why are you showing me now?"

"Not that," Gomzi said. "This."

Crews looked to where Gomzi's finger stabbed a small article at the bottom of the front page.

Ned King's New Bio-theme Park Gets Opening Date.

"That arsehole," Crews said. "Why do we care about that?"

"Just that if his new park is opening, that means media coverage. You know what he's like for self-promotion. And if the media are here and we have an unsolved missing persons case…" He let the rest hang in the air between them.

"Or a juicy half-a-goat mystery," Crews said sarcastically.

Gomzi's eyes widened. "Oh yes! That too! And the Abbott brother missing. Things are hectic around here at the moment."

Crews shook his head. The man was right to be concerned, but he never could tell the difference between reality and a joke. Craig Gomzi himself was a joke. "It could be bad publicity for Blacktooth River National Park, is that what you're thinking?" Crews asked.

"Don't you reckon?"

Crews reluctantly nodded. "You could be right. I

wonder if we should ask the police divers to search further downriver just to be sure. Or call in another dive team."

"Ah! Well," Gomzi said, grinning. "That's where I can give you some good news."

"Is that right?"

"Yep. There's already a new dive team on the scene."

"What the hell are you talking about?"

Gomzi shrugged. "Some old friend of Sophie's. Apparently she called and he came running." He scratched his head. "Steve someone? Ashton? Something like that?"

Crews slapped his hand on his desk, suddenly furious. Gomzi sat back hard, startled. "Sam Aston?" Crews asked through clenched teeth.

Gomzi nodded, made double finger guns across the desk. "That's it. Sam Aston. Nice guy, very friendly. And you should see the sheila he's with." Gomzi whistled and made an hourglass shape with his hands.

Crews barely noticed his deputy's approval of this mystery woman. "Sam Aston," he said, mostly to himself. "This is not going to be good."

Chapter 5

Afternoon drew towards evening, the visibility under the canopy of the rainforest dropping quickly into darkness. The air was heavy, damp with humidity and humming with mosquitoes. JD crept along behind his brothers, watching their backs as the two conversed in low tones, following the bank of the Blacktooth River away from where they'd left their tinny a few hundred meters upstream. He was happy to follow, let Rod and Dicky take the lead. They were the experienced reptile poachers, after all, and they never let him forget it. He was surprised they'd finally agreed to even bring him along this time.

"Come on, Jack Daniels," Rod said over his shoulder, and both older brothers giggled like idiots.

JD ground his teeth but didn't rise to the bait. Their father had named him after the drunken idiot's favorite beverage, and it constantly rankled. So of course, his brothers regularly poked at that particular open wound. Jack Gibson was fine. JD was fine. If he was honest, that's what he preferred. But both his brothers almost always used the full Jack Daniels, just to piss him off. He could understand it more from Dicky. After all, the middle brother had no middle name and Dicky wasn't even short for Richard. Or anything else. He'd been christened Dicky by their weirdly overbearing mother, and even their father hated that. The fact that breast cancer had taken their mother not so long ago probably didn't help. Dicky's very name was a constant reminder of her. It was a terrible name. So Dicky deflecting to JD made a kind of twisted sense. But Rodney Gibson, the eldest brother who should have set a better example, was only too happy to join in. In fact, more often than not, he started the verbal bullying. That bothered JD more than anything else. His eldest brother should look out for him, but both brothers seemed to hate him, more often than not barely tolerating his existence. Then again, they had finally let him come along on a hunt, so perhaps he should suck up the digs and the insults and make the most of it.

"Dad should be here," Dicky grumbled. "He's better at tracking."

"We don't need him," Rod said. "He's already drunk, and he's planning to knock off that new tool kit from the back of the tractor service center after dark, remember?"

Dicky laughed. "Who'll be drunker, Dad or Jimmy Bars?"

"Jimmy is always drunker, even in the morning."

"What if they get caught?" JD asked.

Both his older brothers stopped and turned to look at him.

"Caught?" Dicky asked.

"By who?" Rod said. "There's no alarms, cops probably wouldn't come anyway. Who gives a shit?"

JD shrugged, abashed. Jimmy's surname wasn't Bars, but that's what everyone called him because he kept going to jail for petty theft, driving offences, drunk and disorderly charges, a variety of other charges. So sometimes someone gave a shit. JD wasn't fond of his old man, but he didn't want him arrested. Apart from anything else, it would mean he was alone in the house with his two bullying brothers. Whatever faults his father had, the man did look out for JD. He'd named his youngest son after his favorite drink for a reason, after all.

"Dad'll throw Jimmy under the bus if necessary," Rod said. "That's the only reason he's taking him along. You think he really needs that idiot to boost a tool kit?"

JD shrugged, looked away.

"Now, stop cocking about, " Rod said. "We're inside the boundary of the national park now. The chances of anyone finding us are next to zero, but if someone does collar us, we're in big trouble. This stretch of river, about five hundred meters each way, is our best bet. Let's split up. JD, you go down to the bank here and work your way along. Dicky, you run on ahead another hundred meters or so and start there. I'll go further still and work my way back. We'll eventually meet up again. If no one has found a nest, we move further and do it again, right?" His brothers nodded. "If you do find one, don't go near it, just coo-ee. The others will come and then there's two lookouts while whoever found the nest gets the eggs." He hefted his rifle for emphasis. "Got it?"

Dicky nodded and scurried off through the low bush. Rod looked at JD. "Think you can manage this, Jack Daniels?"

"Yes, of course I can."

JD turned away and started walking before Rod could goad him any more. He heard his oldest brother laugh, then head off along the river.

JD kept his rifle across his chest at port arms, the safety off. Truth be told, he was terrified. This was madness, deliberately heading into croc country, but the money on the black market was good. He knew Rod would want to bag the mother croc too, not just the eggs, to sell for leather and meat. He hoped for that reason tonight's hunt would prove fruitless. Still, if he wanted his brothers to start taking him seriously, he needed to show them he had the right stuff. But his hands shook. He planned to shoot any croc dead on sight, and long before he got anywhere near a nest. He moved slowly, deliberately giving his brothers time to reach the water well ahead of him. He could come running as soon as one of them gave out a coo-ee and not have to do anything but stand guard that way.

It was close to pitch dark under the rainforest canopy as the sun began to drop below the highlands to the west. JD clicked his headlamp on, keeping it on the red setting to avoid startling wildlife. The trees were bathed in a bloody glow as he crept slowly forward. He heard a low splash and stopped dead. Probably just a fish jumping. He swallowed, sweating in the humidity but shivering at a chill that ran up his spine all the same.

He listened hard. Come on, he thought, willing his brothers to find something so they could regroup.

Something rustled through the bush dead ahead of him. His hands began to tremble. The rustling grew louder, something quite large pushing bush aside as it moved through. JD crouched, trying to home in on the direction of the sound. A branch snapped, the sound sudden and stark in the night.

JD gasped, turned, looked side to side. Something dark moved between two trees off at his eleven o'clock. He froze. More rustling, another branch snapping. He half lifted his rifle up in front of him and began to rise from his crouch. He saw movement again. "Christ on a bike!" he whispered, staring in disbelief.

A large, ape-like creature pushed through the foliage, back hunched, arms at its side. One hand carried a huge wooden club that dragged through the damp leaf litter. It looked like a gorilla, but the face was all wrong somehow, even though it was indistinct in the night, bathed in the red glow of JD's headlamp.

"A yowie?" he croaked, in stunned disbelief. The yowie was a legendary apelike creature, Australia's answer to

Bigfoot and the Yeti.

He turned and fled, inconsiderate of any noise. "Rod! Dicky!" he yelled as he ran.

Branches snapped as the beast came lumbering after him. JD began to cry, sobbing as he gasped for breath, branches and vines whipped and slapped at his face, roots grabbed at his feet. He tripped and fell, heard the thumping feet and grunts of effort from the beast right behind him. He felt eight again instead of eighteen, helpless and in a blind panic.

He hauled himself up, realized he'd dropped his rifle but didn't even glance back. He drove forward headlong, yelling his brother's names again and again, as the yowie thundered after him. Pouring with sweat, gasping for breath and close to passing out from the effort, he was forced to slow. The sounds of pursuit, he realized, had ceased. He stood still, looked around himself, drawing great shuddering breaths as his heart slammed against his ribs.

He was alone in deep rainforest. He had no idea where he was, even what direction he'd run. Not towards the river, that was all he knew, as he could neither see nor hear it anywhere close. He thought he'd been running towards his brothers, but couldn't hear them either. Had the thing already got them first? A yowie? Was it even possible? To think he'd been concerned about crocs when the real threat was something most of the country didn't even believe in. But he'd seen it, clearly. And he'd dropped his rifle.

Thinking perhaps the river was directly behind him, if he had indeed run away from it, he decided to turn back at an angle to find it again further upstream. If he managed to get back to the edge of the park, find where they'd tied up their boat, he could wait there for Rod and Dicky. And if they didn't show after, what? An hour? Then maybe he'd fire up the small outboard and head home, get Dad, come back to find them. His dad would know what to do.

He wasn't going anywhere back in the direction of whatever that creature was, that much was certain. He couldn't believe he'd lost the rifle. They'd all give him endless shit about that. He turned and started walking back in what he hoped was the direction of the tinny.

The yowie, more than a foot taller than him, covered in brown shaggy fur, its ape-like face split in a feral grin, stepped out in front of him, its club raised high. JD managed a constricted scream before the club swept down and everything went black.

Chapter 6

"**Maybe I'll do** one more," Aston said, rubbing at his eyes. He was bone tired, the hot sun and humid air sapping his strength even as he rested on the riverbank.

"You sure?" Slater asked. "You're exhausted. We left yesterday, drove and flew and drove and you've been going flat out ever since."

"I know, but I feel like I need to do as much as I can as quickly as possible. The amount of scavengers in an area like this? If there is anything to find, we need to be quick. Honestly," he added in a low aside. "We're probably already too late."

Slater looked out over the sluggish river, eyes narrowed as the afternoon fell towards evening and the light began to soften. "You expect to find a body, though, don't you? I'm mean, you're not looking for evidence he disappeared, or survived somehow?"

"If we find anything, yeah, it'll be a body. Or part of one. People don't go missing in places like this because they get lost in the bush, or because they underestimate the size of the desert like in West Australia. Those are wide open spaces and people get turned around. Here? People get taken."

"Damn."

"So. One more dive. I'll go a little further downstream. You coming in again?"

Slater nodded. "Always safer with a dive buddy, right? You taught me that."

Aston smiled. "Come on then."

They moved another hundred meters down the bank and slipped into the water. The edges were fairly steep, but still the toes of their fins clipped fallen trees and other detritus. The water that looked like coffee with milk in the sun, impenetrable to the eye, was clearer once they were in, masks in places. Tannins from the rainforest tree roots made the water more the color of black tea. Silt drifted thickly, swirling clouds around their hands as they moved. They both wore wrist-mounted flashlights with powerful LED beams, that pierced the gloom with white swords of light. Leaves and bugs and larvae of all kinds twitched and reflected their light back at them, fish shot past in flashes of silver.

Aston moved slowly along the near bank, looking for a fallen log with the right amount of room underneath that a croc might use as a meat locker. The creatures had a habit of stuffing their kills into small places to tenderize the flesh. He hoped he wouldn't be faced with some grisly discovery, but he also knew Sophie would be more upset if he didn't find anything. Losing her brother was terrible, but finding his body would at least provide a measure of closure. Not knowing? He thought that was probably worse. And it would always lead to the hope that maybe, somehow, he'd come back. That sort of thing could wear on a person's soul.

Once he'd searched the steep side of the river, Aston signaled Slater and they began a zig-zag pattern across the riverbed, heading for the opposite bank. They'd quickly established a kind of method, and Slater's main role was watching for crocs to make sure they didn't end up the way they suspected Cooper had. She would frequently surface, scan around for movement, come back down to check on Aston, repeat. All the time he was deeper, looking more closely at the riverbed, she would turn slowly right above him, scanning the silty water. She'd mentioned the whole thing was making her nervous as hell, and he couldn't blame her. These were dangerous waters. But they were also pretty close to town and the chance of an encounter with a croc was unlikely. Though far from impossible, as it seemed poor Cooper had discovered. Aston had laughed when Slater said she was sure she could hear the two malevolent notes of the Jaws theme every time she stopped paying attention.

"That's a shark, not a crocodile," he said, when she thumped him on the arm for laughing.

"So what's the theme for a croc then?" she asked.

Aston launched into the "Never Smile At A Crocodile" song from the old Peter Pan movie, and for a moment the mood lightened. But the seriousness of why they were here quickly settled over them again, and the search continued.

The sun must have dropped below the tree line, Aston realized, as the gloom under the water deepened. They needed to be out of the river soon. He swept his light over twisted roots and logs, blackened and slick, stained by tannins and years, even decades, underwater. Maybe Cooper hadn't been taken by a croc. Did he get tangled in something like this and drown, desperately clawing for the surface above that he could see but not reach? Unlikely, given Izzy had said the young man had stripped off before diving in. What was there to get tangled?

Did he dive to prank Izzy like she'd first suspected and strike his head? Then lay dazed in the water not knowing which way was up until his lungs filled and darkness closed in forever. More possible, but still unlikely. Aston was, he knew, desperately trying to envisage a situation that wasn't a croc attack, because there was something so primevally terrifying about that possibility. Unchanged since prehistoric times, perfect killing machines, gliding effortlessly through the water, opening wide jaws that would clamp inexorably shut, leaving a person with no possible chance of escape.

Growing up here, Aston had seen his fair share of the huge reptiles. He'd swum in the river, here and other places, acting carefree like all immortal teenagers while inside he quaked at the thought of swift, scaled death. Croc attacks were rare, locals knew that and always laughed at tourists and their fears. There was nothing Aussies enjoyed more than scaring foreigners with stories of all the things on land, sea and air in Australia that could kill you. That wanted to kill, especially enjoying the taste of European and American flesh. Euros always tasted like roast pork, and Americans like sausages, was the theory. The best white meat you can get, the local indigenous folks always used to joke.

"That's why I always swim with you, Sam," Aston's teenage mate Clifford always said. "Crocs prefer white meat, so I'll get to swim away while he chomps on you!"

Clifford had died in a car accident when the boys were both only seventeen, and Aston still carried some guilt. It wasn't his fault, but he'd been a part of it, that fateful night. He shook off the thoughts. He needed to concentrate. Attacks were rare, sure, but they did happen. Caution and vigilance were key. That's what kids were always taught.

Something green and bright shot towards him from the left and he jumped, let out a muffled cry around his respirator, but it was only a fish. A hell of a big one, sure, but just a fish. He only caught a glimpse, thought it was probably a jungle perch. He didn't realize they got that big. Must be good water around here.

Heart hammering, realizing he'd been lost in thought, scanning the riverbed on auto, Aston looked around for Slater. She was about twenty feet away on his left, holding herself in place, staring hard. Her outline was blurry at the distance, veiled by the drifting silt, but her body language made him curse. She'd found something. As he thought it, she looked up, spotted him, and gestured frantically.

Shit, Aston thought, and kicked over to her, bracing himself for what he might see. He looked to where she pointed and his heart sank. In the murky water, shadowed by the thick Y-shape of a fallen tree limb, he made out a cylindrical object, maybe thirty or forty centimeters long, pale, almost yellowish. The kind of color human flesh would go in these waters after a short while submerged. White flesh anyway. The tastier kind, according to poor old Clifford. And this looked just like white flesh, in the form of a human forearm.

It was wedged under the wood and Aston moved closer, trying to see where the arm became a wrist and then a hand. How was he going to break this to Sophie?

He swam closer, bit hard against the respirator as he reached out to take a hold of it, twist it to pull it free.

The thing thrashed, whipped around and the end opened up into a surprisingly large mouth packed with razor sharp sharp teeth to snap at him. He whipped his hand away, bubbles escaping with his cry of alarm, as the short-finned eel twisted around itself and shot away into the gloom.

Aston tried to calm his racing heart, cursing his carelessness. Slater was right, he was tired and carrying on was becoming dangerous. Besides, it was late in the day, almost dark. Slater reached out, squeezed his arm and gave him the okay hand sign, her eyes wide and concerned in her mask. She looked sorry too, for leading him to the scare. Aston nodded and gestured up. Time to call it quits for the day.

Chapter 7

JD woke slowly, his head pounding. Spikes jabbed repeatedly behind his eyes and he felt as though he were floating. His heart rate seemed strangely elevated. Had he been drinking? No wait, he was out with his brothers, hunting. Had he fallen into the river? It was so dark, his stomach flexed with nausea. He realized his eyes were still closed despite consciousness returning and he cautiously opened them. It was still almost as dark, but he made out the shapes of tree branches and leaves, a deep indigo sky in between. Something skittered over his bare forearm as he lay on the loamy ground, sharp insectile legs, but though he was aware of it, tensed because of it, he couldn't move to do anything about it. His arms were up above his head, thrown back when he'd fallen. His head throbbed with pulses of blinding pain.

He tried to gasp in a breath, his chest constricted with fear, tears leaking from his eyes. Memories returned slowly, coming out of the mist of his confused mind. A yowie. Its club. Had that been real? His injuries would suggest it was.

As he recalled that wide, leering face, huge furry hands wrapped around his wrists and he was suddenly being dragged. He yelled, somewhere between a scream and shout to stop, as sticks and leaves and dirt gathered in the waistband of his shorts. His heels bounced along the ground. He wanted to fight, to struggle, but his body was jelly, his head a pounding confusion of pain, he was sure he would vomit at any moment.

He tried to cry out again but only managed a croak this time, that sent new spears of agony through his brain. Where was this thing taking him? He tried to twist around, to see his captor, but his head swam with the movement, his vision crossed. He caught glimpses of ruddy fur that looked like shagpile carpet in the low light.

Then he heard voices shouting his name. Rob and Dicky, yelling for him, not with concern in their tone, but anger. He didn't care, at least they were near. It gave him strength to pull back against the hot, hairy hands dragging him along. Despite the surge of pain, he sucked in breath and yelled out. "Here!"

It was barely audible, weak and cracked, but loud enough to carry. Whether his brother would hear or not he couldn't be sure, but still the yowie dropped him. As he slumped to the ground, grunting with a new bolt of pain in his head, he heard it running away through the rainforest, heavy, stamping paces quickly receding. He lay there a moment, trying to get a deep enough breath to call out. Finally he managed another weak, "Here!" And then again, a little louder. He rolled onto his stomach and now the vomit came, hot and liquid, bitter like bile. Coughing it out made his head pound anew and tears fell from his eyes.

As the wave of nausea passed, he sat back slowly, head spinning with dizziness close to vertigo. He thought he would fall down again, but managed to balance himself on his knees, sitting on his heels. Something ran over his cheek from above his left eye. He dragged the back of one hand across his face and it came away red with his blood. He had been badly hurt. Was he in danger of more than a headache?

His brothers emerged from the trees in front of him, and stopped, staring.

"The hell happened to you, Jack Daniels?" Rod said eventually.

Dicky stood back, disdain painted all over his face, as

Rod came nearer and crouched down. He squinted at JD's head. "Quite a whack you've had there, dickhead."

JD swallowed, tried to take a breath, but new nausea prevented him from speaking. He felt that if he tried to say anything it would only come out as more vomit. He stared at his eldest brother in dismay.

"You reckon someone can walk off a belt on the noggin like that?" Rod asked over his shoulder.

Dicky laughed, nodded. "Yeah, 'course they can. Unless they're a complete pussy. Get up, wuss. Walk it off."

They both laughed then and Rod grabbed JD's wrist, put his other hand under JD's armpit, and hauled him to his feet. The world tipped sideways, the trees all around seemed to flex and swim. JD took two steps forward then barfed once more.

Rod danced to one side just in time to avoid it and threw a string of eloquent curses at JD. Dicky laughed even harder. Why were they so bloody amused by all this? JD hated them sometimes, really hated them.

But this time the puke had steadied the world around him just slightly and JD managed to take a couple of fuller breaths. His head still pounded, his legs were weak and shaking, but he stayed standing and thought that was something of a Herculean feat in itself.

"You gonna throw up again?" Rod asked.

"Don't... think... so..."

Rod frowned, shook his head. "Come here, Dicky, get his other arm."

Dicky made his displeasure with that arrangement abundantly clear, but he did as Rod told him all the same. The two brothers draped one arm each over their shoulders and half walked, half carried JD along between them.

"Hell of a concussion you've got there, little brother,"

Rod said. "And you'll probably need stitches, but that's your problem for later. You bloody idiot, what did you do?"

"Was… a yowie," JD said.

His brothers both howled with laughter.

"A yowie!" Dicky said. "That's the sort of thing you see after a whack on the head, not before!"

"Seriously. Huge, hairy… and brown. Had… a big club. Wooden… club."

"Are you drunker than Dad?" Rod asked, still laughing. "A fucken yowie hit you on the head with a bloody club?"

"You're tripping, Jack Daniels," Dicky said. "Was probably one of the Abbotts. Those meth heads are little more than apes. We've had enough run-ins with them over the year."

"Don't be stupid," Rod said. "Why would they be out here and why would they whack Jack Daniels with club? Actually, I heard one of them went missing. Murdered in a bad deal, I wouldn't doubt. It's not the Abbotts. Jack Daniels here is confused, can't remember things straight. You got lost again, didn't ya, dickhead? Freaked out and came running like a baby, straight into a tree. That's what happened, eh? Cracked your stupid head on a low tree branch, and then you dreamed of yowies."

Both brothers devolved into laughter again. Anger swelled through JD, but he was having enough trouble simply putting one foot in front of the other and had no energy to argue. Let them think whatever they wanted, he knew what he'd seen. If they'd have been a few seconds earlier finding him, they would have seen it too, dragging him along behind itself. It didn't matter. What mattered was the thing was gone and his brothers had him safely in hand. With any luck they'd all be back home again soon.

It seemed like hours, but was probably no more than ten

minutes, before they came back to the river and their small metal boat tied up to a fallen tree that lay half in and half out of the water. Rod helped JD in and he sat on the middle bench. The gentle rocking of the tinny did nothing for his nausea, but he was certainly glad to not be standing any more. Dicky sat on the small bench at the back and Rod sat in the narrow prow. Dicky whipped the rope up and over to unhook it from the stubby branch, then shoved the craft clear of the bank. JD felt as though he were recovering his wits a little as Dicky pushed hard against the fallen tree to set them drifting out into the middle of the river.

"I'm telling you, it was a yowie," JD said. "Bloody huge, face a bit like a gorilla, but not exactly. Kind of a gorilla crossed with a bear." He scrunched up his face in thought. The face had seemed wrong somehow, not entirely right in some indefinable way. The darkness, the fear, then the whack on the head, all combined to make recall difficult.

"Gorilla crossed with a bear!" Dicky said with a hoot of laughter. "In Queensland!"

"Shut up," Rod snapped.

"Oh, come on," Dicky said. "You don't believe him do you?"

"Shut up!" Rod said again, his voice hard, eyes scanning left and right over the water. "Something's out there."

JD immediately thought of the Yowie and looked to the riverbank, wondering if the things could swim. Would it be able to reach them in the boat now they were five or six meters from the bank? But Rod's face had hardened, his eyes had that steely intensity that both brothers knew brooked no interruption. He got that look from their father. They sat watching as Rod watched the water in a tense silence.

Something bumped the bottom of the boat.

Dicky frowned, JD suppressed a gasp. He began to feel

sick again.

"Underneath us?" Dicky breathed.

Another bump, harder this time. The tinny rocked slightly.

"Dicky," Rod said quietly. "Get us the fuck out of here, bro."

Dicky dropped the outboard down into the water and yanked the starter cord. The motor coughed to life and he cranked it up to full. Normally they puttered along, not straining the small Honda BF2.3 four-stroke. It was barely over 50cc and pushed them along comfortably enough at a slow walking pace usually. Nobody was in much of a rush in Queensland. But now Dicky had it howling and it still seemed slower than swimming. JD chewed his bottom lip, breathing down the nausea. No matter, they were moving, that's what counted. And the angry sound of the motor would surely scare away any animals that might have shown an interest in them.

Then the motor sputtered and fell quiet. The boat drifted. Rod looked at Dicky with fury in his eyes.

"Shit," Dicky said.

"You didn't fill the tank." Rod's voice was dangerously quiet. It wasn't a question. JD remembered Rod telling Dicky to fill the tank from the can in the tin shed, about an hour before they planned to leave. Dicky had said, "Yeah, yeah, I'll do it," but had carried on playing GTA on the PS4. He'd obviously forgotten.

JD looked from one to the other and back again, then stopped moving his head as another wave of nausea washed over him. Dicky sat silent, lips pressed into a flat line.

"I told you to fill the tank," Rod said. "It was the only thing I asked you to do before we left."

"Forgot," Dicky said weakly.

"You prick." Rod looked over the water again, taking out a large Bowie knife from its sheath on his belt. Dicky had his rifle across his knees. JD thought maybe they hadn't noticed yet that he'd lost his.

Rod stood, the boat wobbling and lurching to one side. JD had a vision of Rod stumbling, disappearing into the murky water, but he bent his knees and steadied the boat, squinting out across the river. He was no stranger to their tinny, had been using it with their dad since he was a toddler.

The night was still, almost full dark and silent. Even the usual sounds of nightbirds and the susurrations of insects were absent. The boat hardly moved, almost as if even the river held its breath. JD wondered how far away they were from the nearest habitation. There probably wasn't another human soul for miles around.

Rod slowly sat down. "Dicky, change places with JD and row us to shore."

He called me JD, JD thought numbly. He must be really preoccupied. Not preoccupied, his hindbrain whispered. Scared. And if Rod was scared, JD was terrified.

"Why me?" Dicky said.

"Because you're the idiot who forgot the petrol."

"Jack Daniels should do it–"

"He's got a bloody concussion, you dill. Look at his head bleeding! Start rowing!"

JD and Dicky clumsily changed places and Dicky picked up the wooden oars from the floor of the boat, locked them into place, and started rowing. He stared daggers at JD as he leaned and pulled, leaned and pulled, thankfully able to use the slow current to help them along.

"I reckon we must be close to the park boundary," Rod said. "Head for the bank. We'll tie up the boat and hike home. You can walk back with a petrol can tomorrow and fetch the tinny."

Dicky grumbled under his breath but angled them in towards the shore.

Something bumped hard underneath the boat again. All three froze, Dicky sitting forward with the oars up out of the water, dripping.

"Keep going!" Rod hissed.

Dicky grunted in fear and redoubled his rowing efforts, face a grimace of effort. JD almost leaned over the side to help paddle with his hands, then imagined what might grab him and pull him in, and quickly sat back up. His head swam again. I have got to stop moving, he thought miserably.

They closed in on the shore with agonizing slowness, despite Dicky's furious effort. JD watched the muddy bank draw nearer and nearer. He finally drew a breath to say, "Nearly there!" when something smashed into the boat from beneath the stern. The tinny flipped up and over and suddenly JD was airborne, arms and legs flailing for one heart-stopping moment before he splashed down into the warm water. Despite its warmth, the water was a shock to his system. He gasped, then coughed as he sucked in the silty water. The coughing made his head pound anew and he thrashed around, heedless of his thumping head, and his shin cracked into something hard. The pain made him look down and he realized it was a tree branch. The riverbank was only a couple of meters away. Thankfully he'd been thrown towards the bank, not the middle of the river. He drove his foot down onto the hard wood and leapt forward, splashed into water and mud and in moments was crawling on his hands and knees on solid ground.

He dragged himself several meters from the river then turned, sitting with his hands behind himself, trying to blink away the shards of agony blinding him. He sucked in breaths, desperately suppressed nausea. Dicky stumbled from the water nearby. The tinny was upside down, back out in the middle of the river, its belly a silver curve in the night. Rod was nowhere to be seen.

"Rod!" Dicky yelled.

"Rod, you there?" JD shouted.

They looked at each other, then out over the water again.

There was a splash and some bubbles from the edge of the upturned tinny. JD and Dicky both flinched, then Rod popped up from under the boat. His face was twisted in anger. "Pair of dickheads!" he spat at them and started swimming hard for the bank.

A V-shaped ripple appeared in the water zipping toward Rod. It was between him and the riverbank and JD yelled out a warning. Rod turned and swam fast back towards the boat. Did he intend to climb onto it? Try to right it and get back in? There was no time!

In his fear-fueled, concussed state, JD had trouble processing what he saw. Something huge surged up out of the murky water. Dark and scaled, massive beyond imaging, with giant teeth and loud, snapping jaws.

Everything fell still and silent once more. JD used both hands to clear river water and tears from his eyes, then stared in shocked disbelief. His brother was gone. He wanted to believe he'd imagined it, maybe tonight was all about imagined monsters. Perhaps he was home, in his bed, dreaming nightmares. But their boat sat crooked in the water with a gaping rip in the gunwale right where Rod had been aiming for. What kind of creature could take a huge bite like that out of a metal boat? And that massive, deep-headed thing was unlike any croc JD had ever imagined. He looked at Dicky in dismay.

His brother sat in the mud, face pale as the moon, shaking his head slowly side to side. "Let's get the hell out of there," Dicky said. "No, Jack Daniels! Bloody run!"

Chapter 8

The Black Stump Restaurant was nearly empty when Aston wandered in. It was a small place with simple décor and a menu to match. Burgers, meat pies, sausages, and chicken parmigiana. The special of the day was lobster ravioli, probably from the frozen foods section of the nearest supermarket. None of it sounded appealing. What he craved was a drink. He took a seat at the bar and ordered Scotch whisky.

Only one other patron sat at the bar. He was a powerfully built man of early middle years. His chestnut hair was bisected by a line of gray running through the center like a part. He stuck out like a sore thumb, but that was no worry of Aston's. Their eyes met and Aston did not miss the way the fellow took a fraction of a second to look him up and down, assessing him, before giving a curt nod of greeting to which Aston replied by raising his glass.

"To drinking alone," Aston said.

The corners of the man's mouth twitched and he raised his own glass. "Always."

"Is that Samuel Aston?" a voice called.

Aston grimaced. He had chosen the Black Stump because he figured the locals would all be hanging out at the pub. Apparently he was wrong.

A tall, skinny man with a high forehead and ears like satellite dishes sat down on the barstool next to Aston. He wore a cheap suit and his breath stank of cigarettes and poor dental hygiene. Some things never changed.

"Hello, Rhys," Aston said.

Rhys Abbott was a lowlife. In their youth, he was in

constant trouble with local authorities for a variety of low-level crimes like burglary and selling weed. Aston doubted the man had changed his ways in the intervening years.

Abbott clapped him on the back. "Sam Aston! Little white Sambo! How long has it been?"

"Not long enough."

Aston heard a little chuckle from the man at the end of the bar. Rhys flashed an angry glance at the man, then returned his attention to Aston.

"You always had the sharp wit," Rhys said. "Kind of a bully with it if you ask me."

"Bully? I wasn't the one committing strong-arm robberies in the toilets."

Rhys shrugged. "I picked on weaker people; you picked on dumber people. My therapist explained that to me."

"You have a therapist?" Aston asked.

"Court appointed. A little misunderstanding with one of my science labs."

Aston nodded. So it was meth. No surprise there.

"What are you doing back in town, Sammy boy?"

"Just helping a friend with something." Aston took a sip of whisky and wished the man would go away.

Abbott flashed a sly grin. "You heard about Sophie's brother. You trying to get back into her good graces or back into her pants? Or both?"

Aston gritted his teeth and mentally counted to five before replying. "I'm here with my girlfriend."

Abbott made a show of looking around. "I don't see her. Is she like that 'girlfriend' you had in Cairns back in the day?" He bracketed the word in air quotes. "The one who went to another school."

"She's back in the hotel. She had work to do." Aston wondered why he was explaining himself to this moron. "If you'll excuse me, I'd like to enjoy my drink in peace."

"Still the same prickly fellow you always were. You probably don't even care that Terry up and disappeared. He's probably dead." Terry was the older of the Abbott brothers and by far the cleverer and more vicious of the pair.

"One down, one to go," Aston said.

Abbott froze and he glared at Aston. "You still think you're better than everybody else."

"Not everyone. Just some people." Aston half hoped the man would take a swing at him. He could use an outlet for his anger and frustration. This town held nothing but memories of pain and loss for him.

Abbott smirked. "I'll find better company to drink with. Maybe Pepe LePew down there will buy me a round." He slid down off the bar stool and approached the big man at the other end of the bar. "Hey, skunk hair. I'll have what you're having."

The man didn't look up.

"Don't take it personal. Just having a little fun," Abbott said. "Just looking for a drinking buddy. I had a recent family tragedy."

"Go away." There was ice in the man's words.

Abbott was not about to be rebuffed twice. He jabbed a crooked finger in the man's face. "Listen here, White Stripes…"

The man struck like a viper. He seized Abbott's skinny wrist in one hand, and with the other, he bent Abbott's index finger backward. There was a sharp snap and Abbott let out a shriek of pain. The big man gave him a shove that sent him flying into a nearby table, then returned to his drink as if nothing had happened.

"You son of a bitch!" Abbot sprang to his feet and drew a combat knife from inside his jacket.

Now he had White Stripe's full attention. Calmly, the man abandoned his seat and adopted a fighting stance. Aston could tell by the way the man moved that Abbott was in big trouble.

"He wants to be left alone," Aston said.

"Screw you, Sambo. He can't disrespect me like that."

"I don't want any trouble in here," a thin voice squeaked. The bartender, who also happened to be the owner of the restaurant, was a short, round man with curly hair and squinty eyes. Aston couldn't recall his name. Clive something. He was holding a cricket bat, but showed no signs of coming out from behind the bar. "Rhys, if you don't leave, I'm going to call the authorities."

"Do it, Clive. And I'll tell them what you sell along with your carry-out orders."

Clive blanched. "There's no call for that."

Abbott turned to say something else to Clive. That was when White Stripe attacked. He feinted a right cross and then jabbed Abbott in the eye with the extended fingers of his left hand. Taken by surprise, Abbott yelped and lashed out with an awkward slash of his knife that cut only air. With a sharp kick, the man sent the knife flying, then followed with an overhand right that buckled Abbott's knees and sent him crumpling to the floor. But White Stripe was not satisfied. He grabbed Abbott's collar, lifted the woozy man's head off the floor, and struck a vicious blow to the temple.

Aston had no use for any of the Abbotts and firmly believed the world would be a better place without them, but he would not sit by and witness murder. And a couple more punches like that would be the end of Rhys Abbott.

"Hey!" he shouted. White Stripe glanced at him, then drew back his arm to deliver another blow. Aston hopped down off of his stool and tackled the larger man. They hit the ground hard, scrambled to their feet, and came up, each ready to defend himself.

"Let it go," Aston said.

But the man wasn't ready to let it go. Instead, he tried the same feint he'd used on Abbot. Aston easily danced out of the way and countered with a jab that caught the man on the chin, then followed with a sharp leg kick. Seizing on his brief advantage, Aston pinned the man against the wall.

"Just stop. He isn't worth the calories you'd burn punching him, much less the jail time," Aston said.

"It was self-defense. No jury would convict me," the man said. Aston could tell the fellow had a lot more fight left in him and he wondered at his chances of getting the better of the big stranger again.

"This is a small town and his family has connections. You'd die mysteriously in your cell, probably before morning." Aston was bullshitting, but he really didn't want to fight this guy.

"Just go. Your drink is on the house," Clive pleaded, his voice reedy.

"I don't know what your business is in Blacktooth River, but I'm sure it didn't involve crooked cops and a family of meth cookers," Aston said.

"Alleged," Rhys slurred. He was conscious, but still lying on the ground. All the fight had gone out of him.

The man took a long look at Rhys, then his eyes met Aston's. Finally, he relaxed.

"Let me go."

Aston released him and took a couple of steps back. To his relief, the fellow showed no sign of wanting to continue the fight. The man reached into his pocket, withdrew a fat roll of cash, and peeled off several large bills. He strode over to the bar and held the cash out to Clive.

"We don't need to tell anyone about this, do we?" It clearly wasn't a question. Clive nodded eagerly and accepted the money. The man took a moment to drain his unfinished drink before departing. He locked eyes with Aston on the way out, but did not speak.

When he was gone, Clive let out a breath like a punctured tire. "Thanks, Sam. Next round is on me."

"I appreciate it, but I'd better be going. I've got an early morning tomorrow." As he headed for the door, Abbott called out to him.

"You know something? Crews is right about you. Wherever you go, there's trouble."

Chapter 9

Craig Gomzi cruised his daily patrol along the Blacktooth River in their new Sailfish Catamaran S8. The snub-nosed trailerable fishing boat was about the only thing of any value in the entire national park, beyond the wonders of nature. Gomzi still wasn't sure how Rusty had managed to convince the Queensland government to finance it but their old launch was literally sinking every time he took it out, so it wasn't like they didn't need a new one. He was glad he didn't have to stop every few minutes to bail out the one thing that kept him separate from whatever else might be in the water. The new launch was nearly eight meters long with twin Honda outboards and more power than he'd ever need on the river, but it was fun too. He longed for a chance to take it much further upriver where there was less boat traffic and he could open up those twin engines. But Rusty was unlikely to allow that.

"Someone in an office somewhere had a budget they needed to spend," Crews said with a wink when Gomzi had asked how the hell they'd scored such an expensive new toy. "Always ask for new gear right before the end of the financial year, son. People will go to many lengths to avoid paying taxes and to make sure they don't get a budget reduction the following year. You can take that advice to the bank."

This boat was Gomzi's office and he loved it. Rusty was happy to sit on his arse in the ranger hut, feet on the desk, dreaming of past glories, but Gomzi was an outdoors kind of man. That's why he'd become a ranger in the first place, after all. He couldn't bear the thought of spending all day, every day trapped inside to earn a living. He knew he wasn't the most capable ranger, but he loved his job and he always tried to do his best. And if he did it well enough, Rusty would continue to sit on his arse all day and stare out the window, lamenting all he'd lost. Gomzi had no idea why the man didn't do something else. Honestly, if Gomzi had to sit through another retelling of Crews' footie glory days... Well, it suited him fine. Rusty in there and himself out here, and the park pretty much took care of itself ninety-nine percent of the time. However miserable Crews might be, Gomzi considered himself a lucky man.

He did feel bad for Sophie Cook, though. Losing her brother like that was awful. Having fairly recently lost his own brother, Gomzi could relate. The New South Wales government seriously needed to start being more honest about that killer kangaroo and what happened in Morgan Creek. No roos here in the rainforest, killer or otherwise, but if it happened there it could happen anywhere, right? Bloody weird business from start to finish. Rusty reckoned it was really a person, a serial murderer, not a roo, and Gomzi couldn't help wondering if there was something to that. Something bloody fishy was going on, that much was certain. Here though, and Cooper Cook? That was just bad luck. The dumb kid should know better than to swim in the river, especially alone, especially at night. Well, not alone, that young cracker Izzy had been with him. But two teenagers out that late at night, it was asking for trouble. What happened to sneaking off into the trees and canoodling like in in his day? Then again, Gomzi thought ruefully, he'd been dumb enough to get in the river at night when he was younger too. Perhaps Cooper Cook had just been unlucky.

Gomzi's rambling thoughts were interrupted by sun glinting off something up ahead.

He killed the motors and drifted silently up to the

wreckage of an old tinny, half-submerged in the middle of the river. A fallen tree, little more than a silhouette in the murk, was just visible below. It looked as though the capsized tinny had caught up on it, preventing it from sinking or moving further with the slow-flowing river. Gomzi frowned. He recognized this battered old thing. Or what was left of it, at least. It belonged to the Gibsons. He'd chased them off in it a few times over recent months. Always sneaking around the park, those rednecks, usually trying to poach one thing or another. Gomzi had heard tell they did a decent trade in crocodile eggs, and skins too when they could. It looked like they'd had a hell of an accident this time. He scanned around, half-expecting to see a battered corpse washed up on the riverbank. But there was no one about, both banks of the river empty and still, the rainforest marching away into shadowy gloom despite the belting sun that hit him, exposed as he was in the middle of the river.

This tinny was more than simply crashed or flipped, though. A massive, ragged hole in one side made Gomzi's blood chill. How was that possible? It looked as though something had taken a huge bite right out of the side of the boat. Something inconceivably large. And how powerful were the jaws to be able to crush the aluminum like that? Long, deep cuts were carved into the metal either side of the hole, and Gomzi imagined great long teeth punching in, carving those lines until the jaws met and a chunk was torn clear. He stared, trying to think what could cause this kind of damage and nothing made sense, except some gargantuan beast. And of course, that made no sense. There were no gargantuan beasts in Blacktooth River National Park. The biggest croc he'd ever seen in these waters was a monster at around seven meters, but even that thing had a jaw a fraction of the size of the hole he stared at. Something yellowish-white wedged low in one of the splits in the metal caught his eye.

He leaned over the side, reached out to take a grip of the exposed whiteness. Like bone, he thought absently. It took some effort, working it up and down, to eventually free it from the metal. He held it up, glistening in the morning sun.

"Holy shit," he whispered. He turned and ran to the radio, keyed the signal. "Rusty, you copy?"

There was static for moment and he was about to key again when Crews answered, voice thick. He'd obviously been caught napping. Again. "Yeah. What's up?"

"Rusty, you gotta get out here. Right now!"

Crews drove the Toyota Landcruiser along a rough fire trail through the rainforest, the big car easily chewing up the bumps and rain channels. Blacktooth River National Park might be about the smallest national park in Queensland but it was still a massive area of land. Everything in Australia was a massive area of land. Hell, they had sheep stations out west bigger than a lot of countries. But despite the size, Crews prided himself on knowing every inch of his park. With his Landcruiser and a GPS he could put himself wherever he chose to be with ease. Gomzi might think Crews was a useless office dweller, but the kid had a lot to learn. Though even with Crews' excellent geographical skills, it would be a bit of a hike from the fire trail down to the river at the coordinates Gomzi had given him. It had better be worth it.

Gomzi had sounded pretty agitated, but the man was easily geed up. He once nearly had a heart attack when a possum got into the bins behind the office one night, sure they were under attack from some monster. The bloke needed to rein in his imagination.

Crews watched the GPS tick over to the spot he needed, then pulled the Landcruiser to a stop. He sat enjoying the AC for a moment more, then, with a sigh, killed the engine. He climbed out into the oppressive humidity, grimacing as he started the kilometer or so hike down the shallow decline to the river.

Within a hundred yards he was puffing and sweat stuck the shirt to his back. His head was a furnace under his Akubra hat. Bloody Gomzi better have found the holy grail down there. He paused as he caught sight of a clump of reddish fur caught on a low, broken branch.

Crouching, he had a closer look. It was glossy and seemed fake to him, reflecting the sun like man-made fibers. He looked around. Hell of a strange thing to find this deep in the forest. He'd worry about it another time. He pulled it free and stuck it into the thigh pocket of his shorts and trudged on.

He noticed occasional footprints in the damp mud where it wasn't covered by leaf litter. A few confused boot prints, but also marks of weirdly large bare feet. They seemed comical in size, way too wide, even though they had the general shape and five toes of a human print. There'd been some hectic activity around here, and quite recently.

Crews noticed a dark spatter across a couple of low, wide leaves nearby and had a closer look. Blood. He took a step back, heart speeding up. That was definitely blood. What the hell had been going on here? What kind of creature had been killed to spray blood like that? He slowly turned, scanning all around, mouth suddenly dry. Sweat trickled into his eyes.

More cautiously, deeply discomfited, he carried on down to the river. Gomzi looked up from the boat as he emerged from the trees. The Sailfish was moored to a nearby stump, Gomzi slumped in the driver's seat under the shade of the canopy, waiting.

His eyes narrowed. "You okay, Rusty? You look spooked."

Crews stabbed a thumb back over his shoulder. "Saw a few things back there." He pulled the fur from his pocket. "Found this, too."

Gomzi's eyes widened and he nodded like he'd seen the answer to everything. "I have it on good authority there have been some reports of yowie sightings in the area."

"Good authority?" Crews asked, letting the sarcasm drip from his words. "You mean Dutton in the pub and internet conspiracy theory forums?"

"Nah. Well, not just that. More people than just old Dutton anyway. I mean, he's a mean old racist prick, but he's been around here a long time. Besides, other people too. Less…" Gomzi shrugged. "Less stupid people."

Crews stuffed the fur back into his pocket. "Yeah, well. Whatever. It's something for another day." He looked past Gomzi to the wrecked tinny, now pulled up on the muddy bank. "Bloody hell!"

"Right? I told you!"

The damage was extensive, more even than Gomzi had led him to believe over the radio. His mind moved immediately to sabotage, because he had trouble believing any kind of wildlife could have done that. "You think KIND might have done this?"

Gomzi tensed, his face angry. "What makes you think of those bloody tree huggers?"

Crews sniffed, thinking, putting together a better

theory. "This is the Gibson's tinny, right?" Gomzi nodded. "Well, the Gibsons are poachers and KIND hate poachers. They hate anyone that even looks at an animal wrong. And they've been around these parts a little bit lately."

"I would think an online petition would be more their speed," Gomzi said. "Some campaign of the triggered." Then his face fell into a more serious expression. "But anyway, I think you're barking up the wrong tree. I've got something to show you."

He hopped down off the boat and handed Crews something. It took him a moment to understand what he was seeing, a smooth, ivory-colored spike the size of a large banana. It appeared to be a huge crocodilian tooth, but that simply wasn't possible. Not something this size. He barked a laugh, shoved the thing back to Gomzi.

"It's a fake. Has to be. Probably planted here by the same people who left the yowie fur." He was relieved by his sudden surety that people were faking everything until he remembered the blood on the leaves and his certainty wavered for a moment, but he pushed on regardless. "It was probably somebody from one of your conspiracy groups."

Gomzi didn't rise to the bait, shook his head. "Take a closer look, boss." He handed the tooth to Crews again, pointed to the root of it. There was small amount of tissue attached to the thick end of the tooth where it had been wrenched free when it was caught in the metal side of the tinny. The organic material was clearly very fresh, washed free of blood by the river, presumably, therefore pale, but still pink. Crews poked at it with his fingertip. It flexed, uncannily convincing, moving exactly like he'd expect flesh to move.

Crews frowned, unable to deny that this huge tooth appeared to be authentic after all. He looked up to the younger man, still standing above him in the back of the new boat. "We need to pay some people a visit, Craig," he said.

Chapter 10

JD Gibson watched out the window as Crews and Gomzi drove away in their grubby Landcruiser. A swirling cloud of dust from their passage floated lazily over the dirt driveway, then slowly settled with hardly any breeze in the hot, humid day to take it away. JD's left eye was swollen almost shut from the massive swelling around the cut above it. He still had symptoms of a concussion, recurrent nausea, slightly blurred vision even in the good right eye. But it was at least a little better than it had been the previous night. The headache remained, however, a sickening pounding behind his eyes that no amount of Paracetamol seemed to change. He did need stitches, he was sure of that, but the nearest hospital was a long way away and the Gibson family had a bad history with the local doctor. So he'd settled for stick-on butterfly stitches they had in the medicine cabinet. It was a shoddy job, and would result in a hell of a scar that regular stitches might have prevented, but it held the wound closed. If he was careful, it would heal eventually.

Of course, the state of his head was the first thing Crews had asked about when the rangers turned up. Regardless, JD had stuck to their story, refusing to admit anything to the two busybodies. No, none of the brothers had been anywhere near the river the last few weeks. Their tinny had been stolen right off the trailer in their driveway a few days before. They had no idea who by. Oh, and this bump on the head? Just an accident at home, that's all. A garage was a dangerous place, after all.

"Who takes the boat and not the damn trailer?" Crews had demanded, pointing to the ute parked by the shed with the trailer still attached. But JD and Dicky had simply shrugged, refusing to be drawn into any further explanation.

"Where did you get the injuries?" Gomzi had asked again, presumably thinking he was being clever by repeating himself.

"Tackle box fell on his head in the garage," Dicky said quickly, his glare daring anyone, even JD, to contradict him.

"Sure it did," Gomzi said with a sneer. "Must have been a tackle box full of bricks, eh?"

"Maybe we should talk to Rod?" Crews said. "Seeing as your old man isn't here, perhaps the oldest brother will make more sense."

"Gone away for a while," Dicky said.

"Gone away?"

"We've got rellies near Darwin. Rod went for a visit."

"That right?" Crews said. "And when do you expect him back?"

Dicky shrugged again. "Bloke goes walkabout, he doesn't make a particular plan to come back. Might be days, might be weeks."

JD thought that was laying it on a bit thick. As if rednecks like the Gibsons ever went walkabout. And clearly Crews didn't believe him. Even that dumbshit Gomzi saw right through it. But there was nothing they could do about it since there was no evidence to the contrary.

And now they were gone, with nothing to tie the Gibsons to any incident. They'd have to officially report their tinny as stolen, Crews had said, but what was the point, Dicky had snapped back. "Given you blokes have done a wonderful job of finding it already and according to you it's wrecked. Not like the thing was insured, so who would we tell? The bloody cops are corrupt as hell and next to useless anyway, so thanks for everything and have a nice day. Don't let the door hit you on the arse on the way out."

"We should have told them more," JD said, turning away from the window.

"Most definitely not. Involving the law only ever complicates things."

"Not the cops. Them. They're park rangers, Dicky. They're not the law."

Dicky made a sound of disgust. "They're just as bad as cops, only without a gun or any real authority. They'll cause us grief, you mark my words."

"Rod is dead, Dicky."

"I know that, ya prick! You think those two galahs can do anything about it? You think anyone can bring Rod back?"

"I just think people should be warned about... whatever that thing was." JD closed his eyes, tried to breathe past his throbbing head. He would give anything for just a few minutes respite from the headache that stabbed constantly.

Dicky turned away, his entire body tense. JD recognized his older brother's mood, spoiling for a fight because he didn't have the answers he wanted. But JD couldn't let it go.

"Seriously, Dicky. Don't you think people should know?"

"Why should we have to tell anyone? Eh? It already got Rod. Let's stay the hell out of it. People will find out without our help, I'm sure."

JD was quiet for a moment, then said, "What was it?"

Dicky turned back to him, face thunderous, but didn't speak.

"My head was spinning," JD said. "Water in my eyes. I couldn't see anything clearly, but it looked... it was so big, Dicky."

"I didn't see much either," Dicky admitted eventually.

"Flung up in the air, water in my eyes too. I just concentrated on getting the hell out of there."

JD stared at him, willing him to say more. Even just a speculation.

"But yeah, it was damned big," Dicky said at last.

The door banged back and their father strode in. It was immediately obvious the man was drunk, even at this early hour of the day. "Bloody Jimmy Bars is such a useless c–" he started, then his eyes fell on JD. "The bloody hell happened to you?"

"Tackle box fell on my head," JD said disconsolately. He was in no mood for one of his father's tirades.

"Where's Rod?" Ray Gibson snapped.

"The Jews took him," JD said sarcastically.

Ray slapped him and JD's head swam like his brain had been hooked out by a fly fisher. He stumbled and fell sideways onto the sofa, a wave of nausea rolling over him. He rolled onto the floor, gasping, then slowly rose to his hands and knees. He sat back on his heels, trying to breathe some equilibrium back as Ray turned to Dicky and asked again, "Where's Rod?"

He looked from Dicky's stricken face to JD and back again, and his eyes narrowed. "What's happened?"

"Rod's gone," Dicky said, face crumpling.

JD hadn't seen his older brother cry since they were all in their early teens, but he thought the young man might now.

"Gone?"

"We had a really bad night last night," Dicky said.

"Gone as in dead?" Ray Gibson demanded. "Are you trying to tell me Rod is dead?"

Both brothers nodded and Ray collapsed backwards into an armchair, eyes wide in disbelief. "What the bloody hell happened?"

"Start at the beginning," Dicky said, looking at JD.

JD frowned, thinking, Why me? He dragged himself up on the sofa and leaned back, then turned his head slowly to face their father. "This wasn't a falling tackle box, Dad. There was something in the bush. I reckon it was a massive yowie. Hit me with a club!"

"A yowie?" Ray's face was a furious grimace of confusion. "Don't be a dickhead, JD. Probably those arsehole meth cookers, the Abbotts. They're a bunch of animals, great big hairy idiots."

"Definitely not one of the Abbotts. Anyway, that's not really the point. Because I got hurt, we went back to the boat, abandoning the hunt to come home. But something attacked the boat."

"Attacked it? A croc?"

Both brothers nodded, and JD said, "But not just a croc. It was a giant, Dad. A monster! Seemed like it was ten times the size of even a big saltie. And it took Rob."

"Bloody hell." Their father stared at the floor between his feet for a moment, elbows on his knees, then he looked up. "How big exactly? They reckon they only get up to about five meters, but I saw a seven-meter bastard near here once when I was a teenager. They get big."

"This thing would make a seven-meter croc look like a caiman," Dicky said quietly.

Ray seized Dicky by the throat and slammed him up against the wall. Dicky stood nose to nose with his father, staring hard into Ray's rheumy eyes. His father's breath reeked of whiskey and stale coffee.

"Liar!" Ray growled. "You boys have always been jealous of Rod, so you did something to him. Admit it!"

Dicky usually caved in the face of his father's wrath, but

not today. "I am not lying," he said. "I wouldn't lie to you about something like this."

"And we would come up with a better cover story than a croc that looks like something out of Jurassic Park," JD added.

Ray frowned, looked from one son to the other. Dicky watched as anger melted into confusion and then dissolved into something like fear. Ray spun Dicky around so he was facing a framed black-and-white photograph of a grinning man holding a rifle and kneeling beside a dead elephant.

"Swear it to your granddad." Ray thrust a finger at the photograph.

Dicky couldn't give two shits about a man who would sneak into a zoo for the sole purpose of killing an elephant, although he admired the fact that the Gibson patriarch had gotten away with it.

"I swear it."

"So do I," JD added.

Ray took a step back, swayed slightly, then found his balance. "Whatever the hell it was, I'm not going to let it live. I plan to find it and I'll have new pair of boots from its bloody hide in memory of my Rod!"

Chapter 11

Karen Rowling waved the last of the tourists goodbye and said joyously, "Spread the message, conservation is everyone's responsibility. Remember to be KIND!" She emphasized the last word heavily to remind them who she was. Who the organization was. It was a cheesy line, but it worked. As soon as their backs were turned, the smile melted off her face. A sense of relief washed through her. She hated the public persona she had to maintain for tour groups, but the organization needed the funds, so it was a necessary evil. She would never enjoy it though.

She turned back to the main building of the KIND Conservation and Research Centre on the edge of Blacktooth River National Park and stepped inside to the welcome air-conditioned comfort. It was going to be a hell of a summer, already starting to swelter and it was only early November. Summer didn't officially start for almost another month and the humidity was already brutal. A part of her loved it, the natural world so constant, so permanently present. Then, at times, she wished for a less in-your-face climate. But regardless of where she was, the work remained important. The mission was everything.

"That was the last group booked in for today, right?" she asked Madeleine who stood behind the counter of the gift shop.

"Sure was. You're off the hook." The girl's smile was wide in her dark face. "I'm on until closing at four, so I'll keep an eye on any drop-ins."

"Wonderful, thank you." Madeleine was a fine asset. A great public face for the shop and the center beyond it, and only too happy to please. Rowling sometimes overused the girl's compliance, but considered herself too important to be bothered by it. That's what staff was for, after all. Rowling needed to concentrate as much as she could on the greater mission of KIND.

She went to tidy up a little in the KIND museum-cum-information center adjacent to the shop. No more tour groups booked in and it was only midday. With Madeleine handling the drop-ins, she could head back into the science center, off-limits to the public, with hours still to go. A rare treat. CCTV would alert her if any tourists did show up and Madeleine would press the bell if she needed help. She would be able to get a lot done, and double check the damage control from last night's little debacle.

But as Rowling turned and headed for the back door behind the shop counter, movement caught her eye. Looking back she was instantly tense, anger bubbling low in her chest as the National Parks Landcruiser pulled to a stop right outside. They didn't even give us a marked parking bay. God, how she hated this pair of clowns.

She considered Crews and Gomzi to be the epitome of useless. The types who turned a blind eye to poaching and other illegal activities while happily taking a salary that was supposed to pay for the protection of the park. The park would probably be better off with no rangers instead of these two.

She smoothed down the short-sleeved olive green shirt and shorts she always wore, and swept her long, black hair back into a ponytail. Rather than give them the comfort of air-conditioning, she went out to meet them, stood waiting while they lumbered out of their vehicle. She hated letting them come inside. Gomzi always touched things, picking them up, scrutinizing them like he would find answers to the great mysteries of the universe. Keep them out in the heat and Crews would keep it short, whatever it was they wanted.

"Morning, Karen," Crews said, smiling broadly.

"It's afternoon," Rowling snapped.

Crews tore his eyes away from her breasts for a moment to glance at his watch. "Ah yeah. 12.04. Only just. Anyway, how ya goin'?"

"I'm fine, thank you. How can I help you?"

"Straight down to business, eh?" Crews let his gaze slide up and down her once more before meeting her eyes. Did he really think she didn't notice his lascivious nature, or did he just not care?

Gomzi was the opposite, eyeing her with undisguised disdain. She knew she was a good-looking woman, but Craig Gomzi obviously didn't think so. He'd called her all manner of things over the years: tree-hugger, hippy scum, triggered snowflake, domestic terrorist even. The man was hilarious in his manufactured hatred for everything she and KIND stood for. Given the absolute nonsense he did seem to believe in, she found the whole situation deliciously ironic.

"I'm very busy," she said icily.

"'Course ya are, 'course. So, couple of quick questions, that's all."

"Questions about what?" Rowling had a bad feeling about this. Something about the bearing of these two clowns had her on edge.

"Just wondering if you know the Gibsons. Dad is Ray, three boys, Rod, Dicky and JD. Know who I mean?"

Rowling nodded. What were these two after? "I know of them, yes. Small town tyranny, isn't it? Everyone knows everyone. I could point them out in a line-up, but I don't really know anything much about them. Petty criminals is what I've heard. Rednecks?" She did, in fact, know all about the Gibsons and hated them passionately, but Crews and Gomzi didn't need to know that. More than once she, or other members of KIND, had chased them out of the park when they'd been poaching. Which reminded her, she would need to talk to Kurt about getting the yowie suit back. He should have been in to work much earlier. She made a mental note to ring him after the clowns had left.

Crews nodded, lips pursed. "Fair, fair." He nodded again. He looked like some kind of mentally unstable donkey. "Yep, that's fair." He looked up suddenly. "You haven't seen them poking around here at all?"

Rowling let out a genuine laugh. "I don't really think the Gibsons are the conservation type, Mr. Crews. Quite the opposite, really. Bloody poachers, I think you'll find. Unless you mean, have they been sniffing around the institute here? To rob us or something? What do you know? Should I be concerned about anything?"

Crews raised both hands, palms out. "Nah, nah, nothing like that. Just wondered if you'd seen them around. You see, there was a bit of an incident out in the park last night, someone got hurt, though they're being cagey about that. Just that it happened not too far from where your place here backs onto the river. You don't know anything about an att... an assault last night?"

"Good grief, man, no I don't! What are you on about? Shouldn't we call the police?" She desperately didn't want the police sniffing around either, but it was a calculated risk. She thought maybe Crews and Gomzi wouldn't want the cops around either, as that would only undermine their own perceived authority. And she really needed to talk to Kurt as soon as possible.

"No, not at all, not necessary. The individual in question denies it was even an assault, but we're keen to cover all options, that's all."

What were these imbeciles talking about? They were terrible at keeping their intentions to themselves, but still managed to make no sense.

"Know anything about yowies in the area?" Crews asked suddenly.

He was clearly trying to catch her off-guard and almost managed it. She covered her surprise well enough, taking a breath and a moment to compose herself before she said, "Yowies, Mr. Crews? Really?"

"What about this, eh?" Crews pulled a handful of long, reddish-brown fur from his shorts pockets and waved it in front of her face. In the bright sunlight it was clearly fake.

"That's obviously not real," Rowling said with a sneer. "So clearly doesn't come from a yowie. Honestly, Mr. Crews, I don't have time for nonsense. Why are you showing me?" She hoped neither man could see her increased heart rate. She felt as though her shirt would be shuddering with it. Where had he found that?

"Ah, no reason. No worries, Karen. Thanks for your time."

Crews started to turn away when Gomzi moved forward and spoke for the first time. "What's the largest croc you've seen around here?" he asked, head tipped slightly to one side.

Her heart rate redoubled. "About four meters, why?"

"And the biggest one you've got in captivity here in your facility?"

"Same, about four meters. They can get up to five or even more officially, you know that, surely? But that's rare. Why are you asking me this? And what does it have to do with," she gestured at Crews, "fake mythical beasts or whatever?"

Gomzi scowled. "We'll ask the questions, thank you."

"Do you think you're bloody Columbo or something?" Rowling snapped.

"How about the largest croc on record? Any idea?" Gomzi pressed on. Crews was watching his deputy with a hooded gaze. "I read it was Lolong, that one they caught in the Philippines."

Rowling nodded, her mouth dry. She needed to distract this line of questioning quickly, but professionalism forced her to answer. "Just over six point one meters, yes. But that was the largest ever in captivity. Anecdotal evidence of larger ones exist. There's Krys, from Normanton in Carpentaria, across Queensland from here. He was apparently shot out there in 1957 and measured a fraction over eight point six meters. Twenty-eight feet, they reckon." She would have loved to see that king alive and moving.

Crews whistled softly. "Eight point six meters? That's a bloody monster!"

Rowling smiled. "But unconfirmed. I believe it though. I think there are lots that have grown bigger than official estimates, but they're smart and avoid capture. That's how they get to grow so big, after all. Being smart." Nerves rippled over her again. She was getting carried away with her favorite subject. "Why are you asking anyway? What's this all about?"

"No reason," Gomzi said, but the look he gave her made her feel faint.

"Well, if that's all then." She paused to give them a chance to say more. "I'm very busy."

"Sure. Thanks for your time," Crews said.

Both men left and she went back inside, watched through the window as they climbed into the Landcruiser and drove away. Feeling like she might throw up at any moment, Rowling turned to the counter. "Madeleine, we have a new problem. A big new problem."

Chapter 12

Aston signaled Slater to surface and they swam together to the river bank again. When he took out his respirator, Aston said, "We're running out of options here."

Slater looked out over the river. "Any remains we might find could be anywhere, right?"

"Yeah, but the river is slow moving. Something would most likely get tangled up, there's so much detritus on the riverbed. But what I mean is, it's been too long. Fish, yabbies, whatever, will have pretty much finished off anything by now."

"Not the bones, though?" Slater asked with a grimace.

"No, not the bones. But how do you identify bones?"

"Eesh…"

"I mean, I'd love to find some bones at this point. Anything would be good, but I think we're pretty much out of options, short of staying for weeks and diving the entire river."

"So what next?" Slater asked.

"Let's take a lunchbreak, then move downriver again. We'll at least keep searching for the rest of today before I break any bad news to Sophie. I don't think we'll have any other news for her, but we'll finish today at least."

Slater nodded, climbing out of the water and shrugging off her tank. "The news is already bad, we all know that. She just needs closure."

"We'll do our best for her, but I don't think she'll get it."

Sophie and Izzy sat on the grassy riverbank not far away. They had been hanging around most of the time during the search, keen to be right there when any news became available. They both looked up with hopeful expressions as Aston and Slater approached.

Aston shook his head. "Sorry, guys. Nothing yet. We'll grab a bite to eat and go back in." He hated to see the disappointment in Sophie's eyes. Izzy had seemed relatively stoic until this point, but today was clearly the final straw. Her eyes filled with tears and she tried to suppress a sob.

Slater crouched beside the young girl, put an arm around her shoulders. "It's bad, I know. We'll keep looking."

"It's my fault!"

Slater leaned back to look Izzy in the eye. "How do you figure that?"

"I asked him to come down to the dock that night. I wouldn't... you know, give him what he wanted and he jumped into the water to cool off." She devolved into tears.

Slater hugged her. "Okay, first thing, you don't owe any man anything. And what they do with their disappointment is one hundred per cent their decision and not your fault. I understand where you're coming from, but this isn't something where anyone is to blame. It's a tragic accident, that's all."

"Are we accepting he's definitely dead?" Sophie asked.

"Officially?" Aston said, as gently as he could. "Not really. That's for the police to decide. They still have a missing person case open. But realistically..." He spread his palms, tried to look as apologetic as possible.

Sophie nodded, looked down at the grass. Izzy's crying increased. Now the dam had broken, she seemed unable to hold anything back.

Slater helped the young girl to her feet. "Come on, let's take a walk."

She flicked Aston a pained look and he nodded. As Slater moved away with Izzy, he sat beside Sophie.

"Nothing good about any of this," he said after a moment. "It's good to see you again, but I really wish this wasn't why."

"Me too. It would have been much better if things carried on like before."

Aston laughed softly. "You didn't miss me at all?"

She looked up at him for a moment, her expression strangely unreadable. "Yeah, of course I did. But you made your decisions and so did I. We managed to live with them well enough for this long, right? I didn't think you'd ever come home again."

Aston drew in a long breath, watching the river. The hours he'd spent in it as a kid, the hours spent wandering the wide, empty streets of Blacktooth River, the boredom in the small school. "I never would have if you hadn't called," he said eventually. "I promised myself I wouldn't. There's nothing here for me except bad memories."

She turned and punched him on the arm. "What the hell, dude?"

He grinned at her. "Yeah, okay. Some good memories too. But you're one of the few good memories and we... well, we didn't quite work, huh? I mean there's nothing left for me here any more."

"You always had your eyes set well beyond this place."

"I would have taken you with me, maybe. If things had been different..." He trailed off. The events of that time were complicated. All of life was complicated, really. There were rarely any easy decisions. Whenever a decision needed to be made, it usually came with costs.

Something softened between them and they shared a quiet moment, smiling.

Eventually, Sophie said, "I might have come too, but probably not. I was always a little scared by what you might lead me into."

"Probably a fair concern," he admitted.

"So I found a way to stay here."

"Whatever happened to you and Rusty anyway?" Aston asked. "You moved onto him pretty quick after I left, by all accounts."

Sophie shook her head ruefully. "I was using him to help forget about you, Sam. The man's an arse. It didn't last long, but he still can't get over it all these years later. Russell Crews might be the biggest mistake I ever made, but it's a mistake that's easy to ignore most of the time."

They turned at the sound of an engine and saw a Landcruiser approaching.

"Talk of the arse and he will appear," Aston said.

Sophie sighed. "What does he want now?"

Crews climbed out of the big car and came towards them. Aston did his best to keep his expression neutral, but was a little shocked at the sight of the man. Rusty had been a rising footy star when Aston left, tall and solid, muscular like a weightlifter, with a full head of long blond hair. It was no surprise Sophie had been attracted to him. Honestly, back then Aston had felt a little threatened by the man's physicality and good looks, even if he had always been a boofhead. Now Crews had truly gone to seed, lumbering along with a slight limp, his big belly stretching the front of his ranger shirt. As he pressed an Akubra onto his head, Aston saw the long locks had gone and Crews was almost entirely bald on top, his pale hair cut short around the sides and back. Time could be a cruel thing. Aston and Sophie stood to meet him.

"Soph, I'm so sorry about Cooper," Crews said.

She nodded, muttered her thanks.

Crews turned to Aston. "Never thought I'd see you

again, Sam."

"Same."

The two men shook hands, but there was a tension between them, like wary lions circling either side of a kill. Sophie looked from one to the other, frowning. Aston didn't want her to be in the middle of any weirdness with him and Crews, so he moved away to let the man talk with Sophie.

There was a moment of muted conversation between the two of them as Aston went down to the water's edge, then Crews called to him. Aston turned.

"I came to talk to you, actually. Spare a moment?"

Aston shrugged. "Sure. What's up?"

Crews joined him on the riverbank and started moving slowly along, away from Sophie, who sat back down, arms wrapped around her knees. "Best to have a little chat in private, mate. Soph is upset enough, eh?"

"If you say so. What's do you need?" Aston hoped this wasn't going to be some stupid high school rivalry stuff, Rusty making sure Aston wasn't back for another shot at a relationship with Sophie. Even though the big man still clearly carried a torch for her, Sophie had made it plain she would never go back to him. And it was none of Crews' business what Sophie or Aston did. And Aston was more than happy with Jo Slater now anyway. Why the hell was his brain racing around like this? Coming back to a home town he'd thought long behind him was messing with his normally level-headed confidence.

"Truth is, I need your help," Crews said.

That wasn't what he'd expected. Aston glanced at him and Crews sneered.

"Don't make this harder than it already is, mate. You can imagine how much I relish asking you for anything. But the fact is, you're more the expert here than I am. I'm big enough to admit it."

Aston nodded, actually a little chastised by the statement. So far, Crews was being the better man. "Yeah, sure, sorry. Happy to help. What is it?"

"I'm investigating something that could be related to young Cooper's disappearance. Here, look. We found this upriver yesterday." He pulled out his phone and flicked through a few photographs of a wrecked tinny, the small boat upside down on a muddy riverbank with a huge whole ripped in the aluminum side.

Aston frowned at the pictures for a moment, then said with a laugh, "If you reckon a croc did that, it would have to be massive. Like, insanely so."

Crews wasn't laughing. His face was deadly serious as he nodded. "Exactly. More like a giant, right?"

Aston laughed again. "You can't be serious, Rusty. No croc could do something like that. I don't know what happened there, but I don't see how I can help."

Crews glanced back to make sure no one was watching them, then pulled something out of his pocket, handed it surreptitiously to Aston. "What about that?"

Aston stopped walking, turning the thing over in his hands. It was a crocodilian tooth, but massively oversized. He became a little uncomfortable studying it. It looked real. It felt real. "Where did you get this?"

"It was wedged in that tinny I just showed you, caught in the metal where it was torn."

Aston looked up, saw Slater and Izzy slowly strolling back towards Sophie. "Hey, Jo," he called. "Got a sec?"

She looked over and nodded, said something to Izzy, and started over. Izzy sat with Sophie, the two women seeming to console each other, happy to ignore the others.

"What's up?" Slater asked.

"Check this out." Aston handed her the tooth.

She looked it over a moment, then said. "Well, shit. This is… this is something, isn't it? From a collection or..?"

Aston shook his head. "From yesterday. Rusty found it in the wreck of a tinny upriver from here. We should do what we can to identify it."

Slater's eyes widened. "Yes. Yes, we should. There's a couple of people I can call." She looked at Crews. "Can I hang onto this for now?"

"Sure, if you keep it safe. I haven't made any official reports yet, so it technically doesn't exist right now. Only you two, me, and Craig Gomzi know anything about it. And keep it just between us for now, yeah? I don't want to start any kind of panic, and I really don't think Sophie and Izzy need to know anything about it until we know more."

Chapter 13

Blacktooth River used to have two pubs and Ray Gibson missed the other one. It had been his favorite, the site of his earliest underage drinking, his earliest drunken brawls, and, in the car park one steamy night, the site of his first clumsy and, frankly, embarrassing sexual encounter. But memories good and bad had a habit of building up into something far greater than individual moments, and the nostalgia for the place was strong. But now the town only had the one place to drink since the old Carpenter Hotel had closed down. It was still there, boarded up and crumbling, a monument to what once had been. A metaphor for his life, Ray might have thought, had he been a more self-aware creature. And Ray would never count the small bar at the Black Stump Restaurant across town as a pub, so there was only one place to drink in Blacktooth River and it was like a second home to him now. He sat on a barstool at the River Hotel, elbow on the polished mangowood bar, one hand wrapped around a double Jack Daniels and Coke, and he fumed.

His son. His firstborn. He ground his teeth. If he was honest, all three of his sons were disappointments in one way or another. Weren't the next generation supposed to surpass their ancestors? His sons weren't half the man he was, but Rod had maybe been the best of them. And now the best of them was gone, taken by a bloody reptile. It was hard to stomach. He'd meant it, he would make that monster pay. He would carve it open to recover his son's bones, and he would wear its skin as boots and belt and whatever else he could think of. He planned to take its biggest tooth and put it on a chain around his neck. He would show that beast that men owned this earth, not the belly crawlers. He just needed a few more drinks first. A little Dutch courage. He wasn't scared, but he always hunted better with a few drinks inside him. It relaxed him. Calmed him. Steadied his aim. Besides, it was always best to hunt at dusk, and he had to do something to get through the afternoon.

He swallowed the last of the drink and looked up to catch Charlie Bartlett's eye. The publican was already heading over, a fresh drink in hand.

"You a mind reader, Charlie?"

The tall, thin publican smiled, his several missing teeth dark holes in his grin. "Not hard to guess you'll want another one as soon as the last is empty, mate. But nah. That bloke over there said to buy you a drink. You can thank him yourself."

Ray looked over with a frown. At the end of the bar was a solid-looking man in jeans and a flannel shirt, but he stuck out like a sore thumb. Looks like an undercover cop at a bush bash, Ray thought. His clothing was clean and crisp, nothing like the weathered attire of locals. He was maybe late forties, his hair cut short and neat, with an interesting wide gray streak right down the middle of otherwise deep brown. Strange way to get old, Ray thought. The man had the physique of an action figure. Military, perhaps, Ray guessed. Special forces? He looked like something from a Hollywood blockbuster, entirely out of place in north Queensland. Why was a guy like that here, and what the hell was he doing buying drinks for Ray? Despite his suspicion, Ray was low on funds, so he decided not to turn down free grog.

He met the man's eye, gave a nod, and raised his glass in thanks. The man returned the gesture. He held a tumbler with a short measure in it, not mixed. Ray looked away. Grateful for a free drink, but not about to be drawn into any conversation if he could help it.

He sat looking at his drink, sipping and planning the demise of the reptile that took his boy. A few seconds later there was movement beside him, and the muscular man took the adjacent barstool. Ray muttered a curse, then looked up and said more clearly, "Thanks for the drink, soldier boy, but you should know I like women."

The man chuckled. "I'm not a soldier and I'm not gay. I'm actually a collector of stories."

"Is that right?" That sounded to Ray like something a gay man might say to start a conversation.

The man nodded, his smile a little unnerving. He acted like he knew things Ray didn't know. As someone who had been treated as stupid his whole life, Ray had learned to instantly spot and dislike anyone who looked down on him like that. He might not have much in the way of a formal education, but Ray Gibson was no fool.

"Well, I don't know any." He gestured over his shoulder to an old, balding man who sat at a table in the corner nursing a schooner of Toohey's New. The man could be found there pretty much every minute the pub was open. "You should talk to Bob Daley over there. He's always got a yarn, and always keen for someone new to tell it to. All of it's bullshit, of course, but if you want stories, he's your man, not me. In fact, you can have him tell you the same story three days in a row and you'll get three different tales."

"I understand you've lived here your whole life," the man said, ignoring Ray's suggestion.

He obviously wasn't going to give up, whatever he wanted. Ray nodded, downed the drink and looked pointedly at the empty glass.

The man waved Charlie Bartlett over. "Another round, please." He looked back to Ray. "Born here, eh?"

"Yep, like my father before me. Our roots go deep here. What kind of stories you want?" Ray suspected the man wasn't military after all, more likely law enforcement. Federal Police, maybe. He needed to be careful what he said. He'd take the drinks and chat a bit, but planned to give this cop nothing. He was pretty rubbish at being undercover, after all, but Ray Gibson was very good at being interviewed but the police. He'd been practicing that since before he was a teenager.

"I'm a cryptozoologist," the man said.

That took Ray by surprise. A spy? "Codes and ciphers and stuff?" he asked.

"No," the man said with a smile. "That's a cryptologist. It's the 'zoo' part that makes all the difference." He laughed at what he clearly considered a joke, but Ray glared. He was being made to feel stupid again. The man's smile faded. "No, a cryptozoologist studies creatures whose existence science has not yet proven. For example, the Loch Ness Monster or a Leftist with balls and a brain."

Ray laughed this time. That aside had scored a bullseye. "Or a son who pulls his own weight," he offered.

The man lifted his glass in acknowledgement and smiled again. "Exactly."

They tapped glasses and drank. Ray made a point of swallowing his in one. The man gestured Charlie over once more, and the publican gave Ray another drink. The stranger had barely sipped his.

"So are there any local legends like that?" the man asked.

"Like what?"

"Strange creatures, unexplained sightings, mysterious disappearances?"

Ray's heart pulsed an extra beat. This bloke couldn't know about his son, not yet. Only him and his remaining boys had any idea. Coincidence, that's all. "There have been alien sightings," he said, to deflect the conversation.

The man grinned. "Of course, as there are everywhere. I'm thinking more terrestrial beasts. A yowie, for example. That's a quintessentially Australian beast and a lot of country towns have their yowie legend. Is there one here?"

"Only those animal rights nutters in costume."

The man raised an eyebrow.

Ray sneered. "Those bastards that call themselves KIND. They have a research and conservation facility on the edge of the national park, backs down onto the river. Bloody hippies and tree huggers, the lot of them. Should go back to the city and their lattes and chardonnay and stop spoiling life for the real country people like us."

"Ah, I see. I haven't heard of them before. Any other monsters?"

"Monsters?"

"Unusual animals, then."

Ray frowned. "Like what?"

"What about giant crocs?"

Ray felt like he'd been slapped. What did this bastard know? The whole line of conversation was getting very uncomfortable. And he refused to be beaten to his act of revenge for Rod. "No," he said curtly, and drained his drink.

He stood and stalked out of the pub, aware of the man turning slightly on his stool to watch him go. But the stranger didn't say any more or call after him. Anger boiled inside of Ray as he thought of his dead son. Time to go bush and find the beast and kill it.

Chapter 14

"**So who exactly** is this guy?" Slater asked.

Aston sighed. "Ned King. He's a self-aggrandizing jackass, really, but I get why Rusty said we should see him. There's probably no one in Australia who knows crocs like he does." They drove along the single lane highway away from Blacktooth River town, towards the edge of the national park, Crews driving ahead of them, leading the way. Aston pointed at a huge billboard by the side of the road. "There he is, in fact. Got a whole new massive park opening any time now, apparently."

Slater grimaced at the garish sign as they passed it. It showed a man of indeterminate middle age waving an Akubra with a hatband of crocodile teeth and wearing head to toe khakis. He also wore a croc tooth necklace, and a Fu Manchu mustache. He had a mullet cut of sandy hair, and the most obnoxious grin Aston could imagine on his chubby face. Big letters in a kind of Disney jungle font across the top of the billboard read Ned King's Crocodile Rescue! Across the bottom of the sign in huge capitals it said, NED KING - THE CROC KING!

"I've seen his face and heard his name for years," Aston said. "He's a bit of an Australian institution, a caricature almost. He's popular as hell for his eccentric conservationist efforts and television specials. He gets involved in just about anything he can manage, nothing is beneath his dignity. In truth, he's an unrepentant self-promoter, always claiming his efforts to raise his profile are ultimately for the good of the animals. But I think he just basks in the fame of it all."

"You don't like him then?" Slater said with a laugh.

Aston grinned. "Look, I'm all for the conservation and by all accounts he really does do good work out here. Has done for years. Decades, really. It's just that when people put themselves before the science, before the animals... well, it sticks in my craw, that's all."

"I can understand that," Slater said. "But Crews thinks he can help?"

"Yeah, and Rusty is probably right. Ned King is the resident expert on all things crocodile, after all. He's claims to be the real Crocodile Dundee, which is patently bullshit, you can tell that just from his picture back there! But he does know his stuff. I'm surprised you haven't heard of him. Maybe his TV specials haven't reached an international audience yet." Aston was reluctant to give the man any credit, but he couldn't deny expertise where it existed. And having seen that tooth and the damage to the boat Crews had shown them? Well, he would be happy to hand the whole thing off to an expert so he could get back to Kangaroo Island. He'd come to help Sophie, and it felt as though he'd exhausted all possibilities there. They'd agreed to take a break from diving the river this afternoon to visit King, and Aston planned one more dive session the next morning to make up for it. After that, he planned to call it done. He'd hinted as much already to Sophie and the look on her face had shown she had begun to accept the inevitable.

Crews indicated and turned into a wide driveway under a huge, bright sign with more jungle writing and another larger than life picture of Ned King. Arcing across the sign in three meter high letters was the word CROCALYPSE!

"Crocalypse?" Slater said, turning to Aston with a frown. "Really?"

Aston laughed and Slater broke into giggles too. "Even by Ned King standards, that is something else," Aston said.

"Holy crap, the man is entirely made of plastic."

"Cheese-filled plastic," Slater agreed.

The car park beyond was huge, room for thousands of cars. A massive swathe of rainforest had been cleared for it. Beyond the car park, the land rose in a natural shallow hill. The park was clearly visible, rides and attractions covering the hill, all surrounded by a high security wall. On the far side, Aston knew, the hill would descend again until it eventually met the Blacktooth River right as it left the boundaries of the national park. King had made good use of the land and the natural rise, his park and epic installment, but it was garish and out of place, a massive wound in the natural beauty of the rainforest.

"Holy crap!" Slater said.

Aston frowned, nodding. "I didn't realize this new park he built was so big. I didn't realize it was such a major attraction. He must have dropped some heavy bribes to the Queensland government to pull this off."

"How much did it all cost?" Slater said.

Aston shrugged. "There are rumors that King is independently wealthy, old family money, and he turned that into a new fortune with his public work. I get the feeling he'd spend his last dollar if it meant a good TV spot though."

They drove to the front of the huge lot where a few dozen cars and campervans were parked. Ahead was a large building, more pictures of King, more ten foot high letters declaring him THE CROC KING! More slogans yelling about how this was the most awesome park in the world and only going to get better. The park itself rose above the building, climbing the hill behind the high wall. The center front of the building was all glass, with huge letters marking ENTRANCE stenciled on. A smaller set of doors off to the right had EXIT stenciled inside and Aston saw a massive gift shop beyond. There wasn't an attraction left in the world, he mused, where you could leave without passing through a gift shop. Or a grift shop, as he preferred to call them.

"He's opening on Saturday," Rusty said as they walked from the cars towards the large glass double doors. "He's been developing this new, expanded 'experience' as he calls it, for months. There's a whole big thing happening this weekend to officially open it, special guests and all that."

They went inside to find a row of ticket booths and a zig-zag path to them marked out with tape like an airport check-in line. Giant fiberglass crocodiles hung from the high atrium ceiling, cassowaries and other beasts roamed the corners. A big sign reading WELCOME TO CROCALYPSE! hung above, and everywhere was Ned King's grinning visage, always with his trademark Akubra on his head or held like a welcome sign.

King himself was right there, chatting to a woman behind the first ticket booth. Two large doors at the back were marked ENTRY in large letters, and a cement path led beyond them up the shallow incline into the park. Immediately either side of the path were brightly colored stalls, inert but ready.

"Ah, Russell!" King said, striding over, one hand outstretched. "Good to see you, mate. Who are your friends?"

Crews shook hands then turned. "Sam Aston, a local boy returned home for a spell." Aston shook hands. The man's palm was hot and clammy. "And this is his partner, Jo Slater."

"Hi," Slater said, moving aside slightly so she didn't have to shake hands.

Nice move, Aston thought.

"Well, hi! I'm the Croc King, but youse can call me Ned.

Rusty said you wanted a chat. How about a look around first?"

Crews had warned them about this and suggested they endure a brief tour before they talked in the hope it would put King off from talking about himself too much afterwards.

"Sure," Aston said. "But we don't have time to see the whole place. It's way bigger than I expected."

"Bigger and better than anyone would ever guess!" King agreed, like Aston's comment had been a compliment. "But there's an easy way to take a tour. This way!"

He turned and led them away from the ticket booths to the other side of the large lobby. A door of opaque smoked glass, which Aston hadn't noticed, led from that side of the building. King looked back, "Delilah, if you would?" he gestured at the door.

"Certainly, Ned." The woman behind the counter smiled and reached down to press something. She was maybe in her thirties, short of stature, with long brown hair tied back. She had the most piercing blue eyes, Aston noticed, so pale they were almost white. The door ahead of them clicked open.

"That's Delilah," King said, loud enough to make sure she overheard. "Invaluable woman, will handle all the front of house stuff. We'll have a lot more staff on board come Saturday when we open, and she'll be in charge of all the ticket and shop gang."

Delilah smiled. "Nice to meet you all."

As King put a hand to the door Delilah had opened for them, two men came through the entrance door from the park and headed directly for King. They immediately put Aston at ease. They had the kind of faces and bearing it was easy to instantly trust. Both looked strong and a little rugged, but with soft, kind smiles.

"Ah," King said. "Excuse me just a moment. Here's two of my finest hands. With the smaller place we had before we got a lot of seasonal workers coming through, helping in the busier months, and these two are the best of them. I'm glad they've returned in time for the opening of this new place. Penry, Ringo, this is Rusty Crews, the national parks ranger here, and his friends Sam and Jo."

Friendly greetings were made all around and then King excused himself for a moment to chat with the two men. After he'd sent them on their way, he returned to the group. "Excellent workers, those two, absolutely lovely blokes. Lots of last minute things to shore up before Saturday, so they're invaluable. And they've been wonderful caring for our crocodiles and other animals, especially during the move from the original habitat here into all the expanded areas. Good enough to be zookeepers or something, but happy to cruise with us. Now, let's go through here and I'll show you what we've been so busy with the last year or two."

He pushed open the smoked glass door and stepped back to let them through. A stairway went up. "After you all, please," King said.

The room the stairs led to was huge and high up, the far wall was clear glass looking out over the park. A huge poster hung on the wall by the door and showed the impressive layout of the theme park, with crocodiles all over it, Ned King's grinning face, of course, and across the top in bold letters, CROCALYPSE! The name was everywhere. In the center of the room was a large glass table surrounded by chairs, and in the middle of the table a detailed 3D model of the park itself.

Aston snickered, gesturing at the poster. "You're a fan of B-movies?"

King laughed along, not at all offended. There was certainly something off about the guy, but Aston couldn't help but find him endearing in his own way. "It's all about the marketing, Sam! You see, we need a lot of money to really care for the animals we're responsible for. The government certainly helped build this place but sadly, conservation is criminally underfunded by the government. Tourism is a hell of a drug, eh? I don't mind playing to the masses to make enough money to do good work. Look here."

He led them to the far wall, looking out over the park. They saw several croc enclosures nearby and Aston had to admit they looked well-maintained, and more than big enough. The animals were well cared for. Penry and Ringo moved along one side of the nearest area, checking fence lines. He saw they had their names stenciled in bold capitals on their backs. They met up with two more men, ARNOTT and COSTELLO on their backs. So close! Aston thought, remembering the old "who's on first, what's on second" gag. That never got old.

Beyond the nearest enclosures, the cement paths led up the hill to all kinds of attractions, including huge enclosed reptile houses, a log flume ride, even a kind of fake mountain in the center with a flat cement viewing platform and picnic tables on top.

"Lady and gentlemen, I present Crocalypse!"

Crews whistled through his teeth. "Quite something, Ned. Really quite something. You really think we get enough tourists up here for something this size?"

"No!" King admitted, the grin evident in his voice. "But something this size will bring enough tourists here, you watch. Look, this gives you a good idea of what we have going on."

Aston turned to see King gesturing at the 3D model of

the park on the table. The place was even bigger than their current view showed, an intriguing cross between a reptile park and a theme park. Along the far side was a roller coaster, obscured by the hill, and not far from that, lower down, a river ride.

Slater pointed to the river ride. "That's obviously a rip-off of Disney's Jungle Cruise," she said with a grin.

King laughed. "It most certainly is! When something works, when it's popular, why try to reinvent it? I've taken the most popular attractions from theme parks all around the world and incorporated them here. This tiny backwater of Queensland is going to become a force to reckon with, I promise you that. Blacktooth River might be the smallest national park in Queensland, but I'm going to make it world famous."

Aston believed him. The scale of the project here was astounding. Near the start of the log ride was a whole section with children's rides and play areas, even a creche. Along with the attractions, dotted throughout the massive park were habitats for crocodiles, alligators, and caimans. The building marked Reptile House was vast.

When King saw Aston lean forward for a better look at that, he said, "More specimens in there than any other reptile park in the world, Sam. Took a long time to build up our collection. We've only just moved our existing animals into that new habitat."

In the center of it all was the tall peak marked Croc Mountain. King pointed to it and said, "This is my answer to Sleeping Beauty's castle, my centerpiece. It has views all around the park from several platforms, plus slides on the inside and outside. At the top is the picnic area and café that can seat five hundred people."

"This is really quite impressive," Slater said. "I've never

seen anything quite like this outside the US. Hong Kong or Paris, maybe…"

"Oh, I do nothing by halves, Jo." King grinned, pointing to a large OPENING SOON! poster on the wall. "Including the opening ceremony this Saturday. You'll all come, won't you? Free entry, of course, for Rusty and his friends. There'll be big-name celebrities in attendance, it'll be broadcast online too. I'm expecting most TV stations will send a crew as well. We're big news, believe me."

Aston read the poster, recognized the names of some of the celebrities – a retired rugby league player, a B-list actor, and a former singing show contestant. Not exactly marquee names on a Hollywood scale, but maybe not so bad at a domestic level.

"What's this here?" Slater asked, pointing to a large structure at one end of the 3D model, on the far side from them. It showed an amphitheater facing a deep pool, the water represented by a kind of clear resin.

Ned sighed, then rolled his eyes. "The one major attraction I didn't manage to pull off. That was going to be an orca show, but KIND and their fellow do-gooders raised such hell about it that I had to cancel those plans at the last minute."

Aston was pleased to hear it. Whatever else King might do well, there was never an excuse to keep orca in captivity. They were invariably depressed and unwell without a wide ocean and their freedom. He hoped King didn't plan to replace it with a dolphin show or anything similar. "What do you plan to do with it now, then?" he asked.

"I suppose I'll fill in the pit and use it for live performances. That's a twenty meter deep pool there, it would have been wonderful, but I can still use the amphitheater. I figure we could even put on live music concerts sometimes, opera, theatre productions, stuff like that. We'll find a way to make good use of it. It's a massive footprint in the park, after all, so I won't let it go to waste. It won't be ready for Saturday, that's all, which is a shame. Can't win 'em all, eh?"

"Anyway," Crews said warily. "This is all very impressive, but we actually need your scientific help, not your... er... marketing expertise."

"Of course, of course. Let's go through to my office."

They crossed to the other side of the large conference room and through a plain wooden door. The office was simple, which surprised Aston. He'd expected more opulence.

King smiled at Aston's expression. "All the glitz and bells and whistles are for the public, Sam. I don't need it. In here, I need to work." He sat at his desk and the others pulled up chairs opposite.

"Okay," Crews said. "We need some help to understand these two things. One, this boat." He put his phone on the desk between them, showing the photo of the Gibson's tinny and the ragged hole in its side.

King leaned forward to look and his demeanor changed instantly. He nodded subtly. "Mmhmm. And the other thing?"

Crews put the big tooth on the desk. "Gomzi found this wedged in the metal."

King sucked in a long breath, nodded again. "This is not entirely a surprise to me, Rusty."

"How so?"

"I've recently found evidence of a crocodile of massive proportions around here. Not this massive, at least, I didn't realize it might have been so big. But this doesn't entirely surprise me, no."

Crews' eyebrows shot up. "Why the bloody hell didn't you report it to the ranger's office?"

Ned laughed. "Seriously? What would you have done? Would you even have believed me? I know people see me as a self-promoter, and I've got this new park opening. I reckon a report like that would be taken as a publicity stunt, don't you think?"

"Ned, at least one person is dead already!" Crews turned red with rage. "Maybe more! You can't keep stuff like that to yourself!"

"Rusty, calm the hell down," Aston said. "How could he have known?"

Crews glared at him for a moment, then at King. Finally he let out a held breath. "Yeah, well. Maybe I wouldn't have believed you if I hadn't seen the boat and the tooth."

"Exactly," King said, clearly relieved. "Here, let me show you some stuff I've been collating." He rummaged in his desk drawer and came up with a folder. He opened it and spread out some eight by ten black and white photos on the desk.

"Old school," Slater said with a laugh.

"I have the digital originals. I printed these to study in the meantime."

Each photo showed tracks with a meter stick beside them to provide scale. They were truly enormous, ten times what even the biggest crocodile print would show, maybe more. If Aston hadn't seen the other evidence, he would never have believed these tracks were real.

King put down another photo. "This is a giant wallow. Like, gargantuan. A reptile of inconceivable size appears to have rested here. And look at this." He moved to a cupboard on the back wall and opened it to take out a massive plaster casting of a track. He strained under the weight of it as he placed it atop the photos on the desk. "That's not scaled up.

That's an actual cast."

Aston couldn't deny it looked real. As he inspected it, he noticed something strange. The foot was longer and narrower, the toes thicker, than a regular croc track. And the track itself looked wrong, something about the generalized shape, but he couldn't quite put his finger on what.

Ned saw the look in his eyes and nodded knowingly. "You clearly know your stuff, Sam."

Aston frowned. "Not really. This isn't actually my field. What am I missing?"

"I have reason to believe the thing is bipedal."

Aston, Slater, and Crews all looked up sharply. That was what he'd seen in the print, Aston realized. The pressure angles were all wrong, unless what King suggested was true.

"What?" Slater asked.

"I think it primarily moves on four legs, but is capable of moving on two. Maybe rearing up to attack, or to run."

"Holy shit," Aston said. "What kind of animal are we talking about here?"

"Honestly, I can't say." King gave Crews an apologetic look. "That's why I haven't said anything to anyone else yet. I've been trying to learn more. There have been local legends of giant crocs for as long as there have been people living here, going all the way back to the dreamtime if you talk to the local indigenous population. But the only creature I could come up with that even vaguely fits this evidence is something called a Razanandrongobe sakalavae, or Razana for short."

"Razana?" Slater said quietly. Aston thought there was a strange edge to her voice.

King nodded. "Yep. People called it the T-Rex of crocodiles. Belonged to a group of crocodile ancestors known as the notoschuians, which means 'southern crocodiles'. We're talking Jurassic creatures here, but though they lived at the same time as dinosaurs, they were different. Most notoschuians were light, thin, upright-walking reptiles, about a meter long. Nothing much to write home about. Not Razana though. Razana was a mightier, bigger version, around earlier than most fossils found. There's speculation it could reach seven meters or more, which would dwarf most saltwater crocs today. The accepted top end for salties is about five. But I think they might have been a lot bigger than seven meters. And their physical abilities and T-Rex-like teeth would have made them apex predators."

"And you think that's what we have here?" Crews asked.

Slater had an odd look on her face but said nothing. "Are you suggesting there's a surviving species of this prehistoric reptile here?" Aston asked. He was getting uncomfortable flashbacks to Lake Kaarme in Finland. Perhaps that's what was bothering Slater too, but it looked like she had something else on her mind. He would have to ask her about it later.

King shook his head. "I can't believe a breeding population could have survived this long undiscovered. And besides, the Razana was an African dinosaur, it was never around here. I'm just saying that all the evidence I've found, and now you and your tooth there? Well, something like Razana is the only thing that fits."

"We can't be talking about a dinosaur, or even a bipedal creature," Crews said. "But there sure does appear to be a huge croc out there and I have to do something about it if it's got a taste for people. It's my job to look after this park and all the wildlife in it, but I have a responsibility to the people in it too. Is it possible to trap a croc of this size?"

King nodded. "It is, but not easy. The only safe way probably, would be to tranquilize it. Which is not outside the realms of possibility."

Crews sighed. "Think you could help us?" he asked. "Provide some resources and manpower?"

King grinned. "I thought you'd never ask!"

Crews quickly raised one index finger. "But I remain in charge of the mission. When it comes to the welfare of the croc, Ned, that's your call. But it's in my national park."

"Of course, that's fair. But under no circumstances do we destroy this creature if we don't have to," King said. "It's too important to science."

"It's not more important than human lives. We kill it if we have to, but by all means try to trap it alive if you can."

Slater quirked an eyebrow. "I find that human lives are grossly overvalued."

Aston suppressed a grin and Crews flashed her an annoyed glance.

"I assure you I can do the job," King said. "I'm the most renowned croc expert in the country for a reason, after all. In the world, in fact."

More notorious than renowned, Aston thought, but he held his tongue.

"I'll need some time to prepare," King said.

Crews nodded. "Sure, but the sooner the better." He turned to Aston. "You and Jo in on this?"

Aston laughed, shook his head. He still had memories of Lake Kaarme haunting his mind. "No, thanks. We're only here to find Cooper. One more dive session in the morning and then that's us finished."

Delilah stood with one ear pressed to King's office door, listening to the conversation within with growing horror. She had barely suppressed a gasp when she heard King mention the Razana. Her heart raced and her breath was shallow as she listened to their plans. This was bad. This was all very bad indeed.

Chairs scraped as the people in the office finished their talk and got up to leave. Delilah darted back across the conference room and down the stairs to the cash register. She smiled at them all as King led them back down, hoping they couldn't see the tremble she felt in her lips.

"Goodbye," she said brightly, distracted again momentarily by the sight of the one called Sam. He was a fine specimen of manhood. That Jo Slater better realize how lucky she was. She watched Ned walk them out to their cars. Once she thought they were a safe distance away, she pulled her phone from her jeans pocket and tapped up a call to Karen Rowling. Heart racing, she waited for Rowling to pick up. Finally, she answered.

"Delilah. Everything all right?" Concern laced Karen's voice.

Delilah swallowed hard. Her mouth was dry and her head was spinning. This was precisely what she was supposed to look out for. She just hadn't expected it to happen so fast.

"No, Karen. It's not. I think we have a problem."

Chapter 15

Ray Gibson, buzzing from the multiple shots of Jack Daniels in his system, stalked through the night in the deep rainforest bush not far from the Blacktooth River. He held his favorite .303 rifle tight across his chest, careful to keep his finger outside the trigger guard. He would find whatever croc had taken his boy. His one good son, the only one of the three worth a damn. The other two wouldn't even come out to hunt with him now, the useless pricks, scared of what had happened before. Where was their sense of justice for Rod if nothing else? He had some sympathy for JD, given the head injury and the kid's continued wooziness, but he wouldn't have let that stop him, not at that age or this. A real man pushed on. And Dicky, that useless, middle child piece of shit, he had no excuse. Ray had seen the fear in the boy's eyes and despised him for it. What a pussy.

Where had he gone wrong? He was hard on the boys, sure, but that was to toughen them up, not make them soft. He'd have been better off with daughters than with those two. At least Rod had shown some spine, a willingness to do whatever needed to be done. And it was Rod he'd lost. The world was a hole that sucked all good things away and there was no justice to be found anywhere in it. Except tonight. Oh, tonight there would be justice when he killed that bastard animal that had taken his boy. Before dawn he would be stripping the hide off that fucker.

He came to the river bank and started along it, red lamp on his headband casting a bloody beam out across the water. He would have to watch out for any danger, but if his lads were right and this croc was a giant, he expected it to have a wide territory. It was unlikely there would be anything around except the one he'd come to kill. He was counting on it, in fact.

"Come on," he whispered. "Show yourself."

A lump on the riverbank caught his eye, reflecting scarlet light back at him. Their boat.

His heart rate rose as he moved nearer and saw the damage. He'd assumed JD and Dicky were exaggerating, blowing up what had really happened because they'd been so pussy-scared about it. But seeing the huge hole torn in the aluminum boat, and the long, wide rents around it that could only have been made by teeth almost the size of his forearm, Ray's mouth went dry.

"Jesus…" he breathed.

He crouched beside the boat and looked out over the water again, watched its sluggish flow, silent as it drifted past. There was no breeze, the night hot and humid. Sweat trickled into his eyes. And there was no sound. That didn't make sense. The bush was alive, night and day. All kinds of animals and birds and bugs making noise. But right now the night was still as a church.

Ray tried to swallow but his throat was tight. He pulled a battered hip flask from his back pocket and took a draw. The bourbon burned down his throat, made him wince. He blinked several times. He was maybe a little too drunk for this, after all. Perhaps he'd spent too long talking to that idiot in the pub, had a shot or two more than ideal. Maybe he should come back again another night, with a better amount of booze in his blood.

He remembered JD and Dicky at home, shaking their heads, refusing to come on the hunt. He gritted his teeth and growled. He was acting just like them. He wouldn't find some excuse to quit. He'd set an example and return with his prize. Show them what it meant to be a man.

A branch snapped in the bush behind him.

Ray spun around on one knee, bringing his rifle up as he moved. He swept the dim beam of his red headlamp left and right, but it only highlighted the trunks of gum trees and low, thick bush. The stillness in the night, impossibly, deepened.

"Are ya out there, ya bastard?" Ray whispered, hoping for bravado. The tremor in his voice only served to unnerve him further. He strained his ears to hear anything, but made out the soft burble of the river sliding by behind him and nothing else.

Slowly he got to his feet and began moving along the river, away from the ruined boat. He glanced frequently at the water, just to be sure, but mostly kept his eyes on the bush. Something was there, he was sure of it. His hunter's intuition, that had regularly served him well, was buzzing. His nerves had pulled taut. His tongue felt thick in his dry mouth and he forced a swallow despite the audible click from his throat. He stalked the soft mud of the riverbank in silence.

Another branch snapped.

Ray froze, feeling dizzy from looking so hard into the darkness between the trees. A dry hiss came to his ears, something moving through the low scrub. Something big. Despite his determination, Ray's knees shook. He resisted the urge to turn tail and run away. Who was hunting who right now? The only thing that stopped him bolting was the thought that if he did then whatever was out there would be able to sneak up behind him.

The rustling in the brush got louder, the thing moving more quickly. Some high branches shuddered, snatching Ray's attention, and he staggered back, up to his ankles in the river as he craned his head up to see. What the hell was up in the trees? More branches cracked and Ray's eyes snapped back down. On the ground too. More than one thing?

He whimpered, the sound entirely involuntary and he disgusted himself with his fear. Despite the heat and humidity, the sweat down his back felt cold. Shadows moved not twenty feet away and his red light highlighted a huge limb, scaled and thicker around than his body, longer than he was tall. Huge splayed toes with massive, black claws pressed into the mud.

"What the fuck?" Ray managed as his gaze slid upwards, following the impossible leg to the start of a wide, pale, scaled belly before it disappeared into darkness. Refusing to believe it, he kept looking up, not able to see the monster, but estimating its position from that one giant leg. Was it standing up? A giant croc, standing on its hind legs? Ray almost giggled at the absurdity even as his bladder let go and warmth spread through the front of his King Gee shorts.

His eyes reached the thickly leaved tops of the trees just as they parted and a massive, too wide crocodilian head pushed slowly through, like a ship emerging from fog several meters above him.

"That's not possible," Ray said, tears of terror running over his cheeks. "You're just impossible." He reflexively fired his rifle, shot after shot, hoping to hit that high, wide belly, but he had no idea where his bullets were going because he couldn't tear his gaze from that hideous prehistoric head as it slowly descended.

He screamed as the impossible head split open to reveal a mass of huge, gleaming teeth. Then it shot forward and the last thing Ray Gibson thought was that it smelled appalling, then everything went dark in a maelstrom of agony.

Chapter 16

The hotel room was simple, but clean. They had all they needed, assuming they didn't need anything invented after 1975. Even the small fridge in the corner had to be close to fifty years old. Amazing it still worked. But no, Aston corrected himself, there was air-conditioning and a microwave, so perhaps he should be kinder to the place. The bed was firm enough and the space was private. He had no intention of being here long. One more dive, mainly to satisfy Sophie as well as he could, not because he expected to find anything, and then they'd be away. He looked forward to returning to Kangaroo Island and sharing some time with Jo there. Then again, right now he was concerned. She seemed distracted. Pensive.

He'd tried to get amorous earlier and she'd spurned his advances. Not with any rancor, she was kind and smiled, but had said, "Not right now, okay?" and he respected that. But clearly something was bugging her.

"You've been quiet since we went to see Ned King," Aston said, trying to circle in on his concerns without being too pushy. "He's a weird character, huh?"

Slater nodded. "He really is. Hard to decide if he's genuinely concerned about animals, or mainly a kind of circus ringmaster on steroids, you know what I mean?"

Aston pursed his lips in thought. She had a point. "I hear ya," he said after a while. "But it's also possible he's both."

Slater allowed a soft laugh. "That's true."

Aston was too concerned to beat around the bush any more. "Is that what's bothering you?"

She glanced over, one eyebrow raised. "That obvious,

huh?"

"Well, nothing's obvious, but you clearly have something on your mind." He gestured at himself. "I mean, earlier on you turned down this!" He grinned and was pleased to elicit a laugh from her too. "Want to talk about it?" he asked.

Slater drew in a long breath and nodded. "Okay, I need to tell you about an assignment I had a few years ago, before we met. Five years ago, maybe a little more. Doesn't matter. I was working with an archeologist called Jade Ihara. She has a... prickly personality, but she knows her stuff." Slater threw a sideways glance as Aston. "She's also beautiful and badass. You'd like her."

"Sounds like I would. You'll have to introduce me."

Slater grinned. "Dick. Anyway, I'll give you the cliff notes. The details don't really matter right now. We'd found a tomb... Well, that's not fair. Jade had found the tomb. She'd put months of work into the project and found something never seen before—a tomb not mentioned in any known Egyptian records. We were along for the ride because a friend of a friend put me onto it and I convinced Jade to let me make a documentary. We got to document every step of the discovery, from her following up her notes to actually finding the site, then going inside. It was exciting stuff. The day we went down into the burial chamber itself was kinda tense. Jade was a little spooked. I think maybe she was actually on the trail of something a little bigger. Like perhaps this discovery was only a part of some greater scheme. Honestly, the more I think about it, the more I believe Jade was expecting something else, like this place was only the start of something far bigger." Slater paused, thinking. "Anyway, I'm digressing. The point is that when we entered the burial chamber we saw what I thought at first was a huge sculpture of a crocodile. Then we realized it was actually an actual, mummified giant crocodile.

"I couldn't believe it was the genuine article, something so huge. But Jade was confident it was real and had likely been preserved for centuries. She said maybe crocs did used to get to that size. But Sam, it was like fifty feet long or something."

Aston did quick mental arithmetic to convert to metric. "That's, what, sixteen meters or more?"

Slater nodded, looking at him to see if he believed her.

"And it was real, you think?"

Slater nodded again, looking away, back into her memories. "Jade was convinced and we closed the place up again as well as we could to prevent any degradation and hurried back topside to start making plans. We needed to reassess everything about accessing that chamber, make sure we had all the right gear, call in the right experts."

"Here's where things went wrong then?" Aston guessed.

"Yep. I went with my crew." Slater swallowed, looked at Aston with wet eyes. "Dave and Carly. They were my crew then too."

Aston's mind flashed back to Lake Kaarme and the carnage there. He put a hand on Slater's arm, offered a soft, sympathetic smile. Dave and Carly never made it back from Finland.

"Anyway," Slater went on. "We went back to my room, went over footage and stuff, leaving Ihara to make plans for the next day. Except the next day, the authorities came down on us in a flood. They shut us down completely, took my footage, even our hardware."

"Surely they couldn't do that legally?"

Slater shrugged. "Who knows whether it was legal or not, they did it. We complied or we'd have been thrown in an Egyptian jail, they said. We really had no choice. They compensated us generously. Too generously, really, but nothing could repay the theft of that exclusive. And they made us sign the most punitive NDAs I've ever seen. It never felt right, Sam, despite all that. I never bought into the idea that the people who took control of the dig site were actually with the government, or with anyone... official, you know? I've dealt with enough bureaucrats in my life to have a pretty good idea how they operate. These people acted so swiftly and efficiently. And honestly, I had the feeling they'd disappear us all just as quickly and efficiently if we didn't go along with everything they wanted. It wasn't worth it to fight against them, not for one ancient tomb. Maybe there were riches or secrets there, I don't know. But I do know when to quit. Nothing is worth our lives. But I've never forgotten the mummified croc. The size of it, Sam! I did some casual research in the weeks after and the Razana came up. I started to think maybe that's what it had been, but so what? I had no more access and the research pretty quickly hit a dead end. But today? Ned King right away brought up the Razana. In Australia?"

It looked like Slater was maybe going to say more, but a knock at the door silenced her.

Aston frowned. "We expecting anyone?"

"Don't think so."

He rose and opened the door. A woman stood outside, wearing a short-sleeved olive green shirt and matching shorts, her long, black hair tied back in a ponytail. "Mr. Aston?"

"Yes. Who are you?"

"May I come in for a moment? Just a quick chat."

"I guess so." He stepped back to let her in and closed the door behind her. He went back to sit on the chair next to

Slater and the woman pulled out a steel-legged chair from a small side table under the window.

"Please excuse my interrupting you, I hope it's not too late."

"Too late for what?" Aston asked.

The woman laughed. "Too late in the evening, I mean."

"Ah, right." Aston glanced at the bedside clock, bright green LED numbers. It said 9.08pm. "No, we're still up." Obviously, he thought. This woman put him on edge and he wasn't sure why.

"Well, regardless, I apologize for the intrusion. My name is Karen Rowling. I'm with KIND."

Slater frowned. "KIND?"

Rowling smiled. "We're a conservation group. Knights in Nature's Defense."

Aston winced at the cheesy name. It seemed to him like maybe there were more conservationists around these parts than there were animals or wilderness to conserve, and everything about them was badly named. "And what can we do for you?" he asked.

"I understand you've been working with Ned King."

"No, that's incorrect," Aston said. "We only just met King this afternoon and we're not working together. How would you know anything about that anyway?"

"Let's just say the croc community is a small one, Mr. Aston. Word gets around."

"Okay, fine. You all gossip about stuff. Can't say I'm surprised, it's one of the reasons I couldn't wait to get away from this place. I still don't see why you're here. What can we do for you?"

Rowling smiled tightly. "Well, I'm not sure you can do anything for me, Mr. Aston. For us. But I just wanted to give you a warning."

It was beginning to annoy him how she kept saying Mr. Aston. He found it condescending. And when anyone suggested they were warning him, Aston immediately became defensive. He wouldn't stand being warned by anyone about anything. Slater hadn't said much at all, but he saw from the tightness around her eyes that this woman was annoying her too. In fact, it looked like Jo was entirely more annoyed by Rowling than he was. "A warning?" he said. "Not the kind of talk I like, Karen. Who are you to warn us about anything?"

"Ned King is not what he seems, Mr. Aston."

"Is anyone?" Slater asked, doing nothing to hide her sarcasm. "Are you?"

Rowling smiled again. That was annoying too. "Perhaps not. But King doesn't care about the crocodiles. He only cares about money."

"Are you talking about Crocalypse?" Aston asked. "You find that a little on the nose maybe?"

Rowling barked a scornful laugh. "Who can find it anything but absolutely ridiculous? Conservation, zoos, and amusement parks don't mix, the latter makes a mockery of the former. And animals should not be exploited for profit."

"And yet it's incredibly hard to get conservation funding," Aston said, knowing the industry well enough to know that. "Most conservation projects have to engage in courting the public purse to stay afloat. Surely you KIND people are the same? Or are you privately funded?"

Rowling frowned. "Of course we need public money too, Mr. Aston. But we engage in educational activities. People pay us for knowledge and genuine experience, not fairground rides and cheap thrills."

"You make it where you can, if you ask me," Slater said. "I think maybe Crocalypse, despite the terrible name, will turn a better profit than your educational activities. And then King will have more funds for conservation. Are you worried he'll put you guys out of business, is that it?"

Aston hated to hear her defending the man, but what she said was true and this Rowling woman was obviously getting under Slater's skin too.

Rowling huffed softly. "Certainly not. And his awful new theme park may well be profitable, but it doesn't make it right. Besides, that's not all. King also sells baby crocs, he sells eggs, croc hides, teeth, claws, and meat. He traffics in exotic reptiles."

"So why don't you report him?" Slater asked.

"He's got connections, high up, local and Federal government, who help him cover it up."

"Like who?" Aston asked. "Expose them and you'll expose his illegal activities too, if what you say is true. Surely that would be high on your agenda if you claim to be real conservationists." He made air quotes around the word "real". Much as he disliked King, he had a hard time believing what this woman accused the man of.

Rowling's eyes darkened. "We are a very serious organization, Mr. Aston. But it's not that simple. We have to operate here and there are local authorities on his side too."

Aston popped an eyebrow. "What, like Rusty Crews?"

She shrugged. "It wouldn't surprise me."

As if old Rusty was any threat to anyone. Clearly the woman was prepared to throw around all kinds of accusations, but no names. And she obviously wasn't prepared to front up to actual authorities about any of it. It all sounded like sour grapes to him. Aston wondered what the hell the point of her visit really was. He wanted nothing to do with the conservation politics of the area he'd thought far behind in his personal history. "You know anything about the recent disappearances?" he asked, to deflect the conversation.

Rowling just about managed to suppress a flinch at the question. Aston slid his eyes sideways to Slater and saw from her expression that she'd noticed it too.

"I don't, no. Disappearances, plural? You mean someone other than the Cooper boy? Of course, everyone local has heard about that terrible event."

It was Aston's turn to shrug. He had no intention of giving Rowling any information, but he had a feeling she knew more anyway and was playing dumb.

"Is that all?" Slater asked. "You came to tell us you don't like Ned King and we shouldn't work with him, is that it? Well, lucky for you, we're not working with him. So if there's nothing else?"

Rowling nodded and stood. "I would simply advise you not to join in any harebrained schemes King might concoct. He's an opportunist. He'll use the disappearances as a chance for self-promotion, you mark my words."

"I thought you didn't know about any disappearances."

"I didn't, until you just mentioned them." Rowling smiled snidely.

"Right, sure." Aston stood and opened the door, standing aside to let Rowling through. "I can assure you that Jo and I only came here to help a friend. My only interest is in the search for Cooper's body. So thanks for the visit, but..." He gestured at the open door.

Without another word, Rowling left. When Aston closed the door, Slater said, "Well that was weird. Maybe she should ask to speak to the manager of Crocalypse."

Aston couldn't help but chuckle. "This bloody town, Jo. I told you I couldn't wait to leave it. You starting to see why?"

Chapter 17

The morning was wearing on and Aston began to feel despondent. He knew there was really no chance of finding Cooper alive or dead, but he had really wanted to be able to offer Sophie some closure. Awful as the discovery of a body might be, it was at least something concrete. Something final. He wondered if maybe she would finally turn her back on this town like he had if she had that finality. If they didn't find anything, Sophie might never be able to leave Blacktooth River. But two hours of diving had proven as fruitless as the previous days and this last chance was slipping past too. One more hour, he'd told Slater, then they'd pack it all in.

He surfaced to recheck his position in the loose search grid he and Slater had worked out.

"Sam!"

Slater's voice was tight. She hung in the water looking over at him. She'd clearly been waiting there for him to reappear.

"What is it?"

"I think you should have a look at this."

The tone of her voice told Aston that whatever she'd found, it was serious. He hoped it wasn't another eel, but Slater was unlikely to make that mistake twice. He stayed on the surface and swam over. Her eyes were a little wide and she gave her head a small shake as she pulled her mask back down and put her regulator in. Aston spared a glance to where Sophie and Izzy waited on the shore. They'd both noticed the interaction and were moving forward, eyes intent.

"Shit," Aston muttered, then replaced his own regulator. Maybe he didn't actually want to find something after all. He dived again before Sophie could call out.

He followed Slater's trail of bubbles and found her holding on to a rotten branch of a submerged tree. The wood was solid black, smooth as glass. It had obviously been down at the bottom of the river for years. He followed Slater's pointing finger and his heart skipped a beat.

It was a leg. Without a doubt the lower half of a human leg, specifically, tangled in some weeds just beneath the fallen tree. It had slipped under in such a way that most things of any size would be unable to get to it, yet it still showed signs of being predated on by myriad smaller critters. But not enough that it was unrecognizable. It was obviously a human limb. The skin was fish-belly pale, the toes wrinkled and chewed by small denizens of the river, bones showing through. The muscular calf had begun to get loose, the amputation a clean severed cut just below where the knee would have been. Something powerful and razor sharp had sliced through it, bone and all. On the side of the ankle was a tattoo of a turtle, stylized like the opal pendants the gift shops always sold pretty much everywhere in Australia. That was the kind of identifying mark that would leave little doubt.

Aston pulled up the camera hanging by a cord from his weight belt and snapped a couple of photos, including a close-up of the tattoo. Slater made a grabbing gesture, then pointed up at the surface. Aston recognized the question: Do we take it back up?

He shook his head. They'd need to record the exact location, but the limb would have to be left for the authorities. Police divers would return to recover it. It was a long way downriver from the police search. No wonder they'd missed it. He took more photos, from further away, making sure to include a variety of identifying features of the riverbed to make the job easy for the police. No body part would last long in these waters. This had to be Cooper. Suddenly, Aston didn't know how he felt about the discovery. Poor Sophie.

He gave the thumbs up and they swam back to the surface. He stayed directly above the find and checked his position relative to the riverbank either side. He took a couple more photos to record the spot, then he and Slater swam for shore.

Sophie and Izzy were waiting right by the river, both visibly upset.

"You found him." Sophie's voice was tight with held back tears. It wasn't a question.

"I need to call the authorities first, I—"

"Sam! What did you find?" Sadness flared into anger at his attempt to evade her question. "You found Coop?"

"Whatever you found," Izzy said, "you have to tell the police and Crews. And you know Crews is going to tell us. So cut out the middle man. Tell us now."

Aston licked his lips, pulling his gear off to avoid their eyes, but he nodded. She was right, and surely it would be better coming from him, here and now.

"There's nothing to be gained by making them wait," Slater said, echoing his thoughts.

"Of course." Aston put his gear aside and unclipped the camera. He found the close up of the tattoo, reluctant to show them the entire severed leg. "We found…" There was no good way to share news like this. "I'm so sorry, Soph. We found something, but it's just a part. Just part of a leg."

Izzy gasped and turned away, hand over her mouth. Sophie's face hardened and she nodded once, decisive.

"Show me."

"Did Cooper have any tattoos?" Aston asked.

"Yes, a couple. Show me!"

Aston turned the camera so she could see the small screen, the close-up of the turtle against milk white skin.

Sophie looked, then tears breached. "Oh my God! That's him." She turned away as Izzy's shoulders shook with the increase in her crying. Despite her back being turned, she had heard. Sophie put her arm around Izzy's shoulders and they pulled each other into a hug, crying hard against each other's shoulders.

Aston sighed, heartbroken for them but unable to do anything about it. He looked to Slater. "I guess we'd better call Crews."

Chapter 18

Blacktooth River had one of the last Black Stump Bar & Grill's left in Australia. It might, in fact, be the last one in existence, Aston mused. He remembered how it was always such a treat to come when he was a kid. Any special occasion called for a big feed at the Black Stump. As an adult, and a well-travelled one at that, he recognized now just how awful the place was. Well, maybe that was unkind. It wasn't awful, it filled a kind of niche in Australian cuisine that people clearly still desired. It had been heaven to him as a kid, after all, and sometimes people never outgrew that stuff.

The classic orange and black sign out front had given Aston a distinct pulse of nostalgia. Inside was largely the same too, wooden floors with wooden tables, red and white checked tablecloths, TVs blaring music videos and a long bar at one end that sold a limited selection of beer, wine, and spirits. The place was like a time machine.

He'd ordered a double burger with curly fries and Slater ordered a steak sandwich. They both had a bottle of cold James Boag's beer in front of them, both still a little shaken. It wasn't the severed limb, Aston had realized, that made him so uncomfortable. It was Sophie's raw grief. He'd wanted closure for her, and now he'd given it, he felt like a dick. But there was nothing else he could have done. He hoped in the long run it would prove to help her get on with life. At least now she wouldn't spend the rest of her days wondering what had happened to her brother.

The waitress, her name badge read AGNES, came over with their food, a tired smile fixed in place. She had to be at least 60 and Aston recognized her from his youth. She paused and looked at him for a moment, eyebrows slightly cinched together.

Aston smiled. "You recognize me?"

"I think I do, but I don't know why. You've been here before?"

"Lots of times, but not for years. I was a kid last time I was here. You'd remember my folks, Betty and Harold Aston."

The woman's eyes widened in surprise. "Oh! You're little Sammy?"

Slater snorted. "Sammy?"

He glanced at her with a pained grin. "Shut up!" He looked back to Agnes and nodded. "I'm Sam. Good to see you again. I can't believe you still work here."

Agnes gestured around herself. "What else is there to do, eh? But I'm retiring soon. Going to sell up my place here, take my savings, and buy a little unit on the Gold Coast."

"That sounds like a great plan," Aston said.

"I remember your parents well, Sammy. They were good people. Terrible what happened."

Aston nodded, lips pressed together. He still missed them terribly. "Yeah, thanks."

"The storm that night," Agnes said. "Honestly, even up here in the tropical north, we'd never seen anything like it. There are legends and stories still told about that storm. You know old Bob Daley? He says it was aliens caused it."

"It was a bad time," Aston agreed. "Bob Daley is still alive? He was an old man telling stories in the pub when I was a kid."

Agnes laughed. "He's got to be ninety if he's a day. Probably older. But yep, still going and still spinning his yarns. That storm is one of his favorites."

"It was a bad one for lots of people, not just us."

Agnes's smiled softened into sadness. "Well, I'm sorry to bring it up. Only I went to school with your mum." Agnes looked off into the middle distance a moment. "They were good people. I'm glad to see you again, Sammy. Are you here for long?" she asked, returning her attention to him.

"Leaving any time, actually. Just a quick visit."

"Well. You travel safe, now."

She turned and left them to it. Aston picked up a fry and chewed thoughtfully.

"A bad storm?" Slater asked. "I remember you said your parents died in a car accident, but we never really talked about it."

"Yeah," Aston said, mind drifting back to that fateful phone call all those years ago. "A huge storm. They were driving from Cape York when a storm hit. They should have stopped, but I guess they were determined to push through. Dad would have been anyway, he was stubborn like that. But the storm was massive, they got caught in flash flooding. Washed the whole car away with them in it. Their bodies were never found. I even looked myself. They must have tried to make it on foot, but they were in a remote part of the rainforest."

He heaved a tired sigh. He understood the realities of the rainforest. Scavengers and the warm, damp climate could reduce human remains to almost nothing in a relatively short period of time. What was more, a person could be standing inches from a body and not be able to see it among the dense undergrowth. Still, the fact that he had failed to discover their bodies rankled. He felt that he had let them down.

"Oh, Sam, that's horrible."

"Yeah. Another reason I don't like coming back here, probably. I guess we should make plans to head off after we've eaten."

Slater frowned. "You don't think we should stay until the memorial service? After all, you and Sophie go way back."

Aston looked up, surprised she suddenly cared. "Really?"

"This is your hometown. You know these people."

"Sure, it's my hometown but it's not really home. Hasn't been for a long time, even before my parents died. I haven't stayed connected with anyone here, and for good reason. Sophie's call came out of the blue, I'm not sure I really owe her anything."

Slater's phone rang and she quickly silenced it.

"Who was that?" Aston asked.

"Doesn't matter. You sure you don't want to stay?"

Within a moment of putting her phone down on the table, she got a text.

"Sorry," Slater said. "Just a sec." She left the table and took the phone with her, heading outside the diner.

Aston watched after her. Obviously something was up, she was twitchy for some reason. She was only gone a moment before she returned to the table and sat down. She put her phone away in her bag.

"Spill it," Aston said.

Slater laughed softly, shook her head. "Nothing gets past you, does it?"

"What's going on?"

"Okay, don't be mad, all right?"

"I'll try, but no guarantees."

"I've called in my crew." At his confused expression, she said, "I'm joining the hunt with Ned King."

Aston was stunned, surprise quickly turning to anger. "Were you going to tell me?"

"Of course! It's just that we've had other stuff going on. We found a leg in the river, Sam! I thought you might be off-kilter with that and Sophie being upset and all. I was going to tell you now, over dinner."

"Is that why you're trying to convince me to stay? Pretending to care about Sophie because you see a documentary opportunity?"

"Sam, that's not fair! You don't have to remain here even if I do. I genuinely thought you might want to stick around. For God's sake, Sam, it's a hunt for a surviving prehistoric reptile!"

"Where are your priorities?" Aston demanded. "Do you care about me and Sophie, or just about the opportunity for work?"

"When did it become 'you and Sophie' again?"

"I didn't mean it like that and you know it."

"Forget I said it. The point is, I can care about you and look out for my career at the same time. Don't accuse me of manipulation. I'm not the one who vanished off the grid when I needed you most."

"I thought we were past that!" Aston said, though a pang of guilt stabbed him. "I was protecting you from Chang and his assassins. I cared enough to not want you killed!"

Slater stared at him a moment, then her eyes softened. "Yes, I know. I'm sorry. I don't like that you ran out the way you did, but I do understand why. We have talked about it. But now, here, this is something new. It's an opportunity I can't pass up. It doesn't mean that I won't also be here for you, and Sophie. And if you need to go, I can cope with that too. I'd much prefer it if you did stick around, but I know that has more baggage for you than me."

"You won't come with me if I head home?"

"I'll come soon after. Sam, if I don't jump on this, Ned

will bring in someone else. Probably some idiot like Grizzly Grant."

Aston knew that name, thanks to Slater's many colorful rants about Grant, a rival television presenter whom she considered to be an utter buffoon. He could understand her not wanting a competitor to scoop her story, but this whole situation was surely too dangerous. "Didn't you learn anything from Lake Kaarme?" he said.

Shock was instant on Slater's face. "That's a low blow, Sam."

"Your team was killed there, Jo. The same thing could happen here if you go out into the bush. You might get killed! This is not a safe place."

"I'm not exactly inexperienced in the field," she said. "Dangerous places are where I go, or had you forgotten that?" Her voice had gone cold, the hard edge he recognized. She would dig her heels in on this. And perhaps that wasn't so unreasonable. She was a professional and Lake Kaarme had been strange and exceptional even by dangerous territory standards.

They looked at each other over their food for a moment. Eventually, Slater said, "If you can't accept that this is my career, we're going to have to have a conversation about the future."

Aston wasn't sure what to say to that. At the least, he was conflicted. He nodded slightly, trying to formulate a response, in part trying to decide if he did want to stay in town any longer or just get the hell out, when two people entered the diner and looked around. Aston immediately recognized Slater's camera and audio team. The camera operator was Lynette Forrest, a tall, slim, blonde woman with an athletic build. The sound guy was Barry Caldwell, a small man, but stocky, with a mass of floppy brown curls and a constant, warm grin. They were good people. They spotted Slater and waved, headed over.

"They're here already?" Aston said, aghast. "You must have called them the moment we left Ned King's place!"

Slater shrugged. "It's my job to see an opportunity and jump on it, Sam."

He stood angrily, tossed some bills on the table. "I guess we'll discuss everything later. You obviously have more important people to talk to right now." Without a backward glance, he turned and stalked out.

Chapter 19

Izzy walked the banks of Blacktooth River as the sun went down, lost in thought. The loss of Cooper hurt deeply. She had loved him, she knew that to be true, even though they were young. Her parents didn't seem to really get it, how much she and Coop cared for each other. There was a future there, a potential lost now forever. She couldn't help thinking over and over again about what might have been, what they might have done, where they might have gone. If only she hadn't acted like a teenager and insisted he come down to the jetty that night, they would still have a future.

She hissed softly in annoyance. This shitbox town, she'd been stuck here for so long, desperate to leave, and then she'd found a twinned soul in Cooper and he'd wanted to leave as well. Some people mocked them, said things like, "Sure, you're going to find your soul mate in the same tiny town you've lived in your whole life!" But she had found her other half in Cooper. No one said there was only one perfect match for every person, there could be lots. Even if someone was a one-in-a-million find, that meant there were at least five just in Queensland alone.

They had all kinds of ideas, she and Coop, they were making all sorts of plans. Sometimes she wondered if Cooper really meant it, if he'd ever actually see their schemes through, but she thought he would in the end. He might take a bit more nudging than her, a little extra force to push him out of his small town complacency, but he wanted to be pushed. Now that same small town had swallowed him up, refused to let him ever leave.

Izzy's anger turned to tears again. Swallowed him up

quite literally. Rusty Crews said Coop had probably drowned and then his body was eaten by crocs, but she didn't buy that. Izzy felt sick again, the repeated waves of nausea incessant for the last couple of days. Cooper was a good swimmer. It was hard to think of him drowning. She'd told Rusty as much, but the ranger had shrugged, his eyes apologetic. "Easy to get a foot tangled in this river, the current pulls on you. It's not a fast river, but it's relentless. All moving water is."

Of course, the other possibility was even more awful to think about. Maybe Cooper hadn't drowned and then been eater, but grabbed while he swam. It was a reality in these parts. As long as she could remember, she'd been brought up to respect the waterways, always look out for crocs, never swim alone.

"Never bloody swim at all, if you've got a lick of sense!" her mother would say. But of course, everyone did. And every now and then reports came in that someone else had been taken. And she had felt something that night, brushing past her foot. Had she been within inches of sharing Cooper's fate? Might it have been her instead of him?

Tears fell as Izzy looked down at the ring on her finger. A promise ring Cooper had given her about six months before. Now it signified a promise he would never be able to keep.

Something moved in the bush, a crack of breaking branch and a slithering of leaves. Izzy stopped, sniffed, looked up. It wasn't full dark yet, still a good half hour or so of twilight remaining, but she found herself in gloom all the same. She turned around, saw the last streetlight where the road turned away from the river some hundred meters back. The dock was another hundred meters beyond that, and the small gravel car park where she'd left her mum's car. Lost in thought, she'd wandered a little further along the river than she'd planned.

Another sound from her right made her jump. The river to her left drifted by as sluggishly as ever, though she wondered about the deeper currents Rusty had talked about. The bush to her right was dark already, the canopy making inky shadows. The lit street seemed suddenly distant. Izzy sucked in a shuddering breath as her heart rate climbed, then started walking.

Another rustling and a crackle of twigs. The sound was immediately recognizable, a croc dragging itself along. She must be between it and the water, a dangerous spot, but the creature would want the river most likely. She turned her head, tried to figure exactly where the sound was. Then it came again, a little ahead of her. She took a few steps back to give it room.

"Go on," she whispered, straining her eyes into the shadowy trees. "Back you go, the water's lovely." She stifled another sob at the memory of Cooper saying the same thing not so long ago.

The crackle of dry leaves and twigs sounded again, moving back the other way. Izzy scurried forward a few paces, confused. Then a long, scaled snout emerged from the scrub a few paces behind her. Izzy gasped, stepped further back. It wasn't too big, less than two meters. It would surely ignore her. It walked its stumpy way out of the bush, aiming for the river, then abruptly turned to look right at her. Izzy froze. The croc's mouth opened, emitted a hissing exhalation that she could only interpret as a threat.

As they stared at one another, more rustling in the trees started and another croc appeared, a little bigger than the first. It came to a halt not far from its friend and turned to face Izzy too. They both stared at her.

"What the hell?" she breathed.

A soft sound of water sluicing caused her to look to the river, and two more crocs slid up across the muddy bank. They moved onto the grass and all four made a ragged line, all staring at her. They hissed in unison, startling her.

"What is this?" Izzy said aloud, crying again.

She began walking backwards, away from the crocs, knowing the road, the streetlight, her car were all that way, somewhere behind her. She just had to keep going, but couldn't stop watching the crocs. She quickened her pace as a fifth one, this one a lot bigger, well over three meters, came out of the bush too.

"Am I dreaming?" she said, almost running backwards, too terrified to take her eyes off the things. "This is a nightmare, it can't be real!" Crocs didn't behave like this. They were solitary hunters, not pack animals.

The five began moving forward, short legs powerful against the ground.

Are they chasing me? Izzy thought. Are they herding me?

"Leave me alone, you bastards!" she yelled at them, then turned and ran. Crocs could move fast on land, but only for a short distance. She was young and fit, she could certainly run faster and for a lot longer than these awful reptiles.

She pumped her arms as she sprinted. One thong slipped from her foot, spinning back into the grass, but she didn't care. She kicked off the other one and hammered barefoot towards the road.

Something began running behind her, off in the trees. Not the crocs scrambling their way along on the bellies, but something big, heavy, pounding along. It sounded like a giant taking huge strides. She risked a look back, almost too scared to see what it was, but too fascinated not to know.

Nothing was there except the line of crocs, further from her now, unable to keep up. But she still heard the pounding run, matching the heart beat that thumped in her ears.

This is the part of the horror movie where the person always falls over! she thought manically, but she didn't fall. She ran on, almost to the road. Further along she saw her mum's car, reflecting the streetlight of the small car park by the jetty. Where Cooper had died. She let out a sob as she ran, breath burning in her chest. Whatever it was making all the noise still pounded with her and she heard branches breaking. She realized it was crashing through the trees to her right, overtaking her.

She didn't dare look this time, so close to the road. Almost there, she thought. Come on! Almost there!

Movement beside her caught her eye despite the determination not to look this time, because it was high up. Too high, like the trees were bending down to grab her. Still running, the road only twenty paces away, she looked anyway and screamed. The biggest, widest crocodile mouth she had ever seen swept down from above the trees and engulfed her. She was assaulted by the rank stench of rotting meat, thought, This is a nightmare, then jaws bristling with massive teeth slammed shut.

Chapter 20

Aston wasn't entirely sure why he was so annoyed, but he couldn't shake the feeling off. He knew Slater had a job to do, and she was damned good at it. He knew she would jump on any lead, especially the opportunity to break a story. It was no surprise she'd thought to get on top of Ned King and his strange giant croc theory. Aston supposed it was that she'd done it without telling him that really irked. She hadn't mentioned a thing, just gone ahead and immediately called in her crew.

Of course, she didn't have to tell him anything, but wasn't that what partners did? Discussed their plans? Especially if those plans might mean Aston had to stay in a town he was eager to leave again. He'd put this place behind him once, with good reason, and was keen to do it again as soon as possible.

He knew what Slater would say if he brought that up. She'd tell him he didn't have to stay, to go back to Kangaroo Island, go back to work and let her get on with her job. Hell, he wasn't aware of where in the world she was half the time, her work took her to the craziest places, so this was really no different. But he felt responsible for this place, for this situation. He wouldn't be able to just up and leave her to it. And despite what she might say, he thought perhaps she knew that. And maybe that's why he was so rankled by it all. She wasn't deliberately trying to control him, but indirectly the manipulation was there.

He walked up to Sophie's front door and knocked. He was concerned about her, and thought it would be good to check in. Since he'd stormed out on Jo, he really didn't have much else to do, after all. Sophie had just lost her brother, and would probably appreciate some company, to help take her mind off things.

While that was true, Aston also knew it was a good excuse not to go back to the hotel just yet as well. He didn't want to have to talk to Slater about her plans while he was still so annoyed about everything. He was self-aware enough to realize that he probably needed to straighten his head about how he felt before they talked again or he'd say something dumb that he would regret.

Besides, let Slater wonder where he was for a change, like he spent half his time wondering where in the world she'd gone. There's that dumbass attitude we were just thinking about, he chided himself. But he couldn't help how he felt. He just needed a bit of time to cool off, probably.

Sophie answered the door, her expression strangely blank. "Sam."

He didn't know what he'd expected. Maybe to find her heartbroken, tear-stained, in need of comfort. Not so empty-looking.

"Hi," he said uselessly, at a loss for a better greeting.

Sophie turned away and went back inside, leaving the door open. He followed her, closed the door behind himself. People deal with grief in different ways, he thought. Sophie was probably just numb from it at this point.

"Obviously you're not okay," Aston said as he followed her into the kitchen. "But are you... I mean, do you need anything?"

"Kind of you to come by," Sophie said. "Crews just left."

"Oh. Business or..?"

Sophie huffed through her nose, but it could hardly be called a laugh. Her mouth didn't show any hint of a smile. "He's contacted the coroner's court and they'll send a registrar to inspect the remains."

"A registrar?"

Sophie nodded, shrugged. "Apparently registrars assist coroners in less complex investigations, so Rusty told me. Mostly death by natural causes. It's pretty clear what happened here, so there's really no need for an investigation or anything. Just paperwork."

"Right. That makes some kind of sense, I guess."

"Crews thinks it should be a simple matter." She barked a laugh that was equal parts sob and anger too. Aston was pleased to see some emotion breaking through. "The remains—" She sucked in a quick breath. "The remains will be released in a few days, he reckons, and we can arrange a memorial service or something."

"Must be tough for him to have to be the official in all this," Aston said.

Sophie shrugged again. "Rusty is Rusty, Sam, you know that. He is not a complex guy."

Aston smiled at the truth of it. "I wonder what you ever saw in him."

Sophie rolled her eyes, shook her head. "I often ask myself the same question. And I ask it of myself regarding you too."

Aston winced, like she'd delivered a physical blow. He thought that barb a little unnecessary, but perhaps he shouldn't have ragged on Crews. Sophie obviously wasn't in the mood for any kind of humor.

"I guess no one's perfect," he offered lamely.

She looked at him, one eyebrow raised. "Really, Sam? You vanished from my life after your parents died." She lifted her hands, palms up. "Just... gone."

"Yeah, I tend to do that. It's complicated—"

"It's really not, mate. You could have let me in rather

than shutting me out. But no, you're a big man, a tough guy, you have to go it alone like some kind of gunslinger or some shit."

"Where's this coming from?" Aston said, taken aback. He thought maybe he'd have done better going back to the hotel to face Slater. Perhaps this was some kind of cosmic justice. "Anyway, after I left for uni you moved on to Crews so quickly I didn't have much chance to do anything. I figured you were happy and I was out, so... so that was it."

Sophie stared at him levelly for a moment, then looked away. "I guess we're all maybe a bit more complicated than we like to admit," she said quietly. "Make yourself a cuppa or something. I have to call Izzy."

She stepped away from the kitchen counter and pulled her phone out. "Is she doing okay?" Aston asked.

"Of course not, but she's tougher than she realizes. She keeps going and hanging around at the dock and walking along the river. She still blames herself and she's torturing herself with that. I'll talk her out of it eventually, but maybe not until after the memorial service. People need rituals to help them deal with stuff."

"That's true. Perhaps right now going to the jetty is the ritual she needs to get it out of her system. As long as we keep making sure to remind her it's not her fault?"

Sophie paused from dialing the number, looked up. "Maybe. Strangely insightful of you, Sam. But she went down to the dock earlier and I haven't heard from her since. I told her to come over for some dinner and she said she would, but never showed up. That's not like her. I'm worried."

Aston had a moment's thought of Ned King's theories, of giant crocs and strange disappearances.

Sophie's face hardened. "What is it?"

He shook his head, tried to smile. "Nothing."

"I can read you like a book, Samuel Aston! What's up?"

Aston swallowed. His fears were well-founded, after all. And if something had happened to Izzy now too? It was too much to think about. He took a deep breath and told Sophie all about the attacks and disappearances. Things Crews had clearly not shared with her yet. Why did he have to be the bad guy in all this?

"Why the hell didn't you tell me everything before?"

"It… well, it wasn't for me to say."

"I thought we were friends, Sam!"

That cut him too. "It was Crews' decision to make. I thought he would have told you everything. It's official stuff as it involves deaths—"

"That's crap and you know it! What else?"

Aston shrugged. It was out now, he might as well tell her everything. By the time he'd got to the end of explaining about their meeting with Ned King, Sophie had gone pale. "I mean, it all seems just too far-fetched to be real, you know?" he said as she stared at him. "And given that Cooper was gone either way, I figured what was the point in telling you more? Scaring you more?"

"What's the point? The point is that I would have told Izzy to stay away from the bloody river! I've got to get down there."

She turned and ran from the house. With a curse, Aston ran after her.

Chapter 21

Craig Gomzi hated when Rusty Crews left him alone in the office to work late. Crews was the laziest boss Gomzi had ever known, but he was the boss and Gomzi had to suck it up. Didn't mean he had to like it. If there was one thing he hated more than being in the office, it was being in the office alone, late, when he could be drinking and hanging out with this friends. He was supposed to be filling out a bunch of reports and requisition orders, but he had the motivation of a stoned teenager. Which was to say, less than zero. He also knew that Crews, being as lazy as he was, wouldn't be back in the office until at least ten the next day, despite his contract saying he should be on call from 8am until 6pm seven days a week.

"Being on call doesn't mean being in the office," Crews had said, with an air of officious superiority. "It means being contactable. I have a phone on me at all times."

Yeah, you do, Gomzi had thought, but not said. Except even an air raid siren couldn't wake you before nine, so there's no point in ringing a phone that's on silent more often than not.

Regardless, Gomzi could relax for the evening and make sure he got in early enough the next day to catch up. Everyone thought he was dumb, but Gomzi was clever. There was value in that, his father had taught him, and his dear old dad had taught him well.

The TV set mounted on a bracket up in the corner of the office played an NRL game. Gomzi had never been especially sporty himself, but he enjoyed watching the National Rugby League. Except right now his team were copping a drubbing, the North Queensland Cowboys down more than 20 points to the Melbourne Storm. To Melbourne! It made him mad. Maybe he did care a little more than he was willing to admit.

He leaned back in Crews' chair and propped his heels on the edge of the desk, scowling up at the screen. Almost halfway through the second half, it was unlikely the Cowboys would catch up. But they might. They'd pulled off miracle wins over bigger deficits in the past.

Gomzi jumped when the door popped open. He dropped his feet from the desk and swiveled the chair to see a solid-looking man step in. He wore neat and clean jeans and a flannel shirt, like he'd just bought them and put them straight on. Gomzi guessed him to be a similar age, but that's where any similarity ended. This guy was solid, built like a soldier from an action movie, with close-cropped hair that had a wide gray streak through the middle. His face was hard, square-jawed, but he smiled, softening the effect. He immediately made Gomzi think of undercover cops, but Gomzi was wily enough to see past that to something more sinister. If he'd been a dog, his hackles would be standing on end.

"Evening," the man said with what Gomzi considered a predatory smile.

Gomzi nodded. "Can I help you?"

"I really hope you can." The man flashed a badge in a leather wallet.

Gomzi caught a glimpse of a silver something, an official-looking card opposite with a photo he assumed was of the man himself. He opened his mouth to ask for a closer look, but the stranger plowed on, slipping the wallet back into his pocket.

"I'm with the parks department. Russell Crews is

expecting me."

Gomzi floundered for a moment. He didn't want to look like an idiot, like he didn't know what was going on with his own office, but he didn't believe this bloke for a second. "Right," he said, uncertainly. "It's a little late, though. Rusty... I mean Russell isn't here now. He went home."

The man nodded, made a show of looking at a chunky dive watch on his wrist. "Yes, yes. Of course. Sorry about that, it's been a dog of a day. So much going on, I'm really running behind. But look, I'm sure you can help, no need to disturb Mr. Crews."

"Right," Gomzi said again. "Mr. Crews. And what's your name?"

"You like working here?" the man asked.

Strange question. Was it a threat? "Yeah, it's a good job. Look, what is it you wanted?"

"They sent me up from Canberra. I need to follow up on the recent disappearances around here."

Gomzi frowned. Canberra? Was the guy a Fed? "You mean Cooper Cook?"

The man smiled. "Sure, for one. Want to tell me about that?" He hooked the chair on the other side of the desk out with his heel and sat down, leaned back, entirely at ease.

Gomzi shrugged. "What's to tell? Poor bastard went for a swim at night. Should have known better. We found his leg and Crews called in the coroner. So not really disappeared. Drowned, Rusty thinks most likely."

"Drowned." The man nodded.

Gomzi wondered why he wasn't taking any notes. Maybe he already knew about the Cooper story. And surely he couldn't be thinking about Steve Jackman's missing goat. Or at least, the half that was missing. Gomzi would look a fool if he mentioned that.

"Who else?" the man asked.

"Who else?"

"Sure. Anyone else missing? There's been reports of a dangerous predator in the area, after all."

Gomzi thought about the wrecked tinny he and Crews had investigated, but something told him not to mention that right away. "Steve Jackman's missing half a goat," he said.

"Half a goat?"

Gomzi pressed his lips together, then nodded. "Chopped right through the middle. Don't really know what might have done that." Gomzi winced then, suddenly sure he was saying stuff he shouldn't. He wanted to ask about the man's credentials again, but felt foolish. Regardless, he was an authority here, and he had every right to know. Plus, the man hadn't given his name, despite being asked directly. He needed to be firm. Official. Rusty wouldn't stand for this. "Let me see that badge again, please, Mister...?"

"What about any sightings?" the man asked.

Gomzi was wrongfooted. "What?"

"Anybody report any animal sightings, or evidence of animals that would strike you as unusual or out of place?"

"Unusual or out of place?"

"Sure."

"Animals?"

"Exactly."

Gomzi had had enough. If the bloke was going to play cagey with who he was, he could play that game with Crews. "Look, you probably need to talk to Rusty. To Russell. Mr. Crews. He's the boss here, so he has all the, you know, all the information. You want to leave a business card or something? I'll get Rusty to give you a call in the morning. After all, he's who you were planning to see, right?"

The man gave his soft smile again, only this time it seemed more than a little disturbing. Gomzi couldn't quite put his finger on what it was about the man's demeanor, but it gave him chills. Not the sort of bloke you'd want to meet in a dark alley, as his old dad would have said.

"That's okay, Craig. I'd better be getting along. But I'll be in touch. Thanks for your help."

He turned and strolled from the office, closing the door gently behind himself.

I don't remember giving him my name, Gomzi thought.

Chapter 22

It was getting late and their father hadn't returned. JD Gibson tried not to worry, but too much was going bad lately. He couldn't do anything except expect the absolute worst. After all, if their father had run into whatever it was that had taken Rod, the man had no chance. As if a hunting rifle would ever stop that monster. And he still had a killer headache, worse than any he'd previously known.

"Maybe he just got too drunk," he said, clutching at straws. "You know he always drinks before he hunts. Passed out somewhere."

Dicky scoffed at the suggestion. "You ever known Dad to get too drunk for anything? I've never known anyone who can drink like he can. You ever see him passed out anywhere?"

His older brother had a point. Their father had a capacity for alcohol that seemed almost superhuman sometimes. One time the man had boasted that he'd started early one Australia Day and drunk himself sober then wasted again three times in a row and hadn't stopped until the following morning, when he'd driven right through to Rockhampton for a job. He wasn't boasting, either. The tale had been corroborated by others present. Most people who knew Ray Gibson were in awe of, or horrified by, his alcoholic ability. It was unnatural. And it would kill him sooner rather than later, regardless of his capacity. But JD thought maybe that wasn't such a bad thing. The shadow of their father had loomed over all three brothers their whole lives. He loved the man in one way. It was, he supposed, impossible not to harbor some love for the people who created you, but he hated his father in many ways. Several people would probably be better off if Ray Gibson died. He derailed the thought. One of the brother's lives had already ended, and, despite everything, he didn't want to consider his father dead and gone too. Maybe gone, somewhere far away, but JD wasn't the sort of person who could wish anyone dead.

"You know what I think?" Dicky said, pausing to slug half a can of beer in one go. He was developing a habit to rival their father. He belched. "Fucking KIND."

"What?"

"Dad said he was going to have a few drinks and then go out hunting for the beast that took Rod, yeah?"

"Yeah. And I'm too sick to go and you're... what? Too scared, I guess?"

Dicky glowered, took a threatening step forward.

JD held up both palms. "I'm too scared to go as well! No way I want to go back anywhere near where Roddy died. My injury just gave me a good excuse, is all. Shit, man, you'd have to be crazy."

"Crazy like Dad?"

JD shrugged. "Frankly, yeah."

Dicky grunted, drank the rest of his beer. He stomped off to the kitchen, then returned with a fresh can. "I'm guessing you still don't want one?"

"I can't imagine having a drink with this headache."

"Might make it better." Dicky gestured with the can, trying to entice.

"It's beer, not Panadol."

Dicky slumped back into the sofa. "Whatever."

They sat in sullen silence for a moment, then JD tried again. "So, what about KIND?"

"Knights in Nature's Defense, my arse. They're

terrorists is what I reckon."

"Terrorists?"

"Yeah. They act all high and mighty for the animals, but they just hate people. Bunch of do-gooders who hate poachers, especially." Dicky wagged one finger at JD, pointing at his head. "What happened to you? You reckon it was a bloody yowie?"

"I said that's what it looked like, I don't know what else—"

"It was one of those arseholes, ya idiot. It was some KIND dickhead dressed up like a giant monkey, roaming the bush to scare people away. The fact that they weren't happy giving you a scare but actually clocked you one and tried to drag you away? Terrorists!" Dicky shot his finger up into the air as if in triumph, case closed.

"And what do you think they were going to do with me, assuming it was some KIND soldier all dressed up?"

"Make an example of ya. Hurt ya, scare ya, send ya back home to scare the rest of town." Dicky leaned forward, elbows on his knees, warming to the subject. "Picture this, yeah? They've got some place all set up to look like a yowie nest. This bastard knocks you on the head, drags you back there, makes sure you're good and scared, then turns their back a bit. Maybe wanders off, acting like they think you're asleep or something, to give you a chance to get away. So you think the monster was planning to eat you or whatever, but you escaped. Brave and clever Jack Daniels escaped the yowie! But that's what they wanted you to think, because then you'd come back to town and tell the story and everyone would be too scared to go out there. So KIND manage to keep us and everyone else out of the rainforest, keep it all for themselves."

Dicky sat back, grinning, clearly proud of himself.

JD drew a slow breath, taking a moment to let his fuzzy head process Dicky's idiocy. But maybe it wasn't so stupid. No, check that. Pretty much everything Dicky ever came up with was stupid, but maybe here he'd inadvertently stumbled onto some kind of truth. KIND weren't terrorists, but was it such a stretch to think they'd dress up and try to scare people away? They were extremists of a sort, after all. Then something else occurred to him. "Nah, wait a minute. If someone came back to town with a story like that, every goon with a rifle would go in, deliberately hunting the yowie. Can you image, everyone desperate to be the one who proves they exist? KIND would have to be mad to risk that."

Dicky sneered, waved away JD's logic. "You reckon KIND aren't bloody mad?" He slugged more beer.

This was getting them nowhere. "You know what, Dicky," JD said, to change the subject. "We should tell Crews."

"What?"

"You might be onto something. I mean, the whole fake yowie nest thing is a bit of a stretch, but they might be dressing up just to scare people off. Maybe KIND are getting more aggressive. More dangerous? We should tell Crews everything and let the rangers handle it. Him and Craig Gomzi."

Dicky tipped his head back and laughed. "Why the hell would we tell them anything? Apart from the fact that the Gibson family doesn't talk to the man, to any kind of authority, Crews and Gomzi are a pair of complete losers. Why do think they get posted to a shithole like Blacktooth River National Park? Hardly a plum job, is it?"

JD thought there was some truth to that, but he disagreed with not getting help from the authorities when necessary. The Gibsons spent half their lives in trouble and most of it was of their own making. Well now Rod was dead and their dad was missing. This had grown well beyond Gibson family drama. "You do what you want, Dicky. I'm going to call Crews. And I'm going to see him."

He stood up, a little groggy still, to get his phone. Dicky stood too, blocked his way. "You'll do no such thing, Jack Daniels!"

"It's not up to you! You're not the boss of me!"

"Rod's dead and Dad's not here, so yes I am. That makes me in charge."

"Don't be an idiot, I'm a grown man. I'll make my own decisions, thanks. Get out of the way."

Dicky put a hand against JD's chest and shoved, nearly knocked him down. "You'll do as I say!"

JD saw red, too much pain, too much heartache, too much unreleased anger. With a roar, he drove forward and swung a punch at Dicky's face. His brother registered a moment's surprise, then tried to duck, a moment too late. JD missed the jaw, but his knuckles cracked painfully into the top of Dicky's head. Pain lanced through his knuckles.

Dicky staggered, crying out, and put his hands over his head. JD tried to take advantage, threw one, two, three more punches, battering Dicky's forearms and shoulders. With a grunt of rage, Dicky stood tall again and swung a punch of his own. It was a glancing blow, skimming off JD's cheekbone, but he immediately saw dancing lights and his head whined with pain. He made a weak sound of hurt and distress, tried stepping sideways, but his leg buckled and he fell. On his hands and knees he gasped, swallowed hard twice to avoid blowing chunks. If he wasn't so concussed he would have beat the crap out of Dicky, but he was too dizzy to even look up after one half-arsed shot. He held up a palm as Dicky advanced on him.

"Stop! Stop. I'm too sick for this."

"And too bloody weak anyway," Dicky said. "So accept that I'm in charge and here's what we're going to do. Screw Rusty and Gomzi, they're no use to anyone. You and me are going to find out what happened to Dad. I am not bloody scared, whatever you say, and I won't sit around while Dad might be in trouble. We're gonna find him and get revenge for Rod."

It had been a mistake, JD realized, to accuse Dicky of being scared. "And if Dad is dead too?" he asked.

"Then I suppose we'll be getting revenge for them both."

Chapter 23

It was past 10pm when Aston and Sophie arrived at the car park by the jetty where Cooper had been taken. Aston refused to accept the theory Crews tried to hold onto, that Cooper had somehow got caught up and drowned. He hadn't admitted as much to Sophie, but he thought Crews' theory close to impossible. There was a lot of detritus on the riverbed, he'd seen plenty of that firsthand while diving, and the currents lower down were a lot stronger, but nothing down there could really tangle someone up. Especially a fit young man, who had no clothes on to get tangled. Rocks and logs mostly littered the riverbed, there were some patches of grassy vegetation, but that was about it. He'd spotted a couple of rusty shopping trolleys from the local IGA, but they were no real threat of anything except tetanus should someone get scratched up by one. Aston had quietly decided that Cooper had indeed been taken by something. He was loathe to accept the Ned King giant Razana theory too, but though it pained him to admit, it was a lot more likely than some random drowning. He figured it was largely academic anyway. The young man was dead and gone, and nothing would bring him back. Of course, the idea of a giant killer still out on the loose was something else entirely to consider.

"Oh no. That's her mum's car," Sophie said as she turned into the car park and pulled to a stop.

"What's that?" Aston asked, pulled from his thoughts.

Sophie nodded forward at the only other vehicle there. "Her mum's car. Izzy has a license, but no car of her own yet. Her mum lets her borrow that one sometimes. You can tell Izzy was driving because the P-plates are on it."

Aston nodded, looking at the magnetic red and white provisional driver plate stuck on the back of the car, remembering how young Izzy was. And how young Cooper had been. "So that's good, right? We know she's here somewhere."

"We already knew she came here, Sam. It's where she is now that matters. She hasn't been answering her phone."

Sophie killed the engine and they stepped out into the hot, sticky night. Cicadas sang, shrill and piercing. Somewhere some night bird squawked. Izzy was nowhere to be seen.

"Izzy!" Sophie yelled, briefly silencing all the nightlife with her volume. "Iz? You here?"

Aston winced at her shouts, but what else was there to do? He'd left his hire car at the restaurant for Slater and walked in a huff to Sophie's house. Now he felt a little under-equipped. He had a small belt knife and that was it beyond his phone, which was turned off because he was in a mood, and his wallet.

"You got a torch?" he asked.

Sophie nodded, leaned in the passenger side to open the glove compartment. She pulled out a small Maglight, twisted it on. "Come on."

"Maybe you should wait in the car," Aston said, reaching for the torch.

Sophie paused to turn a raised eyebrow to him, her face otherwise blank in pure disdain. "Really, Samuel?"

He withered under the look. "Fair enough. Which way?"

"Let's go upriver first, back towards town."

They walked slowly, shining the light, but the road ran alongside the river and there wasn't a great deal of space between the two. After a couple of hundred meters, Aston said, "Doesn't seem likely she'd wander up here. If she wanted to be alone, she'd probably go the other way, towards the bush."

Sophie stopped, lips pursed. "It's not likely she'd wander anywhere really. She usually just comes to sit on the dock."

Aston looked back past the jetty, sticking out into the muddy river. He nodded in that direction. "We found... we found him that way, though."

"Yeah, that's true."

"You think maybe she went down there?"

Sophie sighed. "I was trying not to think about it, but yes, she probably did."

They walked back to the car park, then along the grassy bank heading downriver. Soon enough the taller trees of thicker rainforest began where the road to their left curved away from following the river. The gap between river and bush wasn't large, but it was several hundred meters more before the trees came right up to the riverbank. Regardless, even in the dark, they could see most of the way and there was no evidence of Izzy. No sign of anyone at all.

Aston moved closer to the water, looking at the softer ground there. "Footprints here," he said. They were leading downriver and he followed them. After a while there was a muddle, like the person had stopped, turned around. But they were lost in the mess of grass and fallen leaves.

Sophie shone the torchlight down at the ground a while, then looked up at Aston. "Is this as far she came?"

"In this direction, I think so. She probably turned back, but walked further up the bank, on the grass. Not so easy to see tracks there."

Before Sophie could see the doubt in his eyes, he turned and walked back, closer to the trees. He was almost all the way back to the road when he saw something glistening on the broad leaves of a low bush.

He stepped quickly back, knowing the worst without needing the light. "We should call Crews," he said. "Get some help searching."

"What did you see, Sam?"

Sophie pushed past him and shined her light on the bush. The glistening spatters reflected a deep red.

"No!" she cried, her voice cracking. "Sam, is it blood?"

Already she was crying. She knew it was. He nodded, lips pressed into a thin line. He looked around, cautious of any predator that might still be present. He saw freshly broken branches laying in the grass and looked up. The tops of the trees all around were torn up and battered.

Sophie let out a primal yell of grief and rage. Aston grabbed her into a tight hug, hushed her. "There might be something still here!"

She suppressed her emption, breathed hard and fast in his arms.

"I can't take this, Sam!" she said at last. "This isn't right. This isn't fair! Izzy was a smart, caring, beautiful young woman!"

"I know. I know. I'm sorry. We don't know for sure that's her—"

"Yes, we do!"

He paused, nodded. "I guess it's unlikely to be anything else. Let's get back to the car. Call Crews."

One arm still around her shoulders, Aston guided Sophie back towards the road and the car park beyond. His nerves were on edge, ears alert for any sound. Sophie had managed to get her grief to a quiet sniffing, her sobs mostly just quick movements of her shoulders. Something moved in the bush ahead of them.

Aston froze, pulled Sophie to a halt.

"What is—" she started, but he silenced her with an

index finger to his lips.

She closed her mouth and her shoulders began to tremble under his arm.

Movement again, ahead of them in the bush, between them and the road. Aston moved his finger to tell Sophie to stay put and crept forward, one hand falling to his belt knife. Not that it would be any good at all against a croc, especially a giant one.

He saw a shape in the gloom, his heart hammered. It moved again, something on two legs, as tall as a man. Not a giant, at least. Aston began to slip the knife from its sheath, cursing the shaking of his hand.

Jo Slater stepped from the trees and yelped in surprise. Aston cried out too, then relief flooded him.

"What the hell are you doing here?" he asked.

"I should ask you the same thing!"

Slater's crew, Lynn and Barry, stepped out behind her, casting bemused looks around the small group.

"Seriously, Jo. What are you doing stalking around in the trees at night?"

"We weren't stalking, we were only a couple of meters in. There's no time to lose on a job like this. We're scouting locations, figuring out a shoot, getting angles from inside the trees to the water. This is where..." She glanced at Sophie. "This is where something happened, after all, so we'll want it in the documentary."

"Documentary?" Sophie said, face tight with an emotion Aston couldn't quite decipher. Annoyance, sadness, impotence maybe. "My phone is in the car." She walked quickly away.

"Isn't it a bit unfeeling to do this in front of Sophie?" Aston demanded.

"Sam, I had no idea she was here! Or you. Maybe if you

were answering your phone you could have let me know you were taking a moonlight stroll with your ex-girlfriend."

Aston chewed his lower lip a moment, then nodded. "I'm sorry, Jo. You're right, of course. My phone is off. I was annoyed." He looked to Sophie, almost back to her car now. "It's right here in my pocket."

"I think maybe Sophie wanted to be alone anyway," Slater said. "What's going on?"

Aston took a moment to tell her everything, how he'd decided to check in on Sophie, then Izzy missing, the blood on the leaves.

"And I know you have a job to do," he finished. "This town, it brings out the worst in me. Really, I'm sorry."

He leaned forward, gave her a kiss. Slater was warm in her response.

"Jeez, get a room, guys," Barry said.

Lynn giggled.

"You can be such a dick sometimes," Slater said to Aston, but she smiled with it.

"I know."

Slater glanced back again. "Holy crap, poor Sophie. Poor Izzy! It's really her?"

"Yeah, I think so. I told Sophie we'd better call Crews, get something official happening here."

Slater nodded. "Yeah, good call. And maybe get Ned King in on it, too. He needs all the information he can find to stay on top of this."

"Yep. Sophie will be calling Crews now. I guess I'll call King." He pulled out his phone and turned it on. Several messages from Slater pinged up and he felt like a fool. He knew she intended to document the hunt for Izzy now too, but like she'd said earlier, this was her job. If he wanted to be with her, he had to accept that.

The phone was answered with a muffled, "'Lo?"

"Ned, sorry to bother you so late. I think you need to get down here."

Chapter 24

Aston tried his best to comfort Sophie, but she was inconsolable. Slater and her crew had made themselves a little distant, ostensibly providing space, but Aston knew Slater was also taking the opportunity to work. She had scoped out several angles, had Lynn grab all kinds of stock footage and panning shots of the dock, the river, the car park. She'd done a short piece to camera standing on the dock, the river at her back. It was quite a talent, Aston thought, the way she could put on a nice top and get her hair and make-up fixed in the driver's seat of a car using only the mirror in the sun visor, and appear as beautiful and professional-looking as she ever had, regardless of the documentary budget or crew size. She really was good at her job, a genuine field talent. Now she was heading back towards where they'd found the blood on the leaves. Izzy's blood. He didn't want to believe it, but what else could it be?

"Why, Sam?" Sophie turned to him again after a moment of calm, renewed sobs bucking her shoulders as she cried into his arm. "It's just not fair!"

He stroked the back of her head gently. "It's not. It's really not."

What could he say to the poor woman? No platitudes would help. There certainly wasn't a place for life-is-cruel-and-then-you-die pragmatism. Izzy was only about or eighteen or so, the poor kid had barely started her life.

"We won't let it happen again," he said, wondering if that might go some way to consoling Sophie. "We'll find the thing and—"

"And what?" she snapped, angry. Her wet, red-rimmed

eyes pinned him. "Catch it? How? And then what? And if you do, will any of that bring back Cooper? Or Izzy?"

He shook his head. "No. It won't. I'm sorry, Sophie."

She devolved into tears again, pressed back against his arm. In the distance he saw Slater doing another piece to camera, saw Lynn pan the camera to the leaves with blood on them, then back to Slater.

Car tires crunched gravel and he looked the other way to see a large Range Rover Discovery pull to a stop. Bright white under the single streetlight, the side windows had decals of Ned King's grinning face and a fancy jungle script wrote CROCALYPSE! all down one side. Aston assume the other side of the car was just the same. Ned King hopped out, quickly followed by his top two helpers, Ringo and Penry. Aston felt immediately calmed by their soft, affable faces. A shame more people weren't as balanced as those two seemed to be, he thought.

"Sophie, Ned's here. I'll go talk to him."

Sophie nodded against his arm, still hitching quiet sobs, and turned away. Aston stood and walked towards the Discovery.

Ned raised a hand in greeting. "Sorry to see you again so soon given what you told me."

"Yeah. Sorry to get you up."

"It's okay, I'm usually in bed before nine, and early to rise, but when nature calls you operate by her clock. You want to show me what you found?"

Another car pulled in and parked next to Ned's. The National Parks Toyota Landcruiser looked a bit old and battered next to Ned's gleaming wagon. Crews got out and came to them.

"Hell of a bloody situation we have here," he said by way of greeting.

"Too right," Aston said. "Let's go take a look, shall we?"

"You got a weapon?" Ned asked, looking from Aston to Crews and back again.

They both shook their head. Aston chose not to mention his small knife. Ned gestured at his men, and Penry and Ringo leaned into the back of the Discovery and came up with a high-powered rifle each. They stood comfortably holding the guns, awaiting instructions.

"Just a minute," Crews said. He went over to Sophie where she sat against the dock railing and crouched down beside her. "You should go home. I'll call Gomzi out and get him to drive you, yeah?"

She shook her head, sniffed, and stood up. Aston saw immediately that she'd pushed her sadness and grief down, locked it away under a lid of cold rage. Her eyes were hard, mouth set in a thin line. "I'm going nowhere. Shall we?" She gestured back downriver.

Slater and her crew rejoined them.

"Wasting no opportunity, eh?" Ned said with a grin. "Very good."

"Please, just pretend we're not here," Slater said. "If you can try at all times not to look at the camera, that would be perfect. You all have important work to do, I recognize that, and we'll stay out of your way, so just ignore us, okay?"

For a moment it looked like Sophie would challenge Slater on that. They shared a cool look. Slater's face remained impassive, but Aston saw she was ready to push. He hoped she wouldn't have to.

"Whatever," Sophie said eventually, and turned to walk on.

The group headed downriver, Slater and her crew following quietly.

Crews and King both had high-powered torches with

them, making the search a lot easier. They inspected the blood spatter and damage to the surrounding trees.

"Something pretty massive came through there," King said, pointing into the bush. "I mean, something unnaturally large. Look at the damage to the undergrowth and the higher branches. Nothing we would expect to find around here could do that, especially so high up."

"How would it get so high?" Crews asked.

King turn to him and lifted both arms above his head like some King Kong parody, growling for added effect.

"It stood up?" Crews said, incredulous.

King grinned, dropped his arms and shrugged. "Like I said before, I think it's bipedal. Only explanation I can think of."

"And when it stands up, it's that tall?" Crews asked, pointing above them.

King nodded. "Quite possibly. I mean, if the thing is ten meters nose to tail, it would rear at least five meters tall up on its back legs. And honestly, judging by the evidence, the prints we've found, the wallows, I think it's probably a lot more than ten meters. Fifteen, maybe more. So breaking branches like that eight or ten meters high is no great stretch."

Nerves rippled around the group, everyone looking left and right. Crews played his torchlight out over the river, but there was nothing to be seen.

"Mr. King? Over here."

They looked as one toward where Penry was pointing. Something lay in the grass. Aston moved closer and bent to retrieve it, a dark green thong, the brand RIP CURL clear along one strap.

"Shit!" Sophie spat, her anger rising.

Aston turned to her. "Izzy's?"

She nodded tightly, mouth clenched shut. He saw her jaw muscles twitching.

"And here," Ringo said, a little further away. He help up the second shoe.

"Kicked 'em off while she was running would be my guess," King said. He turned, pointed. "Running hard that way, I suppose trying to get back to her car. But she was..." He paused, glanced at Sophie.

"Don't mind me," she snapped.

King nodded. "She was intercepted here." He pointed at the blood-spattered leaves.

"Wait a minute, though." Aston looked one way, then the other, trying to picture the scene. "If she was caught here, from this side, what was she running from? She must have already been going at a fair lick from that direction before she was taken by whatever came through here."

"Did it go through the trees and flank her?" Crews asked.

King pursed his lips in thought. "Maybe. But that seems unlikely. Perhaps Sam here is onto something. Maybe there was more than one."

"More than one what?" Crews asked.

"That, my friend, is what we need to find out. Let's look further downstream."

As they began to walk again, Aston heard something in the bush to his left. He glanced that way, but King put a hand on his arm, gave a slight shake of the head.

"But something—" Aston started.

"I know, mate. Quiet and calm, we need information. Doesn't sound too big, so let's wait and see."

As they kept moving, Aston became convinced someone or something was following them, but keeping to the trees, just out of sight in the shadows. Definitely not making enough noise to be the beast they imagined, but what was it? His heart rate began to race and his mouth was dry. He looked again at King, who nodded.

"Penry, Ringo?" King said.

"Yes, boss?"

"Go and check it out, eh?"

"I don't know if that's a good idea," Aston said.

But Penry gave his affable smile. "Don't worry, it's okay."

He and Ringo slipped into the trees, silent as shadows, rifles held ready. They were brave as hell, Aston thought. He wasn't sure he'd be game to go into that darkness, knowing something was in there.

Slater quickly moved Lynn into position for a better shot, but she winced as she did so. Aston wondered if some vestige of PTSD existed from their previous encounters and she was anticipating deaths any minute. He had to admit, part of him thought maybe she was right to fear that and he had bad memories too. A shout jolted everyone. King and Crews shined their torches into the trees. Another shout, then more clearly, Ringo calling out, "Penry, your left!"

"Got 'em!" Penry called back.

There was scuffling and a few cracks of branches breaking, a high-pitched yelp that sounded mostly indignant, then Penry and Ringo emerged from the shadows dragging a woman with them.

"What the hell?" Crews said. "Karen Rowling?"

"Knights in Nature's Defense on a night hike?" Aston asked.

"Unhand me!" Rowling snapped, trying to shake off the grips of Penry on one side and Ringo on the other.

King nodded and the two men let her go and stepped back.

"What are you doing out here at night?" Crews demanded.

"Well that's none of your concern. Frankly, I could ask you the same thing!"

"You could indeed, and I'd tell you we're on official business."

"With a television crew? And Ned King? Please! How much is he paying you, Crews? What's in this for you, eh?"

"Now see here," Crews said. "You can't talk to me like that. Mr. King is an expert in his field and he's kindly helping us with our investigation. Ms. Slater is a film-maker who I've agreed can tag along. None of which has anything to do with you. I'll ask again. What are you doing here?"

"It is none of your business, you don't have any authority over me. This is a free country, last I checked. And you're not the police. Isn't there a stray dog for you to round up or something?"

"Hardly the point, Ms. Rowling. You could be hampering an investigation by getting in our way."

"It's a public park and I have every right to walk here."

"Pull the other one! You're not out for a stroll. I can have you escorted out of here very easily."

"Shall we take her back to the car park by the jetty?" Ringo asked.

"You most certainly will not!" Rowling snapped. "Look, I heard about Cooper Cook's disappearance. I'm trying to find his body."

Everyone had a moment of stunned silence at that. Aston thought perhaps she had reached for something, anything, in her desperation to stay and had blurted out that little tidbit. It made no sense at all.

"Why are you looking for a body?" Sophie asked, clearly as confused as the rest of them.

"The body was in the river," Crews said. "At least, the part of it we found was." He clamped his mouth shut, then turned to Sophie. "Sorry, Soph, I didn't mean…"

She waved his concerns away, clearly used to the man only opening his mouth to change feet.

"I was trying to learn all I could about the situation, trying to help," Rowling said. "I was reaching out, psychically. Mentally scanning for an explanation."

At their frowns and noises of disdain, she held up a waxy carved crocodile. "This has power. I don't care if you believe me or not, it doesn't need your credulity to work. And then, if I'm honest, while searching in the bush back there I heard you lot and followed. I was wondering what you were up to."

"Not very good at staying quiet, are you," King said. "More likely to get you hurt."

Aston cut off her retort by saying, "Your vehicle wasn't back there when we left."

"I parked elsewhere to avoid notice."

"You need to leave," Crews said.

"Or what?"

"I'll arrest you."

"You can't do that! You don't have any arrest and detain powers, you jumped-up caretaker!"

Aston wasn't sure if national park rangers did have any authority like that. He thought maybe Rowling was right and Crews was largely powerless here, but he certainly didn't want the woman around. She was crazy and almost certainly trouble. "Ned, do you mind if Penry and Ringo escort Ms. Rowling back to her car?" he said.

King smiled. "Not at all. Lads, would you mind?"

The two men nodded and stepped towards Rowling again. She rounded on them. "Don't you touch me!" Then she turned back to Crews and King. "You can't do this!"

"Try me," Crews said, his eyes hard.

Rowling stared a moment longer, then grunted in barely suppressed fury. "You certainly haven't seen the last of me!"

King smiled obsequiously. "Doubtless. I've never been that lucky in my life."

"I don't need an escort!" she snapped, and stalked off along the river back towards the road.

"Mr. King?" Ringo asked.

King smiled. "Let her go. I don't think she'll try anything else tonight."

The group watched her go for a while, then Sophie said, "Absolute bloody nutter."

"You're not wrong," Crews agreed. "Come on, let's keep moving."

They continued downriver, covering the small gap between the bank and the bush as it narrowed. Almost to the point where the trees came right up to the water they discovered a huge depression in the muddy ground.

"Stop!" King demanded, and the serious tone in his usually jovial voice made Aston's blood chill.

"Is that a wallow?" Aston asked.

King nodded. "And a bloody big one too." He looked around, shone his light out over the river, but they only saw smooth water. He brought the light back to the wallow and it highlighted masses of bright, wet blood, across the grass and pooling down in one edge of the shallow nest.

Barry's boom mic swung briefly down as the man gagged, then he turned and emptied the contents of his stomach into the grass. Sophie put her hands over her mouth and a high, keening wail began to escape.

"This is not good!" Crews said uselessly.

Aston moved forward, trying not to look at the blood.

So much blood! He'd seen something else in the mud at the water's edge. King went with him.

"A print," King said.

"Yeah. And bigger than any croc print I've ever seen." Aston looked up at the showman. "It's like that cast you showed us. You really aren't making any of this up, are you?"

"No, I am not, I'm afraid. There's something big out there. Something really big."

"It's an absolute giant," Aston admitted. "We need to get the hell out of here." He gestured back at Penry and Ringo. "Two rifles against that? Not good odds."

King nodded. "Good idea. We're not prepared to face it now. But what about later? Are you in?"

"On a hunt?"

"Yes. You're a steady head, Sam Aston. We'll need all the help we can get."

Aston sighed. What choice did he really have? If King was going to capture something this size, something this unnaturally huge, he really would need all the help he could get. "Yeah, okay," he said finally. "Guess I'm not heading home any time soon after all."

He tried not to think about the fact that he was already home, and it was more trouble now that it had ever been in his youth.

Chapter 25

It was a little after midday when Aston drove the hire car along the fire trail to the coordinates Ned King had supplied. He glanced at Slater in the passenger seat beside him, wondering if she felt as nervous as he did. She looked calm and collected, but then again, she had a habit of always looking that way. Years of training in front of the camera maybe. Lynette and Barry sat quietly in the back seat, all their gear with them.

Slater lifted her phone, tipped to show Aston the map. "This is it," she said. "Seems like nothing special."

"King said he'd tracked the beast to this area," Aston said. "I guess he chose a safe and neutral starting point. Honestly, I'm not super keen to head into the bush here. I hope he's well-prepared."

"There," Slater said, pointing ahead.

A little further up the trail they saw King's flashy car, a huge decal of his idiot grin in the back window as well. He stood beside the vehicle, Penry and Ringo with him, and two more men Aston recognized from the Crocalypse park, the ones named Arnott and Costello according to their shirts. Now they all wore khaki or camp gear, no fancy park regalia other than King's car in evidence. They looked all business and Aston took some solace in that. The park was the public face of Ned King, but he was a conservation professional too. It was easy to forget with his bright colors and jolly persona, but the group waiting ahead of them looked ready and capable.

Aston pulled in behind and the four of them got out. Greetings were friendly enough, but a little muted, everyone clearly on edge.

"You've met these two," King said, gesturing at Penry and Ringo. "This here is John Arnott and Todd Costello, another pair of good hands at the park. Both handy with tracking and shooting too."

"Shooting?" Slater asked.

"Not to kill. Wait till the others arrive and we'll go over everything."

As if responding to the call, Crews drove up in the National Park Toyota, Gomzi in the passenger seat. Aston ground his teeth when he saw Sophie jump out of the back seat the moment they came to a halt.

"What are you doing here?" he demanded.

"Same as you, Sam."

He took her elbow, led her a little to one side. "You don't need to be here, Soph. This will be dangerous and—"

"Let me stop you right there," she said, pushing him away. "For one, who do you think you are? My dad? Secondly, you're no hunter, you feed fish for a living." That was a bit of a low blow, Aston thought, but he held his tongue as Sophie plowed on. "And thirdly, I'm involved in this to the end. I've lost too much and I plan to see it out, not sit at home wondering what the hell is going on. You got that?"

Aston saw there was absolutely no point in arguing. "I guess so," he said. "But let it be noted that I really, really don't like it."

She sneered at him. "Duly noted. Shall we?"

She pushed past him and joined the others. Aston hurried to catch up. Slater caught his eye as he came, one eyebrow raised. Aston shrugged. He moved next to Crews and elbowed the man's ribs.

"What the hell did you bring Sophie along for?"

Crews let out a short, humorless laugh. "You act like I

had a choice, mate."

"You could have simply refused to bring her."

"I couldn't simply anything with her, Sam, you know that. Besides, it's not your decision either, it's up to her. What are you so concerned for anyway? Worry about your own self and your people." He jerked his head at Slater, Lynn and Barry.

Aston ground his teeth and chose to say no more.

"Okay," King said, rubbing his hands together. "Everyone's here, so let's go over the plan. It's pretty simple, really, in theory. Actually pulling it off, of course..." He raised his palms, grinning. "I've been studying all the intel I've gathered, I've flown over in the helicopter, looked for all the trails I could find and so on. Even spent a couple of hours at first light today with the drone and made some more connections. I think I might even have spotted the beast very briefly, but I can't be sure."

"The drone recorded that?" Aston asked.

"Yes, but it's blurry. Indistinct. The point is, she's out there."

"She?" Crews said.

King grinned. "Maybe? Who knows? Let's just say Razana for now, shall we? Until we know better? I've managed to map out an area Razana seems to stick to most of the time."

"Are we sure that's what we're dealing with though?" Slater asked. "Could it be something else?"

Aston saw she had her crew working already, recording everything.

"I think so," King said. "It's my best guess, but it's an educated one. Despite the unlikeliness. In truth, until we catch it we can't say for certain what it is. All we do know for sure is we're dealing with a BFP and we have to prep accordingly."

"BFP?" Slater asked.

"Big Fucken Predator. It covers a lot of territory. A really big area. But it seems to always return to this region from what I've managed to glean. Presumably it considers it safe here, and no doubt it's established that here is a decent and frequent food source." He paused, glanced guiltily at Sophie.

She returned his gaze with a steely expression. "Don't mind me," she snapped after an uncomfortable moment.

"Okay. Sorry. There are a couple of very big, well-used wallows not far from here, so I think this is the best place to search. We'll break into teams. I'll have Arnott and Costello with me. Sam, you take Ringo and Penry with you. Russell, you and Craig stick together, yeah?"

Crews and Gomzi nodded. Before anyone could say otherwise, Sophie stepped up between them. "I'll go with these two then, that's three teams of three."

King nodded. "Okay then. Jo?"

Slater smiled. "We'll stick with you, Ned. You're the celebrity, after all, and I have to think about ratings."

Sophie made a noise of annoyance but held her tongue.

King beamed and Aston had to suppress a smile. Well played, Jo, he thought. She was playing to the man's ego perfectly.

"We'll stay in touch with these." King handed around small walkie talkies. "Don't let the small size and bright plastic cases fool you, they're decent CB radios with a range of around five kilometres. Stay on channel 51 the whole time. Any sighting, call it in immediately and we all converge together."

"And then what?" Aston asked.

Ned's grin got impossibly wider. "Well, here's the fun

part." He opened the back of his vehicle and began taking out rifles, handing them around. He gave one to Aston, one to Crews, and kept the last one for himself. "That's a rifle with each team," he said. "And each rifle has two darts. The tranq in each of those darts could drop an adult African elephant with ease. Now I recognize this BFP might actually be a little bigger than an elephant—"

"A little?" Crews said sarcastically.

King laughed. Could nothing dampen the man's enthusiasm? "Sure. Maybe a lot. But one of these darts will surely slow it down a lot even if it doesn't stop it. Two of them would have to drop it. I'd be reluctant to hit it with more than three though, as that could prove fatal, so we'll have to be as careful as possible. And the scaled back of the thing will be tougher than even elephant skin, so aim for the soft belly, or low on the side before the real back scales start. High behind the legs is another good spot. If it's coming for you," he added with a sly look, "wait until it opens up and shoot it in the mouth. The soft tissue in there will give us a quick result."

"Are we really trying to take this thing alive?" Crews said. "Why don't we just finish it?"

"Too many reasons," King said. "Not least of which being it's a living thing and deserves its chance. And it deserves our respect. It's simply engaging according to its nature; there's no malice in it."

"You don't solve all your problems by killing them," Aston said. Then he turned to King. "But assuming we do knock it out, you have plans?"

"Of course. I'm all prepared."

Aston nodded. "Of course you are. I'm not sure about splitting up though. Wouldn't it be safer to stay together?"

"It might be safer, but we can cover three times the

ground in three groups and we're likely to be quieter as we do it. Don't forget, we have a large area to cover."

Aston nodded, still unhappy, but he didn't have an argument against that.

"My team will head due north from here," King said. "Russell, you guys head east, Sam you go west. I'll check in on the walkies about every five minutes, so keep any chatter to absolute necessities. Any questions?"

Aston looked around the group. The only people who seemed vaguely okay were King himself, eternally optimistic, and his two men, Ringo and Penry. Those two appeared implacably calm, regardless of the situation. Everyone else had expressions of unconcealed concern. Aston's grip trembled slightly on the tranquilizer rifle. The air between them all seemed a little charged.

"Okay then," King said. "Let's go get us a BFP."

Chapter 26

Karen Rowling tied her long, dark hair back and scooched her chair in closer to the bank of monitors. The cement room deep under the KIND gift shop was lit bright with overhead fluorescents, the hard floor cool under her bare feet. She bent the microphone forward and worked her way around the feeds from the top left.

"Delilah, check in, please."

"Coming through loud and clear," Delilah said. She turned her head to frame her partner, a large, beefy-looking dude called Kurt.

Kurt waved. "Yo!"

Rowling grimaced. The man was a bit annoying, even if he was a good team member. She shifted her gaze to the feed from his headcam so she could look at Delilah instead. Now there was a fine sight, even in grainy cam footage. The woman was doing great work undercover in Ned King's new park, but that meant Rowling had very little time with her. Less than ever. A shame. Rowling loved to look at Delilah in her tight-fitting camo gear. She was fairly sure the spark of interest was reciprocated too, but Delilah was obviously a little shy. Reticent. Neither of them had the courage, it seemed, to test the theory. Not yet anyway. Though Rowling had little doubt.

"Okay, thank you, team one," she said, forcing herself to concentrate.

"Team two, check in, please, Simon."

"Loud and clear," Simon replied. She pictured the tall and thin Englishman as he turned to pan his headcam to the redhead, Keith.

Keith raised a thumbs up. "Yep, I hear ya."

Rowling looked back to see Simon in Keith's feed, laconic as ever.

"And team three, please," Rowling said. "Copy, Lizzie?"

"Copy," Lizzie said. Rowling couldn't help picturing her too, a little rounded, deliciously chubby as her father would have said. Rowling preferred voluptuous as a description. The woman was strong and fit with it.

Lizzie panned to show young, bony Harry. He looked barely old enough to be out of high school, but was actually in his 20s. Just. Rowling looked to Harry's feed to get a look at Lizzie and smiled, then watched Kurt's again, disappointed when the big man looked away from Delilah and out into the rainforest.

"Okay, thank you, teams." Rowling pulled herself together, scanned all the other monitors, each now showing a feed from various cameras secreted around the local bush. Six spots they'd decided might give them the best chance at spotting Razana, but those feeds had been infuriatingly empty all day. At least everything seemed calm for the moment.

"Right," Rowling said, her mouth suddenly dry. She licked her lips. "I think we're ready to go. And you know those other fools are already on their way out there, if they're not already traipsing through the bush. We can't let them get ahead of us. This is essential KIND business, we have to find her first. If the authorities find her, they'll never let her go. It's time to fix our mess and get back in control of this situation."

"We'll be back in time for a few beers," Delilah said.

Rowling smiled. "I'll hold you to that. Let's all focus on a celebratory drink sooner rather than later."

"Copy that," Simon and Lizzie said in unison.

"Okay," Rowling said. "You've got your maps and your routes. Let's get moving."

Chapter 27

JD's head still throbbed. He was sick of it, wondering if it would ever stop hurting. Wondering if perhaps he should be in the hospital. If he moved too fast, a wave of dizziness washed through him that made the nausea rise. His knees were still weak. Why the hell he'd let Dicky talk him into coming out into the bush after this beast was beyond him. No doubt that idiocy was another symptom of the ongoing concussion. He'd looked it up and read that a blow to the head like he'd received could have ongoing effects for days or even weeks. It suggested immediate hospital attention, as there could be damage inside that would get progressively worse instead of better, possibly even causing aneurysms or embolisms at some undefined future point. He'd stopped reading about it then, as he knew there was no way Dicky would drive him the hour or more to the nearest hospital and he was in no state to drive himself. That in itself was something of an ironic state of affairs. Which meant he was really in no state to be walking through dark trees carrying a loaded hunting rifle. He should have gone to see someone else, begged the favor of a lift to the hospital from a neighbor or someone in town. Too late now.

Dicky muttered something, voice slurred from bourbon.

"What was that?" JD asked. He'd had a couple of slugs himself, mainly for courage, and had no idea if the alcohol had eased or worsened his physical and mental state. All he knew was that he'd felt terrible before and he felt terrible now. Degrees of terrible seemed irrelevant.

"I said this bastard's gonna rue the day it crawled out of

its egg," Dicky said. His eyes were red-rimmed, bloodshot, but hard with a barely contained fury. His focus was intense. Fear as much as anger, JD guessed. His brother had always fallen back on rage when he was scared. It was a dangerous defense mechanism. Rod had been the same, but Rod had also had a kind of internal limiter, a pressure valve that gave him some measure of control. Dicky lacked that, and his anger could keep boiling until he exploded. Dangerous for Dicky himself, sure, but often more so for anyone around him. And right now he carried a hunting rifle too.

The sky was a bright blue above where it was visible in patches through the thick canopy, the day as hot and humid as ever. Maybe even hotter. It felt like summer was coming early this year. But underneath in the bush it was gloomy, which meant a slight easing of the oppressive heat. Sweat still poured down JD's back, though, and ran into his eyes to sting and further blur his vision. Shadows seemed to stretch and reach, long branches brushed and scratched. Bright sun lanced through here and there, only making the dark areas more foreboding.

And it was quiet. Day or night, the tropical bush was alive with noise, the murmur and rustle of life, creatures growling and calling, birds hooting, insects chirruping. But right now it was eerily still, like the bush itself was paused, waiting for something.

JD blew out slowly and sucked in a fresh breath at the thought, realizing he'd been almost holding his breath, just taking short, quick gasps. It did nothing to ease his dizziness. He paused, stood still to take a few long, slow lungsful, deep down into his stomach. His skin cooled slightly as he did so, his vision settled a little. His mind too seemed to smooth out. He looked up and Dicky was nowhere to be seen.

Startled, he hurried a few paces forward, the moment's

calm from the deep breathing instantly shattered. "Dicky!" he called in a harsh whisper.

He saw nothing but wide, thick leaves, hanging vines, reaching branches. Vegetation crunched underfoot and snagged at his boots.

JD scurried on, a little left, a little right. "Dicky!" he hissed again. "Where are you?"

Something snapped off to his left and he jumped, dropped into a crouch. Head swimming, he tried to slowly pan his view side to side without increasing his dizziness. He saw pale bark and deep green, shifting shadows.

Something clamped down, hard and sharp on his shoulder. JD imagined teeth slicing in, cried out and jumped up to turn and stagger away.

"Shut up!" Dicky said, face ruddy in the muted sunlight. "Ya bloody idiot, you want to tell the world we're here?"

"Where did you go?" JD hated the tearful waver in his voice. He just wanted to be at home.

"Nowhere, ya dickhead. You're the one who started wandering off sideways. Can't ya walk in a straight line?"

"Right now, maybe not! My head bloody hurts, Dicky."

Dicky rolled his eyes. "You gonna keep going on about your head forever now, are ya? You can't use it as an excuse all the time."

"I'm concussed, you ignorant cock!" JD snapped.

Dicky took a step forward, one hand raised to strike. JD stepped up to meet him, chin raised.

"Do it! Give me the last excuse I need to go home and leave you out here on your own."

Dicky stared, hand still raised.

"Would you like that?" JD asked. "To be out here all on your own? I'm this close to turning around and walking away."

"What was that?" Dicky turned his head to look behind himself.

"You can't distract—"

"Shut up!" The tight fear in Dicky's voice was obvious, he wasn't playing now.

JD pressed his lips together and stepped up beside his brother. They stood stock still, straining their ears.

"Get down," Dicky said, sinking slowly into the undergrowth.

JD did the same. A soft crack sounded off to their right. Both brothers dropped into a deeper crouch, almost to hands and knees, and shuffled up beside the wide trunk of an old tree. Ants walked in a studious column up towards the canopy.

"That way," Dicky whispered, but the rainforest was too thick to see much in the direction he pointed.

JD tore his gaze away from the fascination of the ants and saw a something shift in the deep gloom, a blur of soft colors against the shadows under the trees. Thankfully it was some distance away and only their position on slightly higher ground gave them the sight advantage. It pushed quietly through the trees, leaves rustling against it.

JD felt his brother's movement as Dicky raised his rifle to fire. "No!" JD said, barely loud enough even for his brother's ear right beside him. He put a hand out and forced the barrel down.

"Let me take it out!" Dicky hissed, trying to push the barrel back up.

"If that's the croc, we need a better shot at it. You remember the size of the thing, right? We can't afford to miss and give ourselves away. And I'm not certain it is the croc anyway. Doesn't seem big enough."

"Closer then!"

Dicky immediately began to make his way toward the movement. JD had hoped to convince his brother to give up the hunt, but it was clearly too late for that. He heard Dicky rustling forward out of sight and then crept along behind. After gaining some ground they stopped again, nestled deep in a patch of dense foliage.

A small gap in the canopy let in bright sunlight and they saw movement again, froze. Though still impossible to make out details, it became immediately apparent the shape was on two legs, and not really any bigger than a man.

"Watch your head, Jack Daniels," Dicky whispered, the grin evident in his tone. "Might be another yowie."

JD ignored that and pointed. "Two more behind."

"You reckon it's those KIND idiots?" Dicky asked.

"No." JD thought these people were something entirely different. Entirely more dangerous. "They're wearing full combat fatigues," he whispered. "But charcoal, not camo. And what are those weird, high-tech looking weapons they're carrying? Are they weapons?"

"Looks like something from bloody *Star Trek*," Dicky whispered back.

"You've never watched *Star Trek* in your life. You wouldn't know a Klingon from a Wookiee."

"I know Wookiees are bloody *Star Wars*, ya nong."

"Whatever, those people look like they're not from around here and they look like trouble."

Dicky grunted an affirmative. "I can't argue with that."

The brothers watched as the three strangers moved slowly but confidently away through the bush. The one in front had close-cropped hair with an unusual grey streak right through the middle. They didn't even pause as they pushed forward, but they watched all around themselves the whole time, tense with alertness.

"Something's up here," Dicky said. "Let's follow."

"Are you mad?"

"Got something better to do?"

JD suppressed a tight laugh. "Yes, actually. About a million things better to do than follow whoever the hell they are through the bush when we also know there's a giant killer croc out there somewhere. Sitting at home sticking pins in my eyes would be better, frankly."

Dicky sniggered, but eased out of the leaves and crept forward. "Come on, pussy. We're onto something here."

JD sighed. He was intrigued as well, though he hated to admit it. He'd make sure to keep Dicky in front, between himself and anything else they might encounter. Swallowing his panic, ignoring his thudding heart, he stayed in a low crouch and followed his brother.

Chapter 28

Delilah moved slowly through the bush, grinding her teeth at Karen Rowling's voice incessantly in her ear. Why the woman had the ability to talk on a wide band to everyone or privately to Delilah she didn't know. Karen was such a pain in the ass, the woman was hopeless. And the way she looked at Delilah, it was skin-crawl inducing. The truth was, Delilah liked girls and guys, she was happy to play in any game on that front. For her it was all about the person themselves. But she could never in a million years imagine spending a second of intimate time with Rowling. The thought almost made her gag. She would return the soft smiles and coy eyes as coldly as possible, trying to be polite without any suggestion she reciprocated the feelings, but Rowling never took the hint. The woman was hopeless. Never mind. Rowling was a necessary evil right now because she had enough of a public profile and sufficient connections in the conservation world to give KIND the appearance of authenticity they needed as an animal rescue group. Rowling was not, however, in Delilah's estimation, skilled or driven enough to be an adequate leader. She not only lacked drive, she lacked... well, pretty much everything else. The woman was ignorant to the point of embarrassment sometimes, she subscribed to all kinds of hokey beliefs, she thought people loved her and was utterly blind to their disdain. And that wax crocodile and all the talk of a psychic connection? Delilah shook her head, trying to dislodge the thoughts. Whatever, the woman was in charge right now and gave no one a second to forget it, jabbering away in their earpieces incessantly, frequently switching to the private line just for Delilah to share some snarky comment or piece of inane "insight" about one of the others. In truth, any of the six people currently traipsing through the rainforest was worth three Karen Rowlings at least. Sometimes there seemed to be no justice in the world. Never mind, Delilah's time would come. She would lead KIND one day and the organization would grow exponentially under her guidance.

Delilah's anger with Rowling stemmed also, she knew, from her fear. She was self-aware enough to recognize that. She did not like being out in the bush with Razana out there. Somewhere. Even the hulking presence of Kurt moving silently beside her wasn't especially comforting. She risked a glance sideways. Now there was someone she could imagine spending some intimate time with. He was a bit of a doofus, but he was kind, strong, good-looking…

"Team one, copy," Rowling said.

Delilah sighed. "Copy Knight Leader." Even her call sign grated on Delilah's nerves.

"You're about to cross paths with team three, so hold your fire. Join up and make your way ahead another one hundred meters or so, where you'll regroup with team two. Then we'll fan you all out again."

"Copy that," Delilah said tiredly.

If she had been in charge, she wouldn't have suggested they regroup and waste time. She would have directed her team and team three to go wide, leaving team two central, thereby covering a lot more ground in a fraction of the time. Rowling's directions were as convoluted as the woman's beliefs. But Delilah wasn't in charge.

Suck it up, buttercup, she told herself.

"On your nine o'clock," a voice said.

Delilah and Kurt paused as Lizzie and Harry came through the foliage to join them.

"Dead ahead and regroup with two, apparently," Lizzie said.

Delilah rolled her eyes. "Apparently."

They looked quickly away form each other to make sure Rowling wouldn't see them in each other's headcams, smirking.

"Let's go," Kurt said.

They moved on again, fanned out in a line of four, Delilah and Lizzie beside each other, the men on the outside. The rainforest seemed unnaturally quiet. Too still. The humidity was oppressive, especially in their full fatigues. Every now and then when they passed through a patch of sunlight, the heat was laser-sharp.

"Here, look!" Young Harry's voice was high with concern.

They gathered and looked to where he pointed. Delilah gasped. It was a croc track, and it was massive. Delilah's heart raced, nausea rising. This was all so very real. She hadn't taken part in the initial rescue operation, so hadn't seen Razana then. And since the rescue, the croc had been kept in a secure location known to only a few. Despite all the details she did know, Delilah had yet to see the creature. But the size of the tracks they stared at made her realize the others had not exaggerated its size. This thing was inconceivably huge, beyond anything crocodilian she could imagine. In truth, beyond any other kind of creature either. How could anything be so massive as to leave a print of that size? And the depth of the print, pressing down into the loamy ground, belied the incredible weight of the thing.

"Will this supposedly high-tech knockout gas we're equipped with really do the job?" she asked.

"Yeah, it will," Lizzie said, before Rowling could answer. "We used the same stuff on the rescue mission and it did the trick."

"But she's a lot bigger now, right? Will it still work?"

"She is, but we have more gas, and more of us," Lizzie said.

"Focus please, people," Rowling snapped in their ears. "You have what you need, don't worry."

Several pairs of eyes rolled. Delilah's heart still hammered.

"The gas worked," Lizzie said, smiling. "It'll work again."

Kurt covered his mic with one gloved hand and whispered, "Unless it was really the wax crocodile!"

They all laughed, even Delilah forgetting her nerves for a minute, picturing Rowling with her ridiculous talisman. The woman was convinced it had magical properties.

"What's the joke?" Rowling demanded. "There was background noise on a mic there and I missed it."

"Nothing," Delilah said, grinning at the ground. "Just nerves."

"Right. Then we're back to my previous point. Focus please. Team two, copy?"

"Copy," Simon replied.

"Turn directly south from your position and regroup with one and three. They've got tracks. Team up and move on together."

Delilah took a long breath. That was possibly the first sensible thing Rowling had said all day. They waited quietly, Delilah unable to tear her eyes from the insanely enormous tracks, until rustling in the trees ahead announced the arrival of Simon and Keith. Now the six were all back together again.

"Move out," Rowling said.

Move out, Delilah thought. What an idiot. I'd like to see

her move all the way out. Even out from behind her desk once in a while, or the safety of the center.

The tracks ended in some thick bush by a stand of trees, their trunks crammed together. Looking up, they saw broken branches, some of the snapped limbs lying nearby.

"Let's spread out a little," Lizzie said. "We'll pick the trail up again somewhere around here."

The group of six fanned out a little, scanning the ground. Despite understanding that they would find the trail again more quickly if they moved apart, Delilah stayed close to Kurt anyway. He didn't seem to mind. He gave her shoulder a quick squeeze.

"Pretty tense, huh?" he said, in his low, gruff voice.

Delilah nodded, tried to smile. Her lips quivered with the effort. "So bloody hot too." Sweat trickled down her spine, ran into her eyes.

"Simon, I've lost your camera feed," Rowling said in their ears.

Delilah and Kurt paused. Looking up, Delilah saw movement to their right, where Lizzie and Harry had gone. Keith and Simon had gone the other way. She turned in that direction.

"Simon, copy?" Rowling said again.

Movement to their left and Keith moved into view. At least, his back did as he stepped slowly sideways, looking into the trees.

"He was just here," Keith said uncertainly.

"Simon, please respond. I have no visual and no audio," Rowling said.

Delilah and Kurt moved up next to Keith as the big man pushed aside some thickly-leaved branches.

"I can't re-establish your feed, Simon."

Delilah heard the clicking through her earpiece as

Rowling flicked switches back at the base.

"Boot prints here," Keith said. "Must be Simon."

"Oh, shit."

They looked to where Kurt was staring, open-mouthed. A huge, fresh croc print had pressed the leaf litter flat. Some leaves were still shifting as they rose again after the weight had been removed. Delilah's heart thumped hard. How could it be so quiet? Something that size, moving so close by them, and they hadn't seen or heard a thing.

She saw a glistening spatter across some higher leaves and the pale trunk of a tree. "Blood," she said tightly, pointing it out, bright scarlet in the sunlight.

Kurt stepped around her and pulled aside a mass of vines and leaves. Simon lay there, bent backwards over a low limb. At least, most of him did.

"Had his bloody head off!" Keith said in horror.

Delilah cried out, then slapped a hand over her mouth, stifling both the noise and the potential vomit. She swallowed hard, unable to tear her eyes from the stump of Simon's neck, dribbling crimson into the leaves.

"You seeing this, Karen?" Lizzie asked from beside them. Delilah hadn't heard her approach.

"Yes," Rowling said shortly.

"Now we know why his camera feed went dark," Harry said.

"Jesus, Harry!" Kurt grunted.

"What now?" Lizzie asked.

"The creature must be found," Rowling said. "We cannot fail tonight. This is… unfortunate, but we must press on."

We, Delilah thought in disgust. Rowling would be running for the hills after a sight like this, waving her magical wax crocodile around like a crucifix before vampires. In truth, she wanted to run too. This was insane, the damn thing was right on top of them. It had taken Simon out from under their noses. But she was determined to prove that she was harder, stronger, and more determined than Karen Rowling. Some day she would be the leader of KIND.

"Come on," Delilah said. "We stay together, tight. The tracks go that way."

Chapter 29

Slater stayed beside Lynette, out of shot as her camera operator kept the lens on Ned King. They moved back and forth constantly, used a variety of angles to get the best footage they could as the team crept through the thick rainforest. With some clever editing, they would have a great lead-in with this, assuming led to something happening. But despite the seriousness of the job at hand and the need for quiet, King couldn't help himself and kept up a constant stream of whispered narrative as they moved.

"Despite the unusual nature of what we're after," he said, "even normal crocs are the biggest reptiles on Earth. They're most closely related to dinosaurs and birds, which is a truly astounding thought when you spend a little time with it. Unchanged for millions of years, like sharks, and you know why? Because they work. You don't fix something that isn't broken and evolution has very little to do with something that is so successfully developed. Just a shame humans like their leather boots and bags, eh?"

They moved on, King holding his tranq rifle casually as he paced slowly between Arnott and Costello. After only a few seconds of silence, he turned his head back again. "You know the old saying about crocodile tears? It's based in truth! Crocs really do make tears. But it's not emotional, of course. When they eat they swallow too much air, and that affects the lachrymal glands, which are the ones that produce tears, subsequently forcing tears to flow. Ancient people suggested crocodiles wept in order to lure their prey, or some suggested they cried in sympathy for the victims they ate. It was a story that caught on and spread widely. Even appears in several of

William Shakespeare's plays. Fascinating, no?"

I really am going to have to edit this footage savagely, Slater thought with an internal smile. But some of these facts were pretty interesting. She might use bits and pieces. Always better to have too much material than not enough.

"One more!" King said with a grin. "Crocs have the strongest bite ever recorded. A saltie can slam its jaws closed with 3,700 pounds per square inch, or 16,460 Newtons, of bite force. That's about ten times the force of a lion! But it only works one way. The muscles to open their mouths are very weak, so a human can actually hold a croc's mouth closed easily with their bare hands. Fortunate, no?"

"Saltie?" Slater asked. She knew what it meant, but had to consider her majority American audience.

"Ah. Saltwater Crocodile. The biggest of them all, and what you find around here. Of course, what we're after greatly exceeds even the biggest recorded saltie. I shudder to consider the bite force of the BFP we're after."

"You think it's really a Razana?" Slater asked, remembering the Egyptian escapade with Jade Ihara. How could something from North Africa end up here on the other side of the world?

"Yes, I think it is," King said. "Though I don't know how. Nothing else adds up, given what evidence we have. And another croc fact that I think is particularly apposite in that regard: Crocodiles are not dumb. The brain of most crocodilians is fairly small, but despite that, they're capable of greater learning than most reptiles. We need to exercise great caution."

"Should maybe focus on the job at hand then?" Slater suggested.

King chuckled. "Fair point."

Slater sighed softly, wondering if perhaps it might have

been better to go with Aston after all. She'd thought to get better footage from King, but was already growing weary of him. His ego far exceeded that of even Grizzly Grant, which was saying something.

"Here," Arnott said, pointing.

Lynn moved quickly to get the angle, zooming on a set of massive prints.

"Holy crap," Costello said. "That can't be real."

They followed the prints with their eyes, to the point where they went between trees and were lost in shadows.

"Very real, Todd," King said, suddenly serious. The jovial edge to his tone had vanished completely as the man switched from media personality to hunter. It was quite a dramatic transformation. Even his face looked different. "On your highest alert, lads. John, get your rope ready. Todd, the canvas."

The two men moved out a little to either side, widely flanking King who lifted his rifle to the ready. Arnott took out a large square of canvas and Costello lifted a coil of rope that he'd been wearing bandolier-style.

"What are they for?" Slater asked.

"Remember I mentioned the jaw strength?" King replied, eyes scanning ahead. "Well, the rope is to wrap around the snout a few times and that'll stop it snapping at us. The canvas is to cover its eyes. They become more docile when blinded."

"Will that strategy work on whatever the hell this is?"

"I'm operating on the assumption that the creature will behave like any other croc," King said, creeping forward. "A reptile is a reptile, yes? I suppose we'll find out."

Slater considered that a dangerous assumption, but King had little else to go on.

"They are capable of learning more than most," King

went on, "but they aren't particularly bright in terms of general intelligence."

"Sounds like a lot of people I know," Slater said.

A smile twitched the edges of King's mouth, but was instantly flattened out when Costello spoke.

"Dead ahead," the man said.

The group stopped, staring into the shadows between trees. There was definite movement up there, the branches shifting, leaves softly hissing. Lynette moved the camera to look, zoomed in.

"Can't make it out at this distance," she said. "Too much bush in between."

Ned took out a pair of binoculars, stared a moment, and then cursed quite eloquently.

"What is it?" Slater asked, her stomach suddenly cold and empty.

"Bloody Delilah!" King spat, annoyed and confused. "And others."

"From your park?" Slater asked.

Before King could answer, something rustled in the bushes behind them. They spun around as a giant form burst out. Slater's blood ran cold as she finally got her first good look at the creature she had until this moment hoped didn't really exist. She realized all along she'd wanted it to be a myth.

The Razana charged.

It was essentially a crocodile, but its legs were twice as long in scale as a regular croc, enabling it to stand high, belly well off the ground, and run fast. Its head was massive, much deeper than the usually flat profile of a regular croc, its wide maw crammed with huge teeth, each as long as Slater's forearm. It stood a good seven or eight feet high at the shoulder, and had to be at least fifty feet long. It roared as it came.

Ned's rifle was already trained and he fired a shot, but Slater thought he missed. She ran sideways with her team, marveling at Lynn's professionalism as the woman kept the camera on the beast even as she ran for her life.

Todd Costello had the end of the rope already made into a lasso-style loop and he swung it high, once, twice. "Just like roping a big damn steer!" he yelled and sent the rope out flying. Amazingly it went right over Razana's snout and Costello hauled it tight, slamming the beast's mouth closed within ten feet of Ned King. King ran sideways, desperately trying to get a good angle for another shot.

As Costello dragged back on the rope, the beast's head was pulled a little sideways. Arnott ran in, leapt up and threw the canvas across Razana's face. He held onto one side, slid under the monster's jaw and grabbed the other side, pulling the material taut. There was a lot of it and he managed to cover most of Razana's face.

"They're doing it," Slater said incredulously. "They're really bloody doing it! Lynn, you getting this?"

"Sure am!"

"Steady!" King yelled, and raised his rifle for a second shot.

Razana whipped its head sideways with such force that Costello was thrown off his feet where he still held the rope. Why didn't he let go? Slater thought, then Costello hit the ground not a meter from the creature's massive foot. The movement of its head had thrown Arnott aside too and the canvas slipped free. The beast took in the situation in a flash, reared up on its back legs, so incredibly tall, and then slammed down, one massive front foot coming down onto Costello's screaming face.

His scream cut instantly short as his head burst under

the impact. Slater cried out in horror, and looked to Ned King the moment he pulled the trigger. But as he did so, the Razana's huge tail whipped around sideways and slammed into him, sent him flying into the undergrowth, his shot going wildly high.

That's both tranqs, Slater thought with horror. She knew he had reloads, but how long would that take? And was he even okay?

The Razana shook its head, the rope slipping free of its mouth as Arnott scrambled to his feet. Again the beast went up on its hind legs, towering over the tiny humans, and shot forward, snapping its jaws with incredible speed. Arnott's legs stood up for a moment longer, blood jetting up from the remains of his pelvis, but the rest of him nowhere to be seen. As Arnott's legs fell to the ground, the Razana flicked its head up and audibly gulped.

King yelled something incoherent, hauling himself up from the undergrowth, and started to run, but Slater and her team were already on the move. She had no idea how much footage Lynn might have got, but her camera operator and Barry the sound guy were sprinting away from the carnage and Slater was hot on their heels.

Chapter 30

Karen Rowling watched her monitors in rising alarm. The distant screams had come through the team's mics clearly, but they had yet to establish where the attack had happened. They had already lost Simon and she was reluctant to lose any more, especially Delilah, but they had to fix this mess.

"Move in," she told the team. "Slowly and carefully, pan out sideways, but stay in sight of each other."

Rowling's heart raced. The Razana was clearly nearby. She wished she was out there instead of stuck in this basement ops room. She needed to be out in the field, but she was too valuable, too important, and she had to accept that. KIND needed a strong, decisive leader and that was a responsibility she could not shirk.

But she could bond with the creature like no one else, that was a fact as well. She played with the wax talisman absently as she stared hard from one head cam feed to the next. She should be out there.

"People running," Delilah said, snapping Rowling to attention.

"Running? Where?"

"I don't know exactly. We heard footsteps and hard breathing moving away from us. Too bloody dense in here, hard to see anything. More than one person, though."

"Keep moving." Rowling had five live cameras still feeding her information, but it was almost all just bush and shadows. The six others they'd placed in the rainforest were useless, all hundreds of meters away from the action. So much for that planning. She watched the team as each person glanced left and right, ensuring they were still in sight of each other.

"Movement," Delilah said. "Everybody down."

All five feeds dropped into darkness as the team fell into dense cover. Rowling chewed her bottom lip, watching intently. A slight movement in Delilah's feed as she parted heavily-leafed branches and Rowling saw a group of three people creeping cautiously through the bush some fifty meters distant. They wore charcoal fatigues and carried strange-looking weapons.

Who the hell is that now?

She knew Ned King and that busybody Aston were out here, along with Crews and Gomzi and whoever else they'd dragged along, but this wasn't any of them.

She got a better look as the trio passed through a wider gap in the bush. Full tactical gear, carrying those weapons she couldn't identify. Then she recognized a badge on one shoulder as sun lanced across it, the unmistakable insignia.

"SCAR," she said in disgust.

"What?" Delilah whispered.

"They're from SCAR. What the hell are they doing here?"

"SCAR?" Delilah asked. "What's that?"

Rowling made a noise of disdain. "Snakes, Crocs and other Reptiles."

"Shouldn't that be, wait..." Rowling could hear the cogs turning in Harry's young brain. "There should be an O in it. Scay-or?"

"Don't try to make sense of it," Rowling said. "It's a front anyway. They claim to be a reptile conservation group."

"So they're like us?" Delilah said.

"They're nothing like us!" Rowling snapped. "They're a paramilitary, high science organization, and they're nothing but trouble."

"High science?" Delilah said. "What does that even mean?"

Rowling was in no mood to get into a discussion about it. "Make sure they don't see you," she said. "We want nothing to do with them. Let them pass, then move on. We have to hurry. Thankfully they appear to be currently heading the wrong way. We cannot let them bag Razana. We're under even more pressure now."

They gave it an extra few minutes to be sure, then crept quietly away, carrying on in the direction they'd been heading, and away from the SCAR team. After a minute or so they came to a slight clearing, and signs of carnage.

"Is that someone's legs?" Harry squeaked, then turned and vomited.

"This guy had his head crushed to pulp," Kurt said.

Rowling watched Delilah's feed as she hurried up to look. She pointed to the dead man's arm. "Look, it's that dumb arse Mickey Mouse watch. This is Todd Costello, one of Ned King's men."

"You know him?" Rowling asked, cursing the bite of jealousy she felt.

"We fooled around once or twice," Delilah said, and Rowling thought she heard a smile in the woman's voice and that only made her jealousy stronger.

"Well, you won't be playing with him any more," Rowling said. "One less arsehole in the world."

"That's a bit harsh," Lizzie said.

"Ned King and his crew are nothing but trouble," Rowling said. "Any sign of the prize?"

"Not here," Delilah said. "Other than the obvious. She's moved on."

Rowling watched the feeds as the team turned in slow

circles, looking all around. She caught a glimpse of Delilah, looking scared, Kurt, hard-faced but concerned. The cameras panned the still, quiet bush.

Rowling was watching Harry's feed. Keith, the redhead, stood just off to one side as Harry looked into the deepest gloom ahead of them.

"Can't see any—" Delilah started, then the bush burst open.

A massive, toothy maw filled Harry's feed, then Keith was gone from sight. Just snapped away. The screaming started and the team scattered.

You've really grown, darling, Rowling thought, adrenaline pulsing through her veins. "Fight, don't run!" she yelled. "We have to catch her! Deploy the gas!"

But the feeds were hectic, people running every which way. Harry screamed, high and shrill, then went suddenly silent as his feed went black.

She snapped her eyes to Lizzie's feed just in time to see it fill with teeth. Lizzie skidded to a halt, the trees sliding crazily across her vision as she fell back, then nothing but scales and teeth, then more blackness.

Only two feeds were still live, Delilah and Kurt, both dancing with blurry images as the two ran. She didn't know if they were still together or randomly bolting through the bush. They might get lost out there. She felt faint even as the adrenaline surged, gripping her wax crocodile tightly. I should have been there!

"Run, Delilah!" she yelled, all pretense at professionalism gone. "For God's sake, run!"

Chapter 31

Charles McEvoy checked left and right to make sure his SCAR squad mates were still close by. He refused to let this excursion prove fruitless. Since he'd spoken to Ray Gibson in the pub and then Craig Gomzi at the Ranger's office, he had become convinced this was the right place. Both of them had been hiding something, both reluctant to speak much. They'd seen through his cover even though they had no idea who he actually was or what he wanted. But regardless of their suspicions, they knew more than they were letting on, and he suspected they had their own reasons for doing so. It didn't matter. Their agenda was irrelevant. He knew all he needed to know, and that was that he was on the right track.

"This is a goose chase, man," Blake Frieza said.

"Totally," Kyle Winkler said. "Just an arse-backwards country town full of bogans, making up stories about monsters."

McEvoy looked from one soldier to the other as they traipsed through the bush, sweating in the humidity of the day, and shook his head. These two grunts had no idea. "Not true," he said. "These people may be entirely country, but they have smarts you city boys wouldn't understand. Yeah, there's nonsense about yowies and drop bears and hoop snakes, but this is different. Keep your wits about you."

"We're chasing rumors," Frieza said, sullen.

"We are not," McEvoy assured him. "We're in the right place to get back what's ours. Those KIND idiots stole her away, and now we're going to get her back."

"Nine o'clock, don't look direct," Winkler said.

McEvoy cast his eyes sideways and saw immediately

what his soldier had spotted. An armed group of four... no five people, armed wearing headcams, dropped out of sight into low scrub.

"They just spotted us," Winkler said. "But I don't think they realized we saw them."

"So keep moving," McEvoy said. "Act like we didn't see them and head for cover."

They crept on another little while then, once McEvoy was sure they had enough bush between them, he gave the signal to double back. Using only hand signs, moving like ghosts, they slowly circled around. They easily saw the group rise from the undergrowth and head south.

They think we've gone, McEvoy thought with satisfaction. He gave the signal to follow at a distance. He didn't know who they were, but maybe they were onto something. Two women and three men, as far as he could tell. One of the guys was huge, muscular. Another looked young, skinny. Details were scant with so much rainforest in between. No matter. Tail them for a little while and see.

The group slowed, and McEvoy gave the signal to drop and wait. They hid.

"Is that someone's legs?" a high voice demanded, then sounds of vomiting.

McEvoy smiled.

There was a little more muffled conversation from the team ahead of them, then all hell broke loose. A roar and screams, crashing in the branches. Something came hammering out of the bush and they raised their weapons but quickly realized it was one of the women, running for her life.

Winkler half-rose to follow, but McEvoy put a hand on his arm to stop him. "Let her go. We know what she's running from and that's what we're here for."

The mayhem stilled as quickly as it had started and McEvoy gave the signal to move forward slowly. He raised his weapon, a next generation assault shock rifle, essentially a high tech taser, with more than enough juice to stop Razana. He hoped. Winkler and Frieza moved soundlessly with him, one on either side, similar weapons at the ready.

"You think this will be enough?" Frieza whispered, hefting the gun, echoing McEvoy's concerns.

"Bit late to worry about that now, mate," McEvoy said. "Anyway, these are the standard stunning weapons we used in the facility to subdue Razana in the first place."

"But they said it's probably bigger by now. A lot bigger."

"It hasn't been that long. Now shut up and—" McEvoy's voice stopped dead as they saw the beast through the foliage. It was indeed massive. McEvoy couldn't be sure how much it had grown since it was in their facility, but out here in the wild it looked a lot more fearsome than behind heavy steel bars. Its huge snout was buried in a ruined corpse and it made a sickening slurping, crunching sound as it tore a large lump free then flipped its head back and swallowed the piece whole.

McEvoy gave the signal to spread out. Winkler and Frieza would get to either side of Razana while McEvoy himself stayed face on. At the signal, they would all fire at once. Three together, the firepower would surely be enough to subdue the monster until they had it bound.

McEvoy watched his men creep into position. He raised his hand to give the signal when a high voice yelled. "I found it! Jesus Christ, it's huge!"

Razana's head whipped up and around.

McEvoy cursed. He saw the short, skinny park ranger with the clipped blond hair standing on the other side of the clearing, mouth and eyes wide in shock. The idiot he'd spoken to back at the office.

"Keep it down, Gomzi!" another voice said. "Oh, bloody hell!"

McEvoy saw the older ranger, Russell Crews, step out of the bush not far from Gomzi and freeze.

Razana turned with an ear-splitting hiss and hammered across the clearing, heading for the two stunned park rangers. Gomzi swung a pistol up and fired randomly, five fast, barely aimed shots, even as the front of his baggy khaki shorts soaked with piss. Crews was already off and running, not even attempting to fight.

The bullets seemed to have no effect on the giant croc, but Kyle Winkler made a sudden gurgling Hurk! sound. McEvoy turned to look and saw the operative drop to his knees, blood flooding the front of his fatigues. He turned a shocked, terrified face up to McEvoy, his mouth working, but only scarlet bubbles emerged. His hands came up to try to hold together the ruined mess from Gomzi's stray bullet, then he pitched face first to the ground and lay still.

"Bloody hell!" McEvoy spat, looking back up to see the massive beast bearing down on the small ranger.

Gomzi screamed, clicked his empty pistol a couple more times, then turned and ran.

McEvoy cursed their lost opportunity as the beast put trees between them, compromising their clear shots. He gave the signal to Blake Frieza and the two of them took off in pursuit as Razana grabbed Gomzi in its jaws and kept going. Through the foliage, McEvoy caught glimpses of Gomzi's thrashing legs, heard his high-pitched screams, then a squelching crunch and silence. The legs swung limp, then fell to the ground, detached.

Razana drove into the bush, carrying the rest of Gomzi like a dog with a bone.

Chapter 32

We are probably the worst hunters in north Queensland, JD thought, as he watched Dicky's rising anger. They'd quickly lost track of the three strangers they had been following, they'd seen no sign at all of the giant croc they were after, and now they were also thoroughly lost. A person could easily get turned around in this dense rainforest. But if they carried on they risked getting so lost, they might never find their way out again. They wouldn't starve for a while, the bush provided in plenty assuming a soul wasn't averse to eating some pretty gross stuff, but JD knew he and Dicky weren't cut out to be wild men. And it was hot as hell.

"Well?" Dicky demanded.

"Well what?" JD was exhausted. His head pounded, he still felt nauseated. Spikes of pain drove into the backs of his eyes. All he wanted to do was lay down and go to sleep. He could do it too, right here on the damp leaves in this humid hellhole, wherever the hell they actually were.

"What do we do now?"

JD laughed. "You're asking my advice now? Mate, I've got nothing. My advice was to stay the fuck home. You insisted we come traipsing out here, so I'm all out of suggestions." He jabbed one finger up to interrupt his brother. "Scratch that. I do have one suggestion. We go home."

Dicky scowled. "Righto. So which way is that?"

JD sighed, shook his head. "Stick it up your arse, Dicky."

Dicky turned a slow circle, scanning the seemingly endless rainforest all around. "Pick a direction and try it, I reckon."

"That way then." JD pointed off to his left.

"Why that way?"

"Because its sloping slightly downwards. Down might take us to the river. If we find the river, we can follow it out of the park."

Dicky raised his eyebrows. "Maybe you've got a brain, after all, little brother."

"I've got more bloody brains than you, Rod, and Dad put together. Trouble is, I never seem to use them. If I did use my head, I'd have buggered off from you lot and this shitbox town years ago."

Dicky laughed, mean and guttural. "You'd never have the guts. Come on, loser."

He set off in the direction JD had suggested and JD trudged disconsolately behind. He might not have had the guts before, but he did now. He'd had a gutful, in fact, of everything and everyone Blacktooth River had to offer. He was leaving, first thing in the morning. Assuming they ever got out of this godsforsaken forest, he'd be out of town by lunchtime the next day. He'd hitchhike if necessary. He had a mate who'd moved to Townsville, Archie Barrington. Archie would give him a couch to crash on, he was sure. He'd find a job and start a new life.

Fatigue dragged at JD like anchors as they walked. He'd never been so depressed and his head would not stop pounding. He wanted to cry, and probably would have except he knew Dicky would be entirely unsympathetic. Would actually make it worse, in fact. Then his spirits rose ever so slightly when he heard a splash.

"That the river?" he asked.

Dicky paused, head tipped to one side, then pointed. "This way."

Another fifty meters and they were standing on a

muddy bank, watching the sluggish river slide by in the bright sunlight.

"Okay, that's a good start, Jack Daniels. I'll give you this one, you had a good idea. Now which way do we go?"

JD sighed again. "Have we crossed the river yet today?"

"No, of course not."

"So it should be obvious which way we need to go."

Dicky frowned, like he'd been asked the hardest mathematics question by a particularly cruel teacher. "Should it?"

"Jesus Christ," JD muttered, and pointed. "This way. Come on."

They started moving again and JD's blood ran cold at the sight of something deep green and scaled in the undergrowth directly ahead on the riverbank. He stopped dead, raised one hand to point a shaking finger.

Dicky followed the gesture, then whipped his rifle up to aim.

"Wait," JD said, sucking in a relieved breath. "It's not the big one. That's a regular croc. Let's just move away from the river a bit, go around it and and keep heading this way. We can check in periodically without staying too close to the water."

They stepped sideways, aiming to move well aside of the croc in the undergrowth, but it moved too, turning on the spot to watch them.

"What's it doing?" Dicky asked. His voice was a little high. JD took some pleasure in his brother's discomfort. His humor drained swiftly away when he saw a second croc slide up out of the river and move towards them. "Shit," he said, pointing. Then a third moved along the bank and lined up with the first two.

"Come on, let's just get moving," Dicky said, moving a

little further away from the river.

"This is weird," JD said, fascinated despite a deep urge to run for his life.

"What are you on about?"

"This isn't normal croc behavior, Dicky."

Dicky barked a harsh laugh. "What are you now, David Attenborough? You're an idiot. Come on."

"Dude, something strange is going on."

"Get a grip, Jack Daniels. That knock on the head has got you going crazy."

JD turned on his brother, anger flaring. "You don't think this is strange?"

"So fucken what if it is?" Dicky yelled. "So what?" He whipped an arm out, giving JD a back-handed slap across the face, just like their father always did.

JD's head spun and he saw red, hauled back his free hand and socked his brother right across the jaw. Surprise more than pain rocked him and Dicky staggered backwards several paces, eyes wide in shock and fury. He went to stride back at JD, then stopped, mouth falling open as he looked past JD towards the river.

Neck tickling with gooseflesh, JD slowly turned. Four crocs were now lined up together and all slowly made their way forward in formation. Almost like they were trying to herd the two men in a particular direction. But at least it wasn't the giant beast that had taken Rod, which was what JD had first suspected given his brother's shocked expression.

"We need to get out of here," JD said, turning back to Dicky. "I think they're trying to force us in that direction." He nodded behind Dicky.

Dicky threw both arms up into the air in exasperation. "Why the fuck would crocs try to—"

His words were silenced by the impossibly huge head of the giant monster bursting out of the trees right behind him. Those massive jaws snapped over Dicky's head. As the beast raised up again, the headless body of Dicky continued to gesticulate wildly for a moment as blood fountained from the cleanly sliced stump of neck. Then Dicky collapsed like a toy suddenly switched off. His blood soaked the loamy ground.

JD got one shot off, wildly in the vague direction of the giant croc, then he was sprinting through the bush, dizziness threatening to send his feet out from under him, roughly following the direction of the river. His knees were like rubber as he ran, largely unaware that he was screaming like a steam train whistle as he went.

Chapter 33

Aston, Penry and Ringo crouched in deep foliage, listening to gunshots and screaming. There had been a few shots and shouts, then a minute or two of silence. Before they could figure out which direction the mayhem had sounded from, more shots started and then a howling voice of pain that Aston couldn't help thinking had to be Craig Gomzi.

Every time Aston and his buddies started in one direction, more shouts came from somewhere else. Fear and indecision gripped him.

"What do you think is going on out there?" Penry asked in his soft voice.

"Nothing good," Ringo said, eyes narrowed.

Aston couldn't help but agree. He keyed the shortwave radio. "Ned King, do you copy? Slater? Crews? Anyone out there?"

He was on the channel King had suggested, but all he got was static. He'd been trying repeatedly since the first voice had cried out distantly, but hadn't got a single response.

"Ned is a cheap bastard and the radios are crap," Penry said, with a wry smile. "He claims they're the best, but they're not. In fact, he does that with pretty much everything. Claims it's top notch when it's average at best."

"We'd be better off with children's toy walkie talkies, probably," Ringo said.

Aston admired the calm, steady way the two men had about them. They were unarmed, carrying only rope and canvas, but had a quiet confidence. An unshakable sense of purpose he respected. If they didn't look so different, he would have thought they were twins.

"Are you two brothers?" he asked, suddenly curious despite the situation.

The men shared a quick look, then laughed. "No," Ringo said, and Penry just smiled, shook his head. But they offered no more information than that. Aston was tempted to press them a little more when they heard pounding feet crashing through the bush. At the same moment, more screams erupted.

Aston turned and saw a glimpse of sunlight reflect off Lynn's camera. He stood and Slater barreled right into him. He grabbed her in a hug and she gripped him back, gasping for breath, trembles wracking her body.

"What's happening?" Aston asked.

Penry and Ringo went to Barry and Lynn, checked they were okay.

"You were right," Slater said between gasps.

"About what?"

"We shouldn't have come. This is no joke. We found the Razana... well, it found us. It's huge, Sam. Not just a big croc, the thing is more like Godzilla!"

"Oh, shit. Maybe we should just get out of here." He looked over to Penry and Ringo and they nodded.

"Ned King?" he asked Slater.

She swallowed, sucking in deep breaths to steady herself. "Bolted. Ran away. I don't blame him, the thing killed Arnott and Costello."

Aston stared at her, lost for words.

"It really is a Razana," Slater said. "How the hell is some African dinosaur running rampant in the North Queensland rainforest, Sam?"

"I don't know. And you know what? I don't care. Let's get out of here. We need to try to raise Sophie, Crews, and

Gomzi, find King if we can, but mainly, we get out. Come on."

He headed back the way they'd come, keying the crappy radio as he went, doubtful he'd hear from any of the others.

Chapter 34

Delilah pounded through the rainforest, tree limbs and hanging vines whipping and snagging at her. Rowling's voice in her ear screaming, "Run! RUN!" had become white noise. Delilah thought her heart would burst, but that was all that would stop her from running now.

Gasping hot breath into her lungs, her body drenched with sweat, she cursed the oppressive humidity of Queensland as she stumbled on. She should reach the KIND property any time, why wasn't she there already? The complex abutted the park boundary and they hadn't been all that far away when... She saw again the carnage. The blood. Simon's neck pumping into the leaves, Keith vanishing whole down that gargantuan maw, Lizzie bitten clean in half.

Delilah let out a cry of horror, pushed the thoughts from her mind and kept running. Just get out. This was beyond them. She had no idea what the next step was, but it certainly involved more than a small team from KIND. Maybe those SCAR people Rowling had been so disgusted with could help? Gods knew, they needed all the help they could get.

She skidded to a halt at the sight of sun glinting off muddy water. She walked slowly forward again. The river? Why the hell was she at the river? That was entirely perpendicular to where she should be.

Holding back a sob, Delilah turned in a slow circle, scanning the forest all around her. She'd got turned around in her panic, that's all. If the river was here, she could simply turn and follow it. Not a problem. A much longer journey, but at least she knew where she was now. She'd thought she had known before, but no worries. Don't panic. Now she definitely knew.

Rowling was strangely silent in her ear, but she chose to take that as a blessing. She turned and walked along, keeping a few meters of bush between herself and the water. Her legs were jelly, her lungs tight. She blinked sweat from her eyes every few seconds. She would have killed for an air-conditioned room with thick cement walls.

Razana lay in a patch of sun dead ahead.

Delilah froze, pressing her lips together to prevent a cry escaping. The huge beast had bloodstains around its mouth, up the sides of its long, deep head. It lay in a half-curl, like some giant, scaled dog, basking. And it was between her and where she needed to go.

She looked side to side, mentally planning a route around, a way to give the thing a wide berth but not get turned around and lost again. At least she knew where it was now, and that it was resting, digesting her colleagues.

"Do you still have your weapon?"

Delilah jumped, let out a tiny gasp, at Rowling's voice, clear and excited in her ear. "What?" she managed, barely above a whisper.

"Do you still have the gas grenades?"

Delilah felt a wave of fury wash through her. How dare this bitch, sitting in her comfortable, cool bunker, even think of suggesting that Delilah should still try to take on this monster. Alone now, no less!

Then the fury was followed by a sense of shame, that quickly chilled into a cold anger. Wasn't she, Delilah, KIND's most devout member? Wasn't she the type of person who should be in charge rather than Karen bloody Rowling? If she wanted to be the leader one day, as she knew she deserved, she would have to prove it. She would have to be brave. Here was a prime opportunity. And she did have the gas. Lizzie had assured her it would work.

She looked down at the bulky weapon in her hands, gripped in white-knuckled terror throughout her flight. Another sign she was made of sterner stuff than she was giving herself credit for. One gas grenade was locked and loaded in the pipe, three more clipped underneath, ready to be deployed.

She was almost in range already.

The beast lay there, sleeping.

Delilah flicked off the safety and moved silent step by silent step forward.

JD trudged through the rainforest, his mind flatlining. All gone, Dad, Rod, Dicky, all taken by that thing out there. That huge, terrifying beast. What even was it? It didn't look exactly like a huge crocodile, the legs too long, the head more like the T-Rex from Jurassic Park than a saltie. And the size of the thing!

Maybe he was still lying in the dirt somewhere after being brained by a yowie. Perhaps this was all some fever dream and he'd wake up soon to the usual abuse from his father and brothers.

But no, JD wasn't ever that lucky. Never in his life had he experienced anything that could be considered luck, unless he counted being the only one left alive now. So far. He didn't like his father and brothers, a more despicable pack of arseholes was hard to imagine, but they were his family. The only family he had. Despite everything, he loved them. Now they were gone.

He stopped dead at the sight of grey-green scales reflecting sunlight. How had it got around him again? He'd been staggering a lot, he knew that. His panicked sprint away from the monster had been brief before nausea overcame him again and he'd stopped to puke. Then he'd started forward again, thankfully no sign of the beast behind, so he'd simply kept stumbling along.

He'd stopped frequently to rest, his concussed head swimming. Twice more he'd paused to vomit, and whether that was the concussion or the memory of Dicky's headless body waving its arms, or both, he didn't know. Or care. But now there it was, that bastard. Lying there, sleeping like some giant prehistoric baby, right in front of him.

It was at a fairly long range for his rifle, but despite his brothers' relentless mockery, he was a good shot. He would get the revenge the others had been denied. Slowly, blinking repeatedly against the dizziness that threatened to topple him constantly, and the sweat in his eyes, he slowly took aim.

Charles McEvoy and Blake Frieza had chased the Razana as it ran, but quickly lost it in the thick rainforest. The beast was unbelievably fast, and incredibly adept at navigating the rough terrain. Of course, it helped that it could simply stamp flat the kind of bush that people needed to hack through or find a way around. But that also meant that when it was in full flight, it left an easily followed trail.

After a while, the beast had obviously slowed and taken a more cautious path, and then it took McEvoy a little longer to track it down. But finally they'd got back behind it and now there it was, laying in a patch of sun like it didn't have a care in the world.

"It's so bloody big!" Frieza said in an awed whisper.

"Beautiful, isn't she?" McEvoy said with a smile. "Come on, let's get closer."

"Wait." Frieza pointed. "Three o'clock."

McEvoy looked and saw a woman not far from the beast, creeping forward, some kind of bulky grenade launcher raised in front of her. "I don't know what she's got there," McEvoy said. "But I don't want to her to start blowing shit up. We need to stun it. We're in range, let's—"

He didn't finish the thought as a shot rang out from the other side of the clearing opposite the creeping woman. The beast roared as a bullet tore the scales of its face, blood spraying. But the wound appeared relatively minor despite its accuracy.

The Razana surged up even as they heard a rifle crack and another shot rang out. This one caught the beast in the neck, more blood, but that only enraged it further.

"Shock the bastard!" McEvoy yelled.

The agents sprang up from hiding, leveling their weapons, but a high popping sound came from the woman with the grenade launcher. McEvoy's eyes widened as something struck the ground right beneath the Razana's head and exploded.

For a moment he expected the searing pain of shrapnel and explosive death, but the area quickly filled with clouds of thick green gas. McEvoy and Frieza were too close to avoid it. They staggered backwards, trying to get clear, but they were closer than both the woman and whoever had fired the rifle.

They managed only a few steps before the gas overwhelmed them. It tasted slightly sweet, McEvoy thought, then dizziness swept through him and everything went dark.

Chapter 35

Aston had no idea where in the bush they were. He did know one thing, though, and that was that all this had been a terrible mistake. They had all underestimated just how big and how dangerous this monster was. All that mattered was getting the hell out. Let some other authority come and deal with it. The Army seemed the most suited.

They'd heard more shots a little while before and Aston figured them for pistol shots, not a rifle. Who the hell had been carrying a pistol? He didn't expect it would have had much effect. Thankfully it was fairly distant, as was the roaring and crashing through the trees. But everything had been quiet for a while now.

"This way," Penry said. "Not far to the river, then we can move more easily."

They walked on, alert, then heard gasping and running feet. Turning as one, weapons rising, they realized it was Rusty Crews and Sophie.

"Oh, thank god!" Sophie said.

"Gomzi?" Aston asked.

Crews shook his head, eyes haunted.

"It took him," Sophie said. "Just carried him away."

Slater shook her head. "What a mess."

"Ned?" Crews asked.

"Out there somewhere," Aston said. "But Arnott and Costello are dead."

"Holy crap."

Aston turned, kept walking. "Come on, let's just get out of here."

As they moved on Penry and Ringo took the point, calm

and placid but silent, clearly on alert, their eyes searching the bush.

"River that way," Ringo said.

Penry nodded. "We'll get there and walk along the bank. Much less undergrowth to slow us and we'll see anything coming through the water."

Something crashed through the trees towards them, but Aston knew immediately it was another person, not nearly big enough to be a threat, and the huffing and puffing was entirely human. Ned King staggered out into their path. He was filthy, arms and face scratched from numerous branches. He'd lost his weapons and as he saw them, relief flooded his sweating face. He paused, glanced back the way he'd come, and Aston winced at the dark stain in the seat of his khakis.

By a pure force of will, King quickly dragged his composure back. "Ah, there you are! I've been searching for you."

"Running for your life, you mean," Sophie said, doing nothing to hide the disdain in her voice.

"I'm here to lead you to safety!" King insisted.

Aston saw Penry and Ringo exchange a smile, a slight roll of the eyes at each other. Never mind, let the TV icon try to retain some unearned dignity, it made no difference to any of them. They all knew the truth. "We're all together now," Aston said. "What's left of us anyway. Let's get the hell out—"

Not far away, mayhem erupted again.

"Oh shit oh shit oh shit!" Crews moaned.

It started with a rifle shot, then another. A roar they all recognized now as belonging to Razana. Crashing and branches snapping.

"Who the hell is still out here?" Slater asked. "Do we

help?"

The sound moved slightly away from them. Aston chewed his lip, indecision clawing at him. They might be able to stop more killing if they simply distracted the beast. "Let's check," he said.

The group hurried in the direction of the retreating noise. Within moments they came upon a fairly bizarre scene. At the edge of a wide clearing near the river, two men clad in tactical gear lay dead on the ground, but there wasn't a drop of blood. No sign of any injuries at all.

"What's happened to them?" Crews asked.

"You smell that?" Penry asked, sniffing at the air.

They all paused. Aston smelled a sharp, chemical odor floating on the hot air, a slightly sweet edge to it. Whatever it was had mostly dissipated, but someone had used some kind of chemical weapon in the area. "I'm glad we weren't nearer when this happened!" he said.

He crouched, checked the pulse of the two men. He looked up. "They're both dead!"

"Oh dear." Ned King turned a slow circle, looking into the bush.

Aston passed his tranq rifle to Ringo and picked up one of the strange-looking weapons the dead men were carrying. He hadn't seen its like before, but it was pretty obvious how it worked. There was a safety, a trigger, a lever that armed it.

Penry crouched beside him and picked up the other fallen man's weapon. "Looks interesting," he said.

"Shame they obviously never got a chance to use them," Aston said. "But we'll take all the firepower we can get. You hold onto that," he said to Ringo, nodding at the tranq rifle. "Me and Penry'll carry these."

"Who are they?" Slater asked.

Aston realized Lynnette was still filming, the woman

moving in for a close-up of the insignia on their fatigues. Well, if they survived, Slater would have a hell of a show out of this escapade. "No idea," he said, in answer to Slater's question. "Anyone recognize them? Their badge?"

A general shaking of heads was interrupted as more crashing sounded out in the bush.

"That's coming back this way," Ringo said.

They braced, all weapons raised, as a young man came running out of the trees carrying a rifle. He had blood on his face from a head wound. "I shot it!" he sobbed. "Twice! And the gas! But it's still coming!"

His eyes were wild, but he staggered like he was drunk. Maybe he was, Aston thought. Or he'd got a taste of the gas that killed the two at their feet. He had no time to consider it as the crashing increased and Razana came barreling along.

They ran back into the clearing as the beast crashed into trees, running recklessly. Its head swung a little side to side, its footing uncertain, movements clumsy. Aston saw it was bleeding from a wound in its face and another in its neck, but they appeared minor, not enough to affect it this much. The gas, he thought. It must have got a blast of it, just not enough to finish it or knock it out. And who the hell had fired that anyway?

Sophie let out a scream, pulling Aston back into the moment, as Crews moved to protect her and take a hasty shot with his tranq rifle. It missed, going wide and high, but he and Sophie moved out of the path of the giant predator as it staggered into their midst.

Ringo had already moved to the opposite side and took careful aim, fired. His dart struck home right under Razana's jaw, in the pale softer-looking skin there, but it had no immediate visible effect. Razana swung its head left and right as the group spread out in a wide circle around it.

"Keep moving!" Aston yelled. "If you stay still it'll find you."

"This way," King yelled, backing up and moving around behind the beast.

The group moved around either side, Ringo and Crews reloading as they went. Razana raised its head and roared, and Crews fired again. This time, his shot hit the target, right beside the dart Ringo had landed. Razana missed a step, staggered, slowed a little.

"It's working!" King yelled.

Were the tranquilizers taking effect? Aston didn't care. If nothing else, they had bought them a moment's reprieve from the monster's wrath.

"Run for it!" Aston yelled.

The group turned their backs on the creature and bolted.

"How long should it take for the tranquilizers to kick in?" Aston asked.

Ned King ran alongside, puffing and gasping. "No idea," he said. "Never used them before."

Aston's eyes widened. "Bloody hell, mate."

They burst from cover at the edge of the river, hemmed in. Razana had turned and followed, even now crashing drunkenly through the bush in pursuit. Aston looked down at the weapon in his hands. They couldn't risk waiting for the tranquilizers to start working. What if they weren't enough? He had no other choice and decided it wouldn't hurt to try whatever this thing was.

He armed it and readied himself. Penry stepped up beside him and did the same.

The young man with the head wound who had first led the beast into their midst came stumbling through the trees. Aston hadn't realized he'd been left behind when they ran.

But it was too late for him. The giant head of Razana ploughed through the bush right above him and stabbed down. The creature snatched the young man in its giant maw, long teeth puncturing his body. It shook him like a dog with a rubber toy and flung him through the air. He spun over and over, unnatural like a rag doll. Crews cried out, pushed Sophie aside, and the young man's body slammed into him, knocking the park ranger flat.

Aston ran forward, heard Slater yell, "Sam, no!" but he ignored her plea, raised his weapon, and fired. A silver projectile burst through the air and embedded itself in Razana's tough hide, right at the shoulder. The monster roared as blue electricity sparked and arced all over it, the air filling with the smell of burning and an ozone stench.

Razana roared, staggered, then locked in on Sophie as she ran towards the inert form of Crews, still half under the young man's bleeding corpse. It stumbled toward her and she turned, halfway to Crews, frozen in fear. Aston dashed forward and scooped her up just as those massive jaws snapped shut over the spot where she'd been standing. He caught a whiff of its fetid breath, felt the wind of its head snaking past him. He fell to the ground, thinking surely it was about to snap again, and this time it couldn't possibly miss despite its seemingly drunken staggering, when Penry fired his electric weapon.

The silver projectile struck home right at the base of Razana's jaw and electricity arced all across it again. The beast slowed, shuddered and howled. There was a moment of stillness, everyone frozen in terror, then Razana slowly toppled over and hit the ground with a resounding crash.

Chapter 36

Silence hung over the bush as everyone stood still, stunned. Aston, Slater, Lynn, and Barry moved cautiously forward. Lynn had filmed everything and was still going. Aston marveled at her focus, even as her face was chalk white and her hands shook.

Penry and Ringo moved to one side, standing together, watching.

Crews crawled out from under the corpse of the young man, grimacing at the blood, putting one hand to his knee in pain. Sophie stepped up next to him, eyes concerned.

Ned King startled them all with a sudden WHOOP! of joy. "We bloody did it!" he cried.

"We?" Aston asked, half turning back. Then he shrugged it off and crept closer to the beast. Penry and Ringo looked at one another and shook their heads.

Razana's sides shifted in spaced out, shallow breaths. The air rasped in its narrow nostrils.

"It's still alive," Aston said.

Ned moved forward. "Penry, Ringo, still got those ropes?"

Both men nodded, heavy loops of nylon climbing rope looped across their bodies.

"Right, let's wrap it up. Jaws first!"

The two men stepped up and began tying up Razana's jaw, looping the rope back around its head to ensure it wouldn't slip off. Then they did their best to truss its legs together as it lay on its side, the rope barely long enough to reach, but they managed a cursory hobbling of the creature. The whole time, King walked around it, supervising. He must be unaware, Aston thought with a grin, of the wide crap stain in the seat of his khakis.

Lynn moved in, filming more closely as Penry and Ringo blindfolded Razana, then King moved in for a closer look. "Breathing strong," he said after a moment. "It's out cold. Not sure for how long, but this situation should hold it."

"Those men with the weird guns had rope on them too," Ringo said.

King smiled. "Well spotted, that man. Go get it and we'll truss this monster up some more. Can't be too careful."

As Penry and Ringo trotted back the way they'd come, Slater stepped forward. Disheveled, but ever the professional, she asked Ned a few questions, then stepped aside to give King the full frame of the camera as he launched into a lengthy description of the Razana's capture.

"Bit bloody distasteful to make documentary out of all this," Sophie said, watching with a frown. "How many people died today? And there he is hamming it up like he's on a game show."

"Everything is reality TV to these people," Crews said.

"Yeah, maybe," Aston said. "But after a highly traumatic situation, one of the ways people remain sane is to do things that feel normal. Doing their jobs falls into that category, I suppose. And apart from that, I reckon whatever is happening here is something people need to know about. At least with all this incontrovertible footage, the government won't be able to deny what happened."

"You think the government would want to cover this up?" Sophie asked.

"No idea. I mean, where did this creature even come from? It's amazing that we've managed to catch it, but we really haven't answered any questions yet. If anything, we've simply got more questions to add to everything we already don't know."

Sophie pursed her lips. "Including where the hell that gas came from?"

"Yep. And who were those guys with these weapons?" Aston hefted the weird taser.

"Speaking of doing our jobs," Crews said, and held out a hand for the electric gun.

"Really?" Aston said.

"Really. What, you think you can keep that?"

Aston didn't particularly appreciate the request, but he recognized he had no right to the thing. And even apart from that, it was evidence now in everything that had happened. He handed it over and Crews moved to stand guard over the unconscious creature, positioning himself between Sophie and the beast.

Penry and Ringo returned and added more rope to their already intricate trussing. The best writhed weakly as it began to come around, but all the fight was clearly knocked out of it for the time being.

Slater thanked King and told her crew to take a breather. Lynn and Barry sank thankfully to the ground and King turned back to his prize.

"I need to get back to my car and radio everything in," Crews said. "We need to report these deaths." His voice shook with fatigue and shock.

"We'll take you out," Penry said, as he and Ringo moved toward the ranger.

"Good idea," King said. "And get a crew back here, yeah?"

"What now?" Aston asked.

"We're close to the river," King said, jerking his thumb back over his shoulder at the water behind them. "I'll get more staff in and a flat barge and we'll haul this beauty aboard. We can ferry it all the way back to Crocalypse along the river."

Penry and Ringo nodded and headed off with Crews. Sophie went with them.

"Crocalypse," Aston said, with a shake of the head. "Really, Ned? You think that's a secure location?"

"Where the hell is secure enough to hold this killing machine?" Slater asked.

Ned grinned. "Don't you worry about that. I have just the place."

Chapter 37

It had been four days since Delilah watched her squad decimated and she'd only left her room at the KIND compound for food and bathroom visits, talking to no one. She was shellshocked, she knew that. Even after everything else that had gone down, she'd finally got a shot at the beast and the gas hadn't worked. She hated Rowling for that, maybe more than anything else. Sure, Razana had gotten groggy, staggered around a little. Those two mercs who stood up from the bush right by the animal had dropped like puppets with their strings cut. But Razana shook itself and then just went right back to being a ferocious wild beast.

It looked drunk as it took off through the bush, but was no less deadly for all that. The only blessing had been the animal had focused on the young man with the rifle. He'd got two good shots in, from what Delilah could tell, but they were no more effective than the gas had been.

Despite Rowling yelling in her ear to chase the beast, because surely it would drop any minute, Delilah had had enough. She went the other way, followed the river back to KIND and locked herself in her room.

Rowling had been attentive since her return. Too much so, truth be told. The woman was clearly besotted with Delilah and seemed to think the feelings were reciprocal despite all evidence to the contrary. Meanwhile, Rowling kept up a running commentary of their efforts to track Razana down again. The beast had disappeared, as far as they could tell. Rowling thought it had moved deeper into the rainforest, away from Blacktooth River despite the readiness of food there. Maybe they would never find it again, but

KIND had a responsibility to account for the thing. They had been responsible for its escape, after all. But all that was Rowling's problem, not Delilah's.

Delilah had been ignoring all calls too, even from Ned King who was obviously missing her at the front of the house in his shiny new park. That was due to open any day now and she had no intention of sticking on a plastic smile for tourists for the benefit of King or anyone else. Let him find some new staff too. He was down a couple of people already. She'd seen their bodies in the bush. Why he'd been out there she didn't know except for the obvious. Surely he hadn't intended to catch the Razana too. How would he have known about it? She thought he was probably out trying to capture regular crocs for his new exhibits and had got caught in the middle.

Karen Rowling shattered Delilah's thoughts by barging in without knocking.

"Dammit, Karen," Delilah started, but Rowling held up a finger.

Her face was all business. "Get up, D."

"What?"

"Get up. No more moping about."

"I'm not in the bloody mood."

"Oh, you will be!"

Delilah narrowed her eyes. Rowling was alive with something, some news had her ready to go. "Have you found her?" Delilah asked.

"We have!"

Delilah immediately brightened. "You caught her? Did Kurt get a new team together?" Kurt had been the only other survivor. He'd found his way out of the bush and back to KIND long before Delilah. He'd then headed back out when he realized she was still out in the rainforest, meaning to rescue her, which she thought was quite a character strength. It turned out to be unnecessary as she'd found her own way back and Rowling had called Kurt back in. But they'd lost the beast and Kurt had spent the last four days helping Rowling search for it. But Razana seemed to have gone to ground. Delilah had overheard Rowling trying to organize aerial searches, booking choppers to look for signs of the beast's movements deeper in the bush. She must have finally seen something.

Rowling twisted her lips in annoyance. "No, we haven't captured her. But she has been captured."

Delilah's excitement drained away. "What? Who has her?"

Rowling sighed. "Ned, the Croc King," she said, like the words tasted bitter in her mouth.

"How did he get her?"

"Turns out the wily bastard has had her all along. We thought she had got away, but him and that Aston character and friends managed to bring her down right after you launched the gas. In fact, I'm in no doubt the massive dose of gas you gave her could only have helped them capture her."

"You're sure," Delilah asked. "Ned King has her?"

"Yep. Been hiding it at that new park of his. Crocalypse!" She spat the word like an expletive.

"So who's seen her? We have a new contact in there?"

Rowling shook her head, held up a flyer. "No, but we don't need one. The official opening of the Crocalypse park is all over the news. Suddenly it's a major event, with network coverage and high profile public figures."

Delilah looked at the flyer without taking it. Ned King's signature high color extravagance. The bit that caught her eye said:

SPECIAL UNVEILING! A PERHISTORIC MARVEL! YOU WON'T BELIEVE YOUR EYES!

"Ned has announced a secret main attraction that will be unveiled live on television this Saturday afternoon," Rowling said. "It's his big bonanza opening event. And in case you've lost track of time during your moping around, that's only two days from now."

Delilah bit back a snappy response to that unsubtle barb, staring at the flyer. "It can only be Razana, can't it?"

Rowling nodded. "What else? Somehow those bastards managed to subdue her and get her to King's park. No wonder we've seen no sign of her since the failed mission."

"So what are we going to do?" Delilah asked.

"There's no time to organize a major operation," Rowling said, pulling out the chair by Delilah's desk and sitting down. "Besides, I think we'll have a better chance of success with a small team, not some major assault."

"We can hardly storm his new complex!" Delilah said. "The place is huge, with high fences, security cams, the lot. King doesn't do anything by half."

"Exactly. So, like I said, a small team." Rowling cast a meaningful look at Delilah, who realized she was not afraid of facing the Razana again.

The thought of Ned King exploiting a one-of-a-kind creature like that was too much for her to take. She swung her legs off the bed and sat up to ask, "Right. So what's our plan?"

Chapter 38

An air of festival was thick in the air at Crocalypse. Green and yellow bunting and balloons hung everywhere, happy music was piped through hidden speakers, frequent announcements touting all the rides and attractions echoed everywhere. User-pay police patrolled the park. King must have gone to a great deal of expense to hire so many. The smell of burgers, cotton candy, and the rich aroma of the rainforest filled Aston's nostrils as he walked hand in hand with Slater. The walkways were busy with people, hundreds of tourists thronging the exciting new park. Maybe thousands. Aston had never imagined this many people gathering anywhere close to Blacktooth River, even for an event like this. Truth be told, it was hard to imagine a park of this magnitude anywhere outside a major center. To have such a thing in this remote corner of North Queensland seemed weird, but he assumed Ned King knew what he was doing. The man was nothing if not a skilled entrepreneur. It felt like a kind of turning point.

"I wish we'd gone home a few days ago," Aston said, wincing around at the crowds and bustle.

"Really?"

"I don't like all this commercialism. I mean, I respect King's vision, but I hate the glitz."

Slater smiled. "I get that. But we're the special invited guests of Ned King the Croc King himself!" She rolled her eyes and Aston had to laugh.

"At least you agreed with me not to attend the great unveiling," Aston said. "I don't think I could bear that, King using Razana like a sideshow freak."

"Well, yeah, I couldn't bear listening to King praise himself and then all the speeches from self-important politicians and actors and whoever else."

"King did manage to get a vastly improved guest list at short notice though. All those B-listers playing second fiddle now to some genuine Hollywood talent and actual government ministers, federal too, not just state."

"He does get things done," Slater agreed. "I've set Lynn and Barry to make sure they get footage of all that. I'll edit it into something bearable later on. It'll be a good closing piece for the documentary. I've had some serious interest already, Sam. This could be really big. Despite everything."

"I'm glad." He meant it, though he remained conflicted.

"If we could do anything to bring all those people back," Slater said. "I'd do it in an instant even if it meant the documentary couldn't exist. But we'll honor their memories. We'll dedicate the piece to everyone who's died this past week."

"Even the ones we don't know?" Aston asked. "Like those dudes in the dark fatigues?"

Slater shrugged. "That's for Crews and the other authorities to deal with, I guess. I'll be sure to ask for a full official list of names."

As they strolled through the main crocodile habitat, the reptiles inside appearing quite small and docile after their recent experiences, despite being some of the biggest salties Aston had ever seen, he asked, "You don't feel guilty taking the day off now? Aren't you stressed leaving it up to Lynn and Barry?" He grinned to show he was teasing.

"Not at all. I think we earned a break. So did Lynn and Barry, to be fair, but that's the life. They can start their holiday tomorrow. Meanwhile, I'm quite enjoying the fact that these predators are all confined. I've had enough of being hunted by giant crocs. I'm happy to walk on cement paths and look at them well contained by bars and toughened glass."

"I hear that."

They walked in amiable silence for a while longer, then Slater said, "Talking of getting things done, it's amazing how fast King turned that orca pool into a Razana habitat."

"Spent a fortune, as I heard it," Aston said. "Had people working around the clock. He said he'd find another use for the amphitheater and pool and he wasn't wrong."

Slater pursed her lips. "You think maybe that was his plan all along?"

"Nah, I think he genuinely wanted an orca show. There's no way he could have known about the Razana before a week or two ago. But King is the great opportunist. To be fair, we all benefit. Who knows what might have become of the thing if he didn't have somewhere to contain her? Probably would have been euthanized."

Slater nodded, expression sad. "Despite all the deaths, that would have been a bad outcome. The beast wasn't malicious, just following her nature. I wonder how well she might have survived out there on her own if she'd been left alone. You know, if maybe she'd been deeper in the rainforest, further from town."

Aston shrugged. "She's the very definition of an apex predator. Can't imagine she'd have had any trouble living a long and happy life out there. All the time she remained undiscovered by people, at least. But that's the thing. She was discovered. You think she was out there for years and only recently blundered into a place where people had made a town?"

"I was wondering the same thing," Slater said. "I mean, where the hell did she come from? I can't make sense of a prehistoric beast that size surviving undiscovered for such a long time."

"Me either. Makes you wonder, doesn't it?"

"What do you mean?"

Aston frowned. "I don't know, exactly. But maybe somebody brought it in from somewhere else? After all, the dinosaur we know about was native to Africa. How would one get all the way here on the other side of the world? How does she even exist in the first place? There's no way a population of those things exists somewhere out there. This is a big, wide rainforest, but creatures that size have an extensive range. It's impossible to think there's an entire population of them out there and this is the first time one has crossed paths with people."

"In which case, you're suggesting this Razana is a one-off and someone brought it here deliberately?" Slater asked.

"Has to be, right? What other explanation is there? But who? And why? It's the only thing that makes sense, but all it does is raise more questions."

"And you don't think it was Ned? Let's be honest, it's in keeping with the kind of thing the greatest showman would do."

Aston nodded, smiled. "It suits him, sure. But I believe him when he says he didn't know about it. I think if he had brought something like that in, he'd have it well secured. He has this entire complex, after all. Something else is going on. Who fired the gas out there the other day? Who were those guys with the electric weapons? In the end, those mega-tasers were the only thing that really worked. Those guys knew what they were doing, but they were killed by the gas. So someone else must have deployed that."

"Two opposing groups, who both knew Razana was out there," Slater mused. "So one of them is probably responsible for it being here. The other group at least knew all about it. We still have more questions than answers."

"I was trying to research the insignia those dead guys with the tasers had on their fatigues," Aston said. "But I couldn't find a thing about them."

Slater shrugged, gripped his hand a little tighter. "Well, we aren't going to solve this mystery today, and really it's not our problem any more, right? So why not have some fun?" She slipped her arm around his shoulders and turned him towards a midway of croc-themed attractions.

"Sure, why not?" Aston said, thinking how thankful he was that they had managed to survive another crazy encounter with unnatural wildlife. It was becoming a habit he could well do without.

Chapter 39

Wearing a stolen Crocalypse security guard uniform and hat, Delilah walked along the side fence of the new park. Inside. She had infiltrated the place with ease. It was an amusement park, after all, not a government facility, and Delilah had a lot of experience with these sorts of things. Plus, she had her passes from working here. Slipping from those areas into the more secure back end of the park was no challenge. She'd broken into a lot of places over the years, and a lot of them were more secure than this. Research labs that were hushed up by both corporations and the government, where animals were treated horribly. Commercial farms with a public front but a much busier, and secret, area hidden from prying eyes. Strolling around in this circus of glitz and glamor was no trial at all.

But she shouldn't be here now, among all these crowds. Despite all their planning, they had run into a hitch almost immediately. In the first instance, the plan was pretty much a repeat of the one they'd used to rescue the Razana the first time around. Admittedly, Razana was smaller then, less crazed, but the principal still applied. They had identified one of many large supply gates all around the Crocalypse compound, and one was not far from the amphitheater where they were sure the croc was being held. Using drones to scope the area, they had established that they could get to Razana via the staff access, outside the main public concourses, and lead her unseen to the large supply gate in question. Assistance would be there to cut the heavy chains on the gate, and a specially equipped truck would be waiting. Load Razana onto the truck and be away before anyone knew she was missing.

But all that was supposed to have happened in the early hours of the morning, under cover of darkness, with no one but a light security detail around. A truck breakdown had set them back several hours and the park had just opened, already teeming with people. Ned King was warming up for his big opening surprise. Already she could hear him droning on, the park's PA system echoing loudly. They had to go ahead, despite the additional problems, or it would all be too late. Once the public knew of the existence of the Razana, they would never get her away.

So Delilah had quickly infiltrated as a security guard and the rest of the plan was intact. They simply had to hope no one was paying much attention to the back of the Razana habitat, what would have been the orca pump room but was now Razana's private quarters, linked by a long ramp to the open habitat right in front of the amphitheater. The deep pool originally built for the orca was a prime location to keep the beast, Delilah had to admit that. There was no way should would be able to climb or jump free, it had to be twenty meters or more from the top where the seats curved around to the bottom where the habitat had been hastily constructed. A heavy tarp had been stretched across the top at one corner to provide shade. The tarp was secured by ropes to metal rings mounted in the sides of the pool. Reluctantly, Delilah admitted the whole thing was pretty ingenious and not a bad home for the beast. But it was still captivity. It was still exploitation. She could not stand for that.

Another guard stood by the gate that led around behind the orca pool, a cement path sloping down the twenty meters or so to an access road that encircled the entire park where it stood on the hill. The public areas were all above and away from this circular roadway, the idea being that any workings of the park were well concealed from public view. It worked to keep the magic of the park alive, and it also worked for anyone aiming to exploit those things. Assuming Delilah could work alone. She was determined to succeed. Their cause was just.

"Hey," she said as she approached the guard, careful to remain casual despite her rapidly increasing heart rate.

He nodded. "Hey, yourself."

The advantage of a new park with new staff, Delilah thought. No one knew everyone yet. "Ned needs you up at the main amphitheater. Says he wants a few more hands up there for the unveiling shortly."

The man frowned. "I was told by Ringo to make sure I stayed here no matter what today."

"Boring assignment, huh?"

The man laughed. "You're not wrong. Everything going on here and I get assigned to the dullest spot in the entire park."

Delilah grinned. "Well, lucky you. That's why I'm here. Ned needs people up there and Ringo sent me to relieve you. I guess he wants strong men on hand and let the weak and feeble women do the boring standing around stuff."

The guard made a rueful expression, then shrugged. "I'm sorry about that, that's actually bullshit."

"You're not wrong. But there it is."

"Okay then. Make sure you don't let this gate go anywhere now, you hear?"

Delilah smiled. She hoped this guy wouldn't get in trouble for leaving his post. He seemed like a decent sort. "I'll watch it with both eyes!" she assured him.

He smiled again and trotted off, heading for the main path back up to the amphitheater. Delilah smiled. That was him taken care of. She slipped through the gate, bolted it behind her, and jogged down the slope to the maintenance road. The wall of the Razana habitat towered above her, concealing everything. And that left the path to the side gate entirely clear. As long as no one looked over the back of the amphitheater stage while they moved Razana, they should escape unseen. The plan was still viable. She made her way to the big double doors at the back of Razana's area and looked them up and down, lips pursed. Assuming Razana wasn't too big to get through here the plan was still viable. She had grown in the weeks since the escape. But these doors were designed to admit the large golf carts and their trailers the staff all over the parks used behind the scenes. Razana might have to scooch down a bit, but she'd get through. Just. Hopefully.

Delilah turned and ran the hundred meters or so around behind the amphitheater. The high cement wall to her right provided excellent cover, the colorful awning at the top covering the stage where even now Ned King waxed lyrical about the wonders of reptiles and how people knew so little about the natural world. The sun beat down hot and the day was humid, but the shadow of the wall provided welcome shade. Delilah pictured the scene above, the huge habitat down in the pool in front of King and the dignitaries and stars on stage, partially concealed by the huge stretched tarp. On the other side, the curved rows of seats rising up, packed with spectators all wondering just what this great unveiling would reveal.

Well, unlucky, suckers, Delilah thought. It's going to unveil a big disappointment.

She reveled in the thought of Ned finally getting to his big reveal and then just nothing happening. No Razana appearing. He'd go down quickly to access this side of the habitat to see why she wasn't coming out and find her gone. The mystery complete, Razana freed.

She glanced up and saw security cameras all around the place. Well, maybe it wouldn't be such a mystery. Even if guards elsewhere saw them though those cameras leading Razana away, they wouldn't have time to react before the beast was on the truck and away.

Delilah reached the service gate and saw Karen Rowling waiting there, outside the fence, hunkered down in the shadow of a large tree. The specially equipped truck, with a trusted member of KIND as driver, was concealed by the trees about fifty meters back into the rainforest, along the rough access road. Big, beefy Kurt waited with Karen. He grinned when he saw her, his eyes alive with mischief. He'd been pleased to see her emerge from self-imposed isolation once they had this new plan and Delilah had quickly realized he rather liked her. She decided she'd make all his dreams come true later on once the Razana was safely rescued. She flicked him a wink as an aperitif and his grin grew wider still.

Delilah looked to Karen Rowling, exulting slightly in the woman's unconcealed jealousy. "Ready?" she asked, to shatter the moment.

"The way's clear?" Rowling asked.

"All ready to go. I'm going back now to bring her through, you get ready to cut the chains on the gate and help me guide her to the truck when we get this far."

"I know the plan!" Rowling snapped.

"You're sure the pheromones will work?"

"Yes. She'll follow them, definitely. This is a far more controlled and short journey than trying to get her out of the rainforest. It'll work."

Delilah grinned again. "Right, let's go then."

As she jogged back to the habitat entrance she heard

Ned King announce Curtis Hamsworth, the most famous of the three Hamsworth brothers, all Hollywood A-listers. Quite what the connection was between a giant prehistoric croc and a vacuous celebrity who played superheroes in the movies, she didn't know. But whatever, it was buying her time.

As she got to the large access doors again, double-checking that the coast was still clear, she dug into the big thigh pocket of the cargo pants for her lock pick kit, then paused. She tried the handle and the door clicked open. She was mildly surprised it hadn't been locked, but then again, she'd worked for Ned long enough to know he wasn't really a details guy in that respect. He was also too arrogant to believe anything he tried could ever fail. It made perfect sense to her that he'd plan the habitat down to the finest detail, but leave security up to a handful of largely incompetent minimum-wage locals.

Delilah entered the concrete bunker and found herself in a large room. The lights were off, one end in deep shadow, the other lit from daylight coming through the cage ahead of her. There was all kinds of gear around, clearly a lot of it for the cleaning and upkeep of the habitat and presumably Razana herself. A row of massive chest freezers sat along one near wall, no doubt crammed with frozen sides of beef. Razana could live on that, but it wasn't what she would prefer to eat. Running down live prey was her natural way. On the far side of the big room was a gleaming silver fence, the cage obviously a new addition, the bars bright silver.

Beyond the bars was the sleeping quarters for Razana, with a lot of hay scattered around, and beyond that a long corridor leading away in a shallow incline to the bottom of the pool that had been built for orca. A heavy gate closed off the ramp, allowing the park to keep Razana contained in this bunker at night. Sunlight blared through from the far end of the slope where it opened into the bottom of the deep orca pool, now Razana's supposed daytime home. Delilah paused, realizing she had a problem. The new cage was night quarters for the croc, the gate on the far side could be opened to let Razana in and out of the new habitat, but access to the night cage from this side was small. They could lock Razana out in the pool habitat in order to get into the night cage, but the opening was not much bigger than a regular door, just for staff to go in and out. It had a rudimentary lock, she could pick that easily enough, but Razana would never fit through it. Whether the doors out to the maintenance road were big enough or not was a moot point. She wouldn't be able to get Razana out this way. Chewing her bottom lip in thought, Delilah suddenly froze. She'd been so concerned with the physical structure, she hadn't realized a fundamental issue.

Where was Razana?

Moving forward, Delilah couldn't see the croc anywhere in the large night cage. Heart racing, she took out the gas grenade she'd been carrying, refigured based on their prior experiences. Enough, she was assured by the KIND boffins, to make Razana docile and compliant. Just in case. In her other hand, she held a large glass bottle of pheromones.

As she approached the barred wall of the cage, Delilah realized that down at the far end in the gloom, where the bars met the concrete wall, it looked wrong. The bars were unevenly spaced. She moved nearer. No, that wasn't it exactly. Some of the bars were missing, and a couple on either side had been bent. They'd been pushed apart.

Delilah's legs went to jelly. "Damn you, Ned King," she whispered, thinking to herself again, He's not a details man. Horrified, she realized several things at once. He'd rushed the build in here, had crews working around the clock, and they'd saved time and money using inferior alloy instead of solid steel. The bars on the far side leading out to the habitat were closed and much sturdier than these. This side didn't match up to that quality. And Razana was most definitely not in the night cage where she should be. Delilah's realization that she faced a problem in bringing the croc out this way suddenly became a far bigger problem. Razana had already come out this way. So where was she? Delilah looked into the heavily shadowed end of the room that she'd ignored when she first came in.

There was a scrape of scaly body on cement and a heavy gust of hot, fetid air huffed over Delilah. Her entire body trembling, Delilah slowly turned, fingers fumbling frantically with the gas grenade. She had no time to do anything with it as from the gloomy shadows of the far end of the room something massive and grey-green shot forward. She saw jaws split wide, huge white teeth glistening with saliva, and Delilah let out a piercing scream.

Chapter 40

Rusty Crews sat with Sophie high in the amphitheater seats looking down over the big main attraction. It was an impressive set-up, especially as it had all happened so fast. The seating made a shallow semi-circle in front of the deep pool that had been intended for an orca show. Deep, Crews assumed, to allow the orca to dive then come up and catch balls or some other horrible spectacle. It appalled him, he hated animal exploitation, making noble beasts do tricks for gawking punters. But it paid off in this case. It had to be at least twenty meters to the bottom of the pool, where a habitat had been constructed with boulders, plants, artificial trees, and a stream running down the middle. Part of the area was obscured by a large canvas shade cloth stretched across one corner.

Off to the left side was a large metal gate, thick steel bars blocking off an access tunnel. Down there, Crews assumed, was a nice secure location for the Razana. He hoped King hadn't scrimped on that part of things and the creature had a comfortable place to be. He couldn't believe Craig Gomzi had been killed by the beast.

The family had been distraught. Craig was the second Gomzi in recent months to be killed by a wild animal, although Crews doubted the stories of a giant roo. He had kept that opinion to himself at the previous day's memorial service. That had been an uncomfortable time. But he didn't hold it against the Razana. The animal was simply following its nature. Now, at least, it was contained. While he hated animals being held for exploitation, generally hated zoos and captivity, there was little else to be done with something like the Razana. No way could they let such a thing run wild. He just hoped there weren't any more of them out there. He chose not to think too hard on where it might have come from.

Regardless, he found himself now sitting with Sophie Cook, the beast contained, the sun shining. He would miss Gomzi, but things had worked out pretty well for him. If he could continue to make himself available to Sophie, be a shoulder to cry on, perhaps they could rekindle what they'd lost. They both needed someone, and someone who knew everything that had happened over the last few days was a bonus.

Crews slipped an arm around her shoulders tentatively and she leaned into him. He smiled. He could even endure Ned King's blather if he got to hold Sophie while the man droned on. On the far side of the large pool habitat was a raised stage, with a stretched canvas roof and footlights. On either side of it was a large PA stack, projecting the microphoned voices of those on stage out across the amphitheater. On the stage were several seats, a lectern in the center. The seats were taken by a variety of dignitaries and stars King had managed to gather. Quite an impressive array, as it turned out.

After his initial speech, King had handed over to the State Premier, and she'd waxed lyrical about the value of conservation and how a park like this would do wonders not only for the natural world, but for tourism in the area and the economy. What about the entire national park I look after, Crews had thought, but chose not to dwell on it.

Then King had talked again. The man clearly had an infinite supply of words and was only too glad to spew them endlessly. He finally handed over to Curtis Hamsworth and Crews had to reluctantly admit he was impressed with that.

A genuine Hollywood A-lister, an Aussie boy made good. The man was a real celluloid superhero. Quite the achievement by King to get that kind of star power to officially open the park.

He sat up straighter, realizing this no doubt meant the fanfare was over and the official opening would happen, with the great reveal of Razana to the public. Hard to believe none of these people had any idea of what they were about to see.

Crews glanced up behind himself and saw Slater's people, Lynette and Barry, recording everything. Slater herself was off with Aston, and Crews was pleased with that. It seemed that Aston was indeed tight with Slater and had no more interest in Sophie.

"So when Ned asked me to introduce this main attraction, I thought he was having me on!"

The crowd laughed and Crews drew his attention back to the event. On the stage, Curtis Hamsworth flashed his million dollar smile, his huge biceps flexing under the tight white t-shirt he wore.

"I thought," Hamsworth went on, "that he was trying to convince me movie special effects were real. He's got some kind of holographic projector, I decided, and he's planning on some kind of Jurassic Park trickery. But no, he promised. 'I'll send a helicopter,' he told me, 'and fly you in to prove I'm on the level.' Well, who can refuse a free helicopter ride, eh?"

You probably take helicopter flights to the bloody toilet and back, Crews thought bitterly. Get on with it.

"And when I saw for real what Ned King had described, I couldn't believe my eyes. Honestly, folks, you have no idea what you're about to experience. It will blow your minds! Ned will tell you all about it in more detail once the gasps of disbelief die down, but for now, it's my absolute pleasure to

officially declare Crocalypse open and introduce you all to…
RAZANA!"

With a grand gesture, Hamsworth turned to the pool in front of him, sweeping an arm towards the large steel barred gate down at one end.

"Open the gate!" King yelled.

The energy built up had become electric and people started applauding immediately, then a roar of excitement rang out. An orange light flashed above the barred gate, a siren pulsed a warning sound, and the gate slid back alongside the wall to reveal the dark square opening of a tunnel leading down.

And nothing happened.

"I think our main attraction has become a little shy!" King said with a laugh.

"We all get stage fright!" Hamsworth said with a self-deprecating smile that did not reach his eyes.

The crowd dutifully laughed.

"I don't like this," Sophie said, and Crews had to admit his nerves were strung tight as well.

"Come on out, my pretty!" Hamsworth said, moving to the end of the stage.

Steps led down from that side of the stage, presumably behind the entire public area to the staff paths that ran around the outskirts of the park just inside the fencing some twenty meters below. Hamsworth stopped at the end of the stage, just beside the steps, and leaned against the PA stack to look over the end of the habitat, down to the empty gate.

"Here, girl!" he said jovially, and made a whistle like he was calling a dog.

Then someone on stage screamed. Chairs scattered as the seated dignitaries leapt to their feet and scrambled backwards, looking in horror at something off the stage.

"Oh shit!" Ned King said, his clip-on mic amplifying the exclamation across the entire park.

Still grinning his million-watt smile, Hamsworth turned to face them. His brow knitted at the sight and he managed to half turn back before Razana surged up the stairs and snatched him up in its massive jaws.

Hamsworth screamed, his amplified voice ringing out over the myriad screams from the crowd. Then blood erupted from one of the most well-known mouths in Hollywood, and Razana shook him like a dog with a rabbit. Parts of Curtis Hamsworth went in at least two different directions, blood spattering bright red across the pale, brand new cement.

"Run!" people screamed, but Crews was way ahead of them. Even in the midst of the carnage, a stray thought passed through his mind. *I wonder who they'll cast as Captain Thunder now?* He grabbed Sophie and the two of them turned to run down the stairs at the back of the amphitheater, leading down to the main park.

The public was in a mad panic, running in every direction. Crews saw one woman pushed and go cartwheeling down the cement steps, screaming at first then falling silent as she went limp but kept tumbling. Another man went down under foot, his arms reaching as foot after foot came down on him. Crews took one look back as he and Sophie started down and saw Razana take the Queensland State Premier in one gulp, Ned King leaping off the far end of the stage, then Crews was stumbling, desperate to keep his feet and hold onto Sophie.

"Not again," Sophie sobbed as they went. "Please, not again!"

Chapter 41

Aston sat back in the strange fiberglass gondola, his arm around Slater as she leaned into him. He had to admit, this was a good day. They were finally relaxing, enjoying time together. He was a little concerned about the job he'd left behind on Kangaroo Island, but they had assured him he could take all the time he needed. He'd framed his sudden time off as being related to a death in the family, which was stretching the truth a little, but not too much. There was a time, admittedly brief, that he'd considered making Sophie his family. His strong desire to get out of Blacktooth River had overridden those thoughts quickly, of course, but it was enough for this rationalization so he decided to roll with it. He'd head back on Monday, be back at work Tuesday, and put this entire debacle behind them. Jo would have the next few weeks filled with trying to cut and edit all the footage she'd gathered into a solid documentary once they'd filmed this last chapter with Razana safe and contained, the star feature of Crocalypse. Plus she had another job to get to before long. Life could return to normal.

The gondola rolled along the fake river, winding its way through a wood and plastic recreation of the rainforests of far north Queensland. Apparently it was supposed to be several million years ago, but it looked much the same to Aston. Lilly Pilly and Casuarina swamp oaks, flax lily and plume rush, the plants were thick and vibrant. Many of them, in between the fake stuff, were real, he realized. A sprinkler system ran through the ground, keeping the roots damp and the soil loamy. The river itself, while made of fiberglass with the gondolas on underwater rails, looked impressive. The banks were decorated with rocks and sandy draws. Aston reluctantly gave Ned King his due. The man spared no expense in making an experience here for tourists.

Native animals populated the trees, but these were thankfully all fake. Animatronic and mixed together in ways that would never happen in the wild. Kangaroos and wombats rocking back and forth on automatic hinges. A cassowary every twenty meters or so, stalking on long legs, its head with the bony ridge dipping towards the boats as they passed.

"That bird'd kill ya with a single kick, son!" said the man sitting behind them. His American southern drawl was pronounced and he simply could not stop offering opinions on everything. He wore a faded John Deere shirt that didn't quite cover his generous belly. "Of course, that's not even a real thing. They obviously made that up, no seven foot bird ever walked these forests."

"Are you sure, dear?" said his wife. "Wouldn't they know?"

"Of course they know, Darlene! They're just making a spectacle for the tourists."

"Aw, come on, Dad!" said the teenage son. "I want it to be real!"

"You believe what you like, Jack Junior." The man laughed heartily, like that was some kind of hilarious joke. His daughter had remained silent the entire time.

Aston thought maybe she was the only one of them with half a brain. "Should I tell him cassowaries still inhabit these rainforests?" he whispered to Slater. "I mean, it would take all of three second's research to prove the man has no idea what he's talking about."

Slater laughed. "Obnoxious American tourists are a feature of every popular location, Sam. If you start correcting them now, you'll never stop."

Aston grinned, shook is head. "Rednecks. We have our own kind right here in Queensland, we don't need to import more."

"I wish I had my guns!" the man suddenly declared. "This place is like a shooting gallery."

Aston glanced at Slater, one eyebrow raised.

She laughed. "He should meet my friend, Bones Bonebrake," Slater said.

"Is that a real person?" Aston asked. "What kind of name is that?"

Slater smiled. "Native American. Cherokee, I think. Bones hates rednecks, too, that's all."

"Well, he sounds like a good bloke," Aston said. "I'll have to buy the guy a beer someday."

They rounded a bend and on the left the river bank smoothed out a little into a wide, sandy beach. Rocks littered the edges and several crocodiles lay sunning themselves, heads moving in rhythmic repeated patterns. Aston could almost hear the cogs turning. Despite the good job he'd made of this, Ned King's Crocalypse River Ride was cheesy as hell.

"What's that one at the back?" Slater asked. "Looks a lot big—" Her hand froze halfway raised to point.

Aston stiffened, his heart racing. "Fucking run!" he yelled, and he and Slater were scrambling up over the back of their seat, almost stamping on the American family behind them in their desire to make a quick exit.

"What the hell is wrong with you people?" the man in the John Deere shirt said, laughing. "It ain't real!"

Aston and Slater landed in the water beside the boat. It came up to their chests and they waded hard, making for the opposite bank.

"That one is!" Aston shouted back, pointing at Razana

as it thrust itself up from the fake undergrowth and took quick, long-legged strides across the riverbank.

It made a beeline directly for the boat Aston and Slater had just vacated. The American family sat frozen in terror, staring. In fact, Aston realized, not the entire family. The teenage daughter hit the water with a splash right beside him and swam hard right as Razana leapt forward. The giant croc came down through the fabric canopy of the gondola, slamming one huge foot right into the big American's rounded belly. His wife screamed and there was a furious snapping of teeth, but Aston wasn't watching any more. He scrambled up the far bank of the river, Slater and the teenage daughter right beside him, and they made a run for it, diving in between the fake trees, desperately hoping there was an access door out of the cheesy boat ride.

Chapter 42

Rusty Crews held Sophie's hand tightly as they made a run for the middle of the park. The main concourse was likely to be where they would have most room to move. People in a panic in tight spaces were more frightening than the Razana they were running from. As the crowds had flooded down from the amphitheater, Crews had heard the screaming and simply gone in the opposite direction. But now things were descending further into chaos. Wails of "What is it?" and "Where is it?" echoed all around.

"Wait!" Sophie shouted, dragging back at his hand.

Crews stopped, looking around. "What is it? We have to keep moving."

"We don't want to just run right into it!"

More muffled screaming started up and they turned. A long building ran the length of the park on one side, big decals declaring Crocalypse River Ride! and Experience Blacktooth River in Prehistoric Times! pasted all over it.

"Is the screaming coming from in there?" Crews asked, but his question was immediately answered as Razana burst out through the wall, debris raining down around its shoulders as it paused and looked left and right. Its thick tongue licked in and out.

From a hundred meters away, Crews and Sophie stared in horror.

"It she looking for something?" Sophie asked.

Razana took off again, long legs making short work of the distance between the ruined wall of the river ride and a large glass-fronted building opposite. Unfortunate tourists who happened to be too close were snapped up, bitten in half, grabbed and shaken to bloodied pieces, or just trodden under those massive, clawed feet.

Shots rang out. A police officer came dashing forward. He froze when Razana turned her head in his direction. He let out a curse and began running backward, firing wildly. A few bullets struck the creature's hide but did no apparent damage.

"This…" Crews gulped, unsure what this was. "This is bloody bad," he said at last.

Razana smashed through the front of the glass wall and a giant sign crashed to the cement below.

"That sign said Reptile House," Sophie said.

More screams rang out, more glass crashing. People continued to run randomly, but the general flood seemed to be heading for the main gates out of the park. Crews couldn't blame anyone for that, but for he and Sophie to get to the gates meant going right by the reptile house. They waited, hoping the beast would find another direction.

After a moment, Sophie pulled on his hand. "Let's go, before she comes out again."

"Too late!" Crews pointed a shaking finger.

Razana dashed out, then turned and started running along the concourse right towards Crews and Sophie. For a moment they stood stunned, mesmerized by the sight of dozens of snakes and lizards pouring out of the ruined reptile house behind her. It looked like the reptiles were following Razana, Pied Piper-style, a bizarre conga line of scales.

"That's… that's impossible," Crews said.

The screaming, panicked crowd broke in all directions, running into one another, pushing each other out of the way. Razana whipped her tail around as she ran, sent people flying to crash into others running by, or break against trees and fences. The snakes and lizards began racing at the tourists, striking and biting, climbing them and constricting.

"They're all on the attack!" Sophie said in a high, panicked voice. "They're all attacking!"

"Impossible…" Crews muttered again.

Razana broke right and bounded away, still some fifty meters from where they stood, but now the way out was filled with a furious hoard of rampaging reptiles.

"This way!" Crews said, and dragged Sophie towards the back of the ruined reptile house. "If we go around we can come out near the path leading out past the crocodile habitat. That's not far from the shop and the exit."

They ran around the buildings, pushing through trees, and came out opposite the glass fronted crocodile enclosure just in time to see Razana already there. The giant creature drove its head into the thick glass wall that kept the crocs in, smashing out a huge section.

Razana let out a serpentine hiss that sounded eerily like communication to Crews. "Is she calling them?" he asked.

"Surely not," Sophie said.

But the crocs all turned at the sound and immediately began lumbering toward the break in the glass wall. Were they really responding to Razana or had they simply noticed an exit to their captivity?

A death adder reared up suddenly from the undergrowth and struck at Sophie. She screamed, leaping sideways, and managed to avoid the bite with the aid of Crews yanking her out of the way just in time. In an act of pure instinct, Crews raised a booted foot and stamped down on the venomous reptile's head.

They ran from the trees, heading for the pathway and the gates, hoping to stay ahead of the emerging crocs, but were slammed by a wave of screaming park visitors running wildly along. Someone heavy bumped into Crews and his grip on Sophie's hand was wrenched free. In the press of people, he lost sight of her.

"Sophie!"

He couldn't see her, and was jostled along by the crowd. There was more screaming as Razana and her gang of crocs turned on the fleeing tourists still trying to sprint past the ruined glass wall.

A saltie at least five meters long came running through, using its head to knock people down, snapping at any who fell close enough, leaving screaming wounded in its wake.

Razana was releasing the reptiles from their habitats, directing them to attack the people. It was undeniable. That required a level of intelligence Crews would have never thought possible from a reptile.

"Sophie!" he yelled again, the crowd carrying him along.

Then he heard her calling his name. He pushed out sideways, following the sound, and saw her scrambling up into one of the giant hollowed out logs on the log ride. It ran along one side of the park, then used the steep hill to drop, then rise and drop again. They had been planning to have a ride on it after the opening ceremony. Was she mad, climbing aboard now?

Then Crews realized she was trying to get to the other side as Razana pounded after her. It slipped and stumbled on broken fencing, giving her a moment, but it wouldn't be long enough. Crews had no weapon. He looked left and right, then picked up a garbage can and hurled it. It sailed through the air, end over end, and clanged off the back of Razana's head when she was only meters from snapping Sophie up.

Razana turned around and hissed at him, her tail whipping sideways into the control panel for the log ride. The log Sophie was almost over suddenly lurched into motion. She screeched and fell, dropping back into the hollow fiberglass log as it went shooting down the flume.

Razana turned again, distracted by fleeing tourists. As she ran down a group of teenagers, Crews sprinted to the ride and leapt into the next log as it went sailing by, thinking only of catching up with Sophie. She might be hurt, unconscious in the bottom of the ride.

People ran and screamed in all directions and Crews felt suddenly foolish, floating along peacefully in a fake log while people were dying all around. But he had to catch up with Sophie. He wondered for a moment if it might be quicker to leap out and swim to catch up, but it was moving faster than he could swim despite its relaxed pace. The course followed twists and turns, travelled under sprays of water and jets from the sides. He was soon soaking wet and frustrated.

Finally, they reached the long climb before the final plunge. Now the logs were creeping along and Crews clambered out, and sprinted up the gangway that ran alongside the track. Sophie sat up groggily, looking around in confusion. Crews shouted for her to get out of the log.

"Quickly!" he yelled. "Before the drop!"

Sophie's eyes widened in surprise but she staggered as she tried to gain her feet and the log crested the rise. With a grunt of effort, Crews sprinted and leaped, just managing to jump in with her as the log seemed to pause briefly at the top of the incline, then they shot down a dark tunnel.

Crews clutched hold of Sophie, both falling back against the seats. Ordinarily this kind of ride would be a thrill for him, but today seemed to have all the wrong kinds of excitement. They dragged themselves into a sitting position just in time to see the circle of light at the end of the tunnel.

Just in time to see Razana's head fill it from one side. She hissed again.

There was nowhere to go and no time to do anything.

Crews shoved Sophie down to the floor of the log and rose to face death.

"No!" Sophie yelled.

All he had was his fists and he shouted, "Come on then, you bitch!" as he leaped at Razana when the log shot out of the tunnel, using his bodyweight to push Razana's head aside. He saw the log shooting away, Sophie wide-eyed as she sailed to safety, then Razana had him by the neck. Claws dug into his body as her fetid breath filled his nose. And then pain like he'd never known before and everything went black.

Chapter 43

Aston and Slater ran hard for the main exit only to find a throng of people in absolute chaos. The way was blocked by bodies, the wounded, and the living, scrambling over each other, fighting each other, and among it all, every kind of reptile in a frenzy of attack. Crocodiles snapped at people, lizards ran everywhere, snakes rose up to strike or strangle.

"Is that the Prime Minister?" Aston asked, aghast, as a huge carpet python dropped from a tree above the man and coiled quickly around his chest and shoulders. The country's leader managed to get out one tight scream, then a sharp cracking stopped the sound and blood poured from his mouth.

"What the hell is happening here?" Slater said, staring in disbelief at body parts scattered around.

"Oh shit." Aston pointed.

Between them and the main gate, Razana appeared, her face bloodstained, her eyes sharp and roving. The huge croc-like dinosaur caught sight of him and turned. Had it recognized him? It was showing signs of intelligence well beyond anything that seemed possible, but one look around the theme park proved that possible and impossible were thoroughly blurred concepts.

A trio of police officers appeared on the scene. Armed only with handguns, they moved into the path of the oncoming creature, but their bullets did not even slow Razana, who snapped up two screaming tourists, then strode onwards again,, still heading in the direction of Aston and Slater. Everyone in their path scattered.

"We have to get it away from the crowds," Slater said,

then screamed and kicked out as a snake rose up beside her. She clipped the snake under its head and it briefly recoiled, hissing.

"That way!" Aston pointed to a security gate that led to the staff-only roadway around the base of the large hill, behind all the exhibits and attractions. He waved his hands at Razana and made loud noises, whoops and calls.

Slater ran ahead, pushed open the double gates, ducking behind one to hold it wide.

Aston led the beast on, past the end of the themed rides. Sophie came stumbling towards him, blood-soaked, dazed. Her eyes widened when she saw him leading Razana along. Aston grabbed her arm, turned her to haul her with him. He tried to push her aside as he ran through the gate, but she refused and stayed with him.

"Help Jo!" he yelled, as he sprinted down the cement path leading to the maintenance areas.

"It got Rusty!" Sophie said, tears in her eyes.

Aston shook his head. And how many others? he wondered, but just kept running.

He glanced back to see Razana pounding after him. It was fast on its long legs and he wouldn't be able to stay ahead of it for long, but he was grateful to see Slater and Sophie pushing a gate each, closing the way back to the main concourse. If he could keep Razana this side of the fencing, there would be far fewer people in harm's way. Of course, that didn't account for all the other reptiles out there, going wild as if directed like an army.

Up ahead, he saw Karen Rowling. She stood with her legs wide, planted firm, and she held up something he couldn't make out from the distance. But he was closing fast.

"Get out of the way!" he yelled. He had no idea where he was leading the beast, but there was nowhere else to go but forward, with high fences to his left and the rainforest beyond that, and a high cement wall to his right, with screaming crowds on the other side.

"Stand aside!" Rowling shouted back. "I've got this!"

"What?"

"RAZANA!" Rowling screamed at the top of her voice, and held the object in her hand up high.

It was a waxy carving of a crocodile, Aston saw. What was this crazy woman doing? He was tempted to crash tackle her as he drew close, try to save her as well, but her eyes were so determined. Like she knew something more than he could imagine.

"That's my girl!" Rowling said, loud, but gentle, as Aston sprinted past.

Gasping for breath, he paused to look back.

Razana had slowed to a slow walk, watching Rowling intently.

"What the hell..?" Aston whispered.

Razana stalked forward, head cocked like a curious dog, eyes flickering from Rowling to the wax effigy in her hand and back again. It stopped only a couple of meters from her, its head a full body length again above her trembling hand. It hissed gently.

"That's my girl," Rowling said again. "You remember me, don't you? Of course you do. I've got a truck waiting to take you home, my darling. Like before, eh? Safe and looked after."

Razana tipped its head the other way, lowering to be almost eye level with Rowling. From his perspective behind the woman, Aston had a moment to contemplate just how huge this beast was, its head almost the size of a small car.

That head shot forward, huge teeth snapping, and Rowling's hand vanished to halfway up the forearm. Rowling screamed as blood jetted from the stump of her arm as she staggered back.

Aston started to take steps backwards, prepared to turn and run for his life again. Rowling be damned, the foolish woman had chosen her fate. What was she thinking? There was obviously history there, and he honestly didn't really care what it was.

An explosion boomed somewhere nearby, made them all stagger. A ball of flame pushed a roiling black could up just the other side of the high wall. Rowling collapsed to the ground, sobbing, her ruined arm clutched to her chest.

Razana turned, then looked up and started to run. Away from them. Back towards the gates Slater and Sophie had closed. Aston became aware of a loud thrumming sound and looked to see what had scared Razana. He saw a news helicopter sweep in low over the wall. A missile shot from it, trailing a hot jet of exhaust from under the helicopter and barely missed Razana, instead blowing a huge hole in the wall. Debris flew. The acrid smell of smoke filled the air. People screamed. Razana ducked through, back out into the main park.

Aston realized it wasn't a news helicopter at all, just painted to resemble one, but equipped with all kinds of weaponry.

Slater and Sophie ran to join them.

"Who are they?" Slater asked, pointing as the chopper banked to chase the giant croc.

"I don't know!" Aston said. "Help me with her!"

He pulled the belt from his pants and quickly looped it to tourniquet Rowling's devastating wound.

"SCAR," she said weakly.

"I should think so," Aston said. "Honestly, a lot more than a scar. You'll never see that hand again."

"No, you idiot." Rowling gasped, face pale. "The chopper. Probably SCAR. Trying to destroy Razana. Cover their arses and protect their intellectual property."

Slater tore away some of her t-shirt and used it to bandage Rowling's bleeding stump. The woman whined at the touch, but accepted the help.

"Their intellectual property?" Aston asked. "What are you talking about?"

Rowling took a few deep, trembling breaths, eyes downcast. "SCAR. Stands for Snakes, Crocs and other Reptiles."

"That doesn't make sense," Sophie said. "It's missing the O."

"Fuck's sake," Rowling hissed. "It doesn't matter. Just listen. That's a front anyway for this weird paramilitary scientific organization. They experiment genetically with animals, mostly reptiles. They grew Razana in their labs, from DNA they found somewhere in Africa."

"Egypt," Slater said quietly. She looked pointedly at Aston and he nodded.

"Maybe, don't know. Doesn't matter. Anyway, we found out about it and raided their facility near Townsville where it was kept. We brought it back here, to our place, to give it a free life away from experiments and whatever else SCAR had planned for it."

Rowling winced, phased out briefly, her eyes rolling up.

"She needs medical attention right now," Aston said.

"I'll take her," Sophie said.

"Wait!" Rowling snapped, coming back to herself. "Important." She sucked in more quick breaths, then said, "Razana grew fast. Too fast. We had to build a new enclosure and move her, but there was a mistake. Long story, doesn't matter. She escaped, out there." Rowling gestured vaguely at the rainforest beyond the fence. "We've been trying to catch her again, but SCAR obviously got wind of what was happening and they got here too."

"The guys with the weird electric guns," Aston said.

"Sure. Probably. Whatever." Rowling gasped again, but seemed to be finding some equilibrium. Aston had to admit, she seemed pretty tough. "What matters now," Rowling went on, "is that SCAR will try to destroy her. Don't let them!"

"They have a chopper with missiles!" Aston said. "I don't think I can do much about that!"

As if to illustrate the point, there was another explosion, a little further away. More smoke boiled up into the sky, more people screaming.

"And I swear Razana is nonverbally directing other reptiles to attack," Slater said. "I can't see how it's possible, but it is. She has to be stopped."

"SCAR messed... with the DNA," Rowling said. "Added dolphin and bee DNA to the mix. They talk about chemical communication... all the time. Maybe it can communicate with other reptiles. And her intelligence is boosted... way up. We were doing problem solving experiments with her. She's at least as smart... as a good dog. Maybe equivalent to a young child."

"Regardless, she's too dangerous!" Aston said. "I'd do anything to see her survive if possible, but the carnage out there!"

Karen dug into her pocket with her good hand and pulled out a glass bottle, pressed it against Aston. "Take this. Pheromones. It'll work, I promise. I thought the wax croc—" She winced, gasped. "Whatever, didn't work. These will, definitely. There's a truck... out behind the amphitheater. That way. Use that. Lead her. Please." Rowling's eyes flickered again and she passed out.

Machine gun fire rang out over the park, then the explosion of another missile.

"They're taking no chances!" Slater said. "How many more people are dying from their relentless attacks?"

"I have to get Razana away," Aston said, staring at the bottle Rowling had given him.

"I've got her," Sophie sad, pointing to Rowling. "Go!"

Aston and Slater jumped up and ran back the way Razana had gone, accompanied by the sound of more automatic weapon fire.

Chapter 44

When Aston and Slater ran back out through the gates into the main park, they were struck by two things. One was the absolute carnage caused in such a short time. Body parts lay everywhere, blood pooled on the concrete and arced up walls and trees in arterial sprays. The other thing was the moment of calm. Other than a few people crying and moaning from their injuries, thankfully being tended to by other members of the public and wide-eyed park staff, the crowds had dispersed. Hopefully the vast majority of people had made it out and away. Aston imagined a speeding convoy of cars and buses careening for the highway and a fast journey far away from Crocalypse.

"Where are the reptiles?" Slater asked.

Aston nodded, realized that was a third thing. The snakes and crocs and lizards were nowhere to be seen. If Razana had indeed been communicating with them, cajoling them to attack, perhaps when she'd stopped giving orders, distracted by the chopper, the other reptiles had simply taken their opportunity for freedom. It would be easy enough for any of them to escape through the fences and gates and take shelter in the surrounding rainforest. Aston wished them well.

The chopper had banked around and came in again, low over them, pressuring them with its downdraft and noise. Aston watched it go, saw it had no more missiles to deploy. That was something, at least. Then the large machine gun mounted under the cockpit roared again, fire spitting from the muzzle. Aston followed the trajectory of the gunfire and saw Razana running full speed. But she wasn't trying to escape the chopper. She ran obliquely, right for Croc Mountain, the tall fake peak in the middle of the park with walking tracks up the side and a large viewing area on top.

Razana flinched as bullets ripped into her hide above her tail and along the ridge of it, a couple of bony plates spinning free. But she powered on, sprinted up the shallow side of the artificial hill and ran across the level viewing platform as the helicopter banked again and came around for another pass.

"Is she—" Aston started, but had no time to finish the thought as Razana leaped from the edge of the wide cement platform, the huge monster's athleticism incredible to behold.

Clearly taken by surprise, the chopper didn't even fire before the enormous weight of the giant croc latched onto one landing runner. The helicopter whined, the engine howling as it tipped and spun in the air. The rotors clipped the railing around the edge of the viewing area and the helicopter slammed into the side of the fake hill with a resounding crash. Flames gouted upwards as both chopper and Razana tumbled out of view behind the hill.

"SAM!" Slater yelled, and yanked hard on his arm, pulling him sideways to fall hard on the cement as a two-meter long section of helicopter rotor whizzed by and chopped down the tree right behind where he'd been standing. The blade thunked into the earth and the tree fell with a crunch.

"Thanks!" Aston said.

They dragged themselves to the their feet and started running again. "You think she survived that?" Slater asked.

"We'll find out."

They took one of the winding paths up the side of the hill and started around when Slater pointed. "Rowling's plan?" she asked.

From their vantage they saw an access road leading through the rainforest to a large double gate. Parked about fifty meters back from the gates, mostly obscured by the canopy, was a truck. Or at least, the remains of one, now little more than a smoking ruin. Two bodies, blackened and broken, lay nearby.

"Looks like SCAR wanted to make sure KIND didn't get Razana back under any circumstances," Aston said.

"That accounts for one of their missiles," Slater said. "I guess they missed with the rest?"

"Missed Razana maybe." Aston pointed to the other side of the park where a black and smoking crater was surrounded by more burned and decimated bodies.

Slater shook her head, lips pressed together.

They came around the side of the hill and saw the burning wreckage of the helicopter. Further down the slope Razana ran, injured and slow, limping as she went but still moving. She was heading for some broken down fencing near the amphitheater.

"Looks like she might be trying to get out," Slater said. "We can't let her, can we?"

Aston pursed his lips. "No," he said quietly.

"But what can we do?"

Aston looked at the bottle in his hand. "Well, I hope Rowling was right about this," he said, and took off in a sprint.

"Sam!"

He heard Slater start after him, but didn't have time to explain. He ran around the flank of the hill and hit the pathway at an angle to Razana as she reached level ground.

"Hey, Razana!" he yelled. "Come on, you beauty!"

He unstoppered the bottle and raised it high. The

strong, acrid smell hit him immediately. Whatever was inside was potent and bitter. Razana snapped her head around. She had been sagging a little on her legs, bleeding from numerous bullet wounds, blackened in places by burns, but the pheromones gave her renewed energy.

"Well, shit," Aston said, and bolted.

He ran the long way around the seats of the amphitheater, the pounding of Razana's scaled feet gaining on him all the way. He heard her long black claws clacking against the cement, heard her labored, rasping breath. He imagined those massive jaws descending on him at any moment, wincing as he ran.

"Come on, come on, come on!" he urged himself.

He came around the far side of the amphitheater and up the sloping path that led to the stage behind the deep pool. He felt Razana's hot breath jetting onto him as he ran, but didn't aim for the stage. He jumped up onto the low wall surrounding the deep pool, heard Slater's scream from somewhere behind, and then he was airborne, launching himself out into space.

"Please hold my weight, please!" he begged as he fell and came down onto the wide, tan tarp stretched over that end of the habitat for shade. It sagged and swung and he stagger-ran, desperate to keep his feet on the taut but shifting material. It held him and he upended the bottle of pheromones and kept running.

"Sam!" Slater screamed again.

He reached the far side of the tarp, vertigo making his head swim as he saw the drop on the other side to the rocks and trees and winding creek twenty meters below. He leaped again, turning in the air as he grabbed one of the thick ropes connecting the corner of the tarp to a metal ring in the wall some ten meters from him. He had gambled everything on the ring being stronger than the tarp.

As he turned in the air he saw Razana leaping over the wall as he'd done, following the scent smeared all over the tarp which would look to her like solid ground. Her long, heavy body writhed slightly in the air before she came down on the thick material. For a moment it held, bouncing her like a trampoline. She lunged forward, her massive jaws snapping shut less than a meter from his face, then a deep, tearing rip sounded and the material shredded away from the metal cleats holding the ropes to its corners. The tarp tore and Razana plummeted down. Aston swung away Tarzan-style. He hoped again for the ring to hold, putting his legs out to cushion his impact against the side of the habitat.

He slammed into the smooth white plastered side about halfway down at the same moment Razana crashed into the rocks below. The torn tarp beneath her did nothing to cushion the blow and she slammed hard to earth. Aston heard her bones cracking. She bucked once, writhed to one side, then fell still. Blood leaked from her slack jaw.

Aston hung on with desperate strength for a moment more, looking down at the unfortunate beast. "You poor thing," he said quietly. "You didn't ask for any of this, did you?"

"Sam?"

He looked up and saw Slater, pale-faced and wide-eyed, leaning over the low wall above.

"Coming," he said with a crooked grin and began to climb hand over hand up the rope. "Get something to pull me up, yeah?"

Slater vanished for a moment, then returned with a bright red rope that had been used to mark off the VIP area to the side of the stage, back when all this was exciting and new. She hung it over the side and Aston reached the metal ring mounted in the habitat wall, pulled himself up onto it, then grabbed the red rope. Slater backed up, pulling, and he wall-walked to the top and fell over it onto the solid ground of the stage.

"That was quite a plan," Slater said, one eyebrow raised.

Aston looked over the side at the body of Razana, then back to Slater. "Not gonna lie," he said with a grin. "I'm honestly as surprised it worked as you are."

Chapter 45

Aston and Slater moved away from the wall into the shade of the covered stage and slumped to the ground.

"What a day!" Aston said. "In fact, what a week."

"That was quite something, Mr. Aston."

Startled, they looked up to see Ned King walking towards them. His clothes were ragged, his face bloodstained. He carried a rifle loosely in one hand. Lynn walked behind, filming, and Barry was with her, his boom mic raised.

"You did not get all that?" Slater asked, incredulous.

Lynn grinned, nodded. "Got it all," she said.

Aston sighed. "Bloody hell."

"You survived again then," Slater said to King.

He raised a hand in acquiescence. "It does appear that way. I've been busy though." He hefted the rifle for emphasis. "I think I managed to take care of the worst of the reptiles that were rampaging. Those remaining are becalmed now, or escaped."

"Gonna take a bit to recover from this," Aston said.

King grinned. "I'll leverage today's events one way or another. It'll cost a fortune of course, but we'll get through it."

"Don't you care at all about how many people died?" Slater snapped.

King became serious. "Of course I do. And I'll do all I can to compensate families and meet their expenses. But this was sabotage, not my fault."

"KIND," Aston said, like it was a curse. "I think maybe Rowling has a lot of questions to answer."

"Indeed," King said.

"She's gone."

They turned to see Sophie coming towards them.

"Gone?" Aston asked.

Sophie nodded. "I sat with her for a moment, after she passed out. I wasn't certain what to do, so I tried to carry her to get help, but I wasn't strong enough. I put her in a shady spot by the wall and ran for help. There were so many people hurt, but I finally found a medic. Lots of emergency services are starting to arrive, by the way."

"That's good," Aston said. "But Rowling?"

"When I took the medic back to where I'd left her, she wasn't there. Must have come around and wandered off."

"We saw her heading into the bush," said a soft voice.

Penry and Ringo approached, both as bloodied and grubby as the rest.

"Ah, you both okay?" King asked them.

"Depends what you mean by okay," Ringo said.

"We're alive," Penry said. "But consider this our resignation."

"Where will you two go?" Aston asked. He felt a strong affinity for the calm pair.

"Wherever the wind blows us," Penry said.

"We like to let life lead us, not the other way around," Ringo said.

Aston smiled, nodded. "I hope our paths cross again."

"You never know," Penry said, and the two men turned and strolled away.

"How does a horrible bitch like Karen Rowling survive when good people like Cooper and Rusty don't?" Sophie said, tears in her eyes.

"Russell Crews was a good man," Aston said. "I'm really sorry, Soph."

"Yeah, me too."

Aston stood. He gestured to Lynnette and Barry. "Got all you need?" he asked Slater.

She nodded. "Yeah, I should say so."

Aston took Slater's hand. "Ned, this is your mess to clean up. We're done here. Sophie, you want to ride with us?"

"Yes, please."

The five of them walked away, heading for an exit. Aston glanced back once, saw Ned King standing there, watching them go. He didn't seem too bothered about anything.

Police and paramedics ran everywhere as they made their way down towards the main gate. There was enough for the authorities to deal with that five able-bodied people were easy to ignore.

When they reached the car, Sophie said, "I'm parked over there. I'll take myself from here."

"You gonna be okay?" Aston asked.

"I doubt it, but I'll live."

"Stay in Blacktooth River?"

She shrugged, gave him a crooked grin. "For now, yeah. But I do feel like maybe it's time to spread my wings."

Aston leaned forward, kissed her cheek. "Good idea. You have my number. Call any time."

"Likewise."

Without a backward look, she walked away.

Aston unlocked their car and he and Slater climbed in the front, Lynn and Barry in the back. "Let's get the hell out of Blacktooth River," Aston said. "I warned you that bad things happen whenever I return to the old hometown."

Epilogue

In a carefully guarded secret location, SCAR scientists studied the tanks in their deep underground laboratory.

"This one?" a doctor asked.

His lab assistant shook her head. "No. DNA corruption succumbed quickly to a virus. We're running more tests. But look here."

She led him to another area, showed a batch of large, smooth eggs. One of them had cracked and a large crocodilian creature squirmed across the sand. It blinked at them with strangely intelligent eyes.

"This batch all died in the egg," the lab assistant said. "Except this one."

"So we've got one?"

"If she survives, yes."

The doctor grinned and leaned close. "Hello, Razana," he said quietly.

Karen Rowling looked at the new prosthetic hand with a creased brow. She flexed her forearm, or at least, what remained of it. Tried to use the muscles like the occupational therapist had taught her. After a moment, the metal fingers shifted, then flexed into a fist.

With a grin, she unfurled the fingers again, reached forward and tried to pick up the paper cup on the table in front of her. She crushed it, water spilling across the polished surface.

"Damn it," she muttered. "Never mind. Try again."

She would master this new appendage and then she would head KIND's next offensive. Firstly, she planned to take out SCAR. If she'd learned anything from this recent debacle it was that KIND needed to be more like that awful organization. They had entirely the wrong philosophy, but they set a good example in might and power. KIND would take out SCAR and replace them. And Karen Rowling would lead them to it. Delilah had died for this vision, and died before she could declare her love for Karen, or Karen really show her love for Delilah. She would take KIND to new, world-beating heights in that brave woman's honor.

Rowling smiled, flexing her hand again. This wasn't over. Oh no, this was far from over.

The End

About the Authors

David Wood is the USA Today bestselling author of the Dane Maddock Adventures and several other books and series. He also writes science fiction as Finn Gray and fantasy under the pen name David Debord. He's a member of International Thriller Writers and the Horror Writers Association, and also reviews for New York Journal of Books.

Learn more about his work at
www.davidwoodweb.com
Or drop by and say hello on Facebook at:
www.facebook.com/davidwoodbooks.

Alan Baxter is a British-Australian author who writes horror, supernatural thrillers, and dark fantasy, liberally mixed with crime and noir. He rides a motorcycle and loves his dog. He also teaches Kung Fu. He lives among dairy paddocks on the beautiful south coast of NSW, Australia, with his wife, son, dog, two lunatic cats, several tropical fish, and a lizard called Fifi. Read extracts from his novels, a novella, and short stories at his website - www.warriorscribe.com - or find him on Twitter @AlanBaxter and Facebook, and feel free to tell him what you think. About anything.